"Oh, Phyllida, it is all so shocking— and exciting," cried Janet.

"Mamma's nephew, Sir Hugh Abingdon, arrived yesterday to ask if he might spend the weekend with us. Have you not *heard* of him?" she asked as Phyllida looked blank. Janet warmed to the scandal, her voice sinking to a dramatic whisper. "Goodness, he is most *tremendously* dashing and wicked."

"La!" teased Phyllida, amused by Janet's expression. "Whatever has he done?"

"Dreadful things—things you and I aren't even supposed to know about they are so bad. But, well, he is devilish handsome, so I thought I should tell you before you meet. Please be warned, won't you, before we go into the Ballroom."

Phyllida smothered a smile as she replied, "I promise, Janet—and I am most grateful."

No one could say Phyllida had not been amply warned, but when Hugh Abingdon's dark eyes met her sparkling green ones across the Randall's ballroom, she could heed no advice. Her heart's thundering beat resounded so, she heard no other voice.

Novels By Caroline Courtney

Duchess in Disguise
A Wager For Love
Love Unmasked
Guardian of The Heart
Dangerous Engagement
Love Triumphant
The Fortunes of Love
Love's Masquerade
Heart of Honor
The Romantic Rivals
Forbidden Love

Published By
WARNER BOOKS

CAROLINE COURTNEY

Forbidden Love

WARNER BOOKS

A Warner Communications Company

Cover design by Gene Light

Cover art by Walter Popp

Warner Books, Inc., 75 Rockefeller Plaza, New York, N.Y. 10019

Ⓦ A Warner Communications Company

Printed in the United States of America

First Printing: December, 1980

10 9 8 7 6 5 4 3 2 1

Forbidden
Love

Chapter One

The afternoon sun poured through the drawing room windows of an elegant house in Bath, where a tall, slender girl was standing beside a great bowl of daffodils. In front of her a very young man had dropped down on one knee.

"Phyllida—I *entreat* you to marry me! I have the consent of your father, believe me, and I swear to love and cherish you all my life. I am run mad with love for you, and your beauty haunts me day and night. Indeed, I can scarce keep my mind even on *hunting,* for thinking of you!" To him this was the most telling proof of his love, for hunting was a very serious pursuit.

Phyllida sighed. It was her fifth proposal in three weeks and she hated having to hurt people—especially one as young as this, who was probably scarcely eighteen, as she was herself.

"Dear Toby, please get up." Her smile was gentle and genuinely sad as she held out a slim hand to help him to his feet; his very new, downy mustache trembled with emotion and his eyes grew suspiciously moist. She went on: "I like you so much but, in truth, I do not love you, so I declare I must refuse this great honor. Oh, pray do not feel too sad—I promise that you will meet many girls prettier than I and one day you will be grateful to me for saying this."

"Never!" he declared dramatically, clapping a hand

to his damp forehead. "My heart will be at your feet for-ever—you are the most exquisite being on earth, Phyllida, how could I find another?"

Quite overcome, he turned abruptly and left the room.

Again Phyllida sighed. She had no conceit whatever and honestly could not understand why so many young men found it necessary to propose to her—they numbered fifteen now, since she had come out into society five months ago. But Toby had spoken no less than the truth, for Phyllida was exquisite indeed: a glowing honey blond, her shining hair was coiled smoothly back into a chignon at the nape of her neck, sparkling green eyes were fringed with unexpectedly dark lashes, and she had a mouth that curled deliciously whenever she was amused—which was often.

Her mother, sitting quietly at her embroidery frame in the back drawing room—for even a proposal must be chaperoned—echoed the sigh. Mrs. Chase was a comfort-able matron in her fifties, married to a wealthy and suc-cessful lawyer. Her life was extremely pleasant except for one ripple that constantly disturbed her composure—worry over her most bewildering younger children. Her two elder sons had been as normal and easygoing as their parents, following their father into the law and marrying most suitable young wives with good dowries. Then, after a lapse of eight years, came Gareth, now nineteen, who cheerfully refused to conform in any way and insisted that he meant to become a painter.

"Such a *disreputable* idea," mourned Mrs. Chase frequently to her husband. "Surely you can put a stop to it?"

"He is young yet, m'dear. Give him enough rope . . ." Mr. Chase was an orderly man and dreaded any commo-tion in his household.

A year after the birth of Gareth came Phyllida, so delicately formed and pretty that she became the apple of her father's eye at a very early age. But her independence baffled her mother and, as she gradually matured into a ravishing creature, poor Mrs. Chase felt a secret awe of her daughter—like a homely duck who has reared a wayward swan. Phyllida was gentle and loving toward her parents, yet threatened to be as difficult as Gareth, possibly because the two were devoted friends and allies.

So Mrs. Chase prayed earnestly that Phyllida would accept quickly one of the desirable suitors who came asking for her hand, and settle down in a home of her own. Her prayers so far seemed to have fallen on deaf ears and now Phyllida joined her in the back drawing room.

"I'm sorry, Mamma, but surely both you and Papa knew that I could never accept Toby! I declare he was more like a puppy begging for a bone!"

"*Really!*" Her mother was outraged. "Before long he is likely to become a viscount. Will you never be satisfied?"

"Oh—sometime, I expect so," and Phyllida drifted out, no doubt going straight up to the bare attic room that Gareth had claimed as his "studio." Really, it was *too* provoking . . .

"Come in," Gareth called cheerfully, continuing to add deft strokes to a portrait of his sister. "Sent another victim to the sacrifice?"

Phyllida laughed and went to look over his shoulder. She studied the sketch closely: "You brute! I look like a bossy Amazon going to war!"

"Well—aren't you?" Gareth swung round on his stool. "This isn't supposed to be an exact likeness, but what we both stand for. You know, I believe we have been born out of our time, you and I—life in Bath is so narrow, while the world outside is wide and filled with exciting possibilities. I mean to travel as soon as I have enough money."

Phyllida sank into the only armchair, her eyes brooding. "And what chance have I—a mere woman—of ever exploring it?" Her soft voice was bitter. "Mamma never stops hinting that she wants me to marry well—and quick-

9

ly, poor dear, because I worry her so much." Suddenly her voice was edged with genuine anxiety: "Do you think there can be something wrong with me, Gareth? All these charming young men come here begging me to marry them, yet, I swear, not one has even kindled a spark of feeling in my heart. They are all so worthy—but so *dull!*"

"Of course there's nothing wrong with you," declared Gareth firmly. "You'll find your man all right—and heaven help him, being saddled with you for life!" He chuckled.

His sister aimed a cushion amiably in his direction. "You're a rotten tease! If I *do* meet him we shall love each other to distraction forever!"

"That really *would* be dull—everyone needs a few fireworks now and then to liven things up."

Gareth had no idea just how many fireworks, heart-aches and dramas awaited his beloved sister—and starting in the very near future. In fact this was possibly the last peaceful afternoon she was to pass for a very long time.

Phyllida was delighted with her new ball gown, cut in the very latest Empire line and exactly matching her golden hair. The undersheath of satin was embroidered with clusters of crystal flowers which shimmered and gleamed beneath an overdress of finest silk muslin. She wore a gold locket studded with brilliants round her neck and a pale gold fillet in her hair.

She was standing in front of a tall mirror examining the overall effect when her mother bustled in to see if she was ready.

"It seems a shame to wear this for anything as ordinary as Lady Randall's cotillion," Phyllida mused. "I should have kept it until the spring season begins next weeks when the Prince arrives."

The spring season was short but very gay, making Bath the third most fashionable city in England. At that time the Prince Regent, accompanied by his courtiers and of course Beau Brummell, showing off his latest outrageous styles, came to take the waters. Not that they took the waters too seriously, though, for they tasted of rotten eggs. The days and nights were filled with parties, outings and other pleasures, but physicians assured His Royal Highness that a course at Bath was extremely wise before the excesses of the summer season in Brighton.

"Nonsense, my dear," said Mrs. Chase, who had a slight migraine and felt a little out of sorts. "Lady Randall is a famous hostess; why, no member of the *ton* would dream of belittling her invitations! Oh!" A wave of nausea caught her unaware and she reached for support. Instantly Phyllida's strong young arms went round the plump figure. Her voice was tender,

"Poor little Mamma—is it one of your wretched headaches again?" Mrs. Chase nodded gratefully—really, Phyllida could be a veritable angel.

"I—I fear that I cannot come with you, my dear. Miss Smith must take my place."

"Don't you worry about this evening—I shall ring for your maid but, first, lean on me while we go to your bedroom."

Phyllida helped the young maid to ease Mrs. Chase out of her overtight gown and high-boned corsets. Then, when she was wrapped in a soft bedgown, helped her into bed.

"Thank you, daughter, I shall soon feel relief now. But before I sleep I shall instruct Miss Smith."

"Oh, Mamma—*must* she accompany me?" cried Phyllida. "It is only a small cotillion to celebrate Janet Randall's birthday—I truly need no chaperone for such a harmless occasion."

"The very idea!" exclaimed her mother, feeling much restored. "We should be the talk of all Bath if you attended such a fashionable house alone! Miss Smith will prepare herself in no time, I assure you."

Yes, thought Phyllida, who heartily disliked Miss Smith. An acid little woman of uncertain age, she had once been governess to Phyllida and then stayed on to do fine sewing, run household errands, and escort Phyllida on daily promenades or to any function that did not appeal to Mrs. Chase. She certainly would take little time to get ready for the evening, since she would merely change her gray alpaca for a rather dusty black velvet, long out of fashion. Her gray hair was always severely scraped back into a bun anchored by large iron hairpins and, as she often said, she "knew her place"—which was to melt into any background and remain practically invisible though ever watchful. For all her intelligence Phyllida was still too young to understand that Miss Smith clung to her employment with the Chases because she had nowhere else to go, and not because she was particularly fond of the family. But then she was fond of no one.

And so, ten minutes later, she accompanied the radiant Phyllida down to the carriage and they set off for Lady Randall's magnificent mansion near the center of the city.

Lady Randall's daughter, Janet, was waiting eagerly for Phyllida's arrival. The two girls were the same age and had once attended dancing classes together, but there any likeness ended. Gareth dubbed Janet "a silly goose" when he met her and, indeed, she was—but a good-natured goose who felt no jealousy toward her more attractive contemporaries. Now, as Miss Smith took Phyllida's cloak off to the cloakroom, Janet drew her into a small sitting room, her eyes like saucers and her voice breaking into nervous giggles as she spoke,

"Oh, Phyllida, it is so—so shocking and yet, I declare, it is terribly exciting as well. Mamma is quite put about, I can tell."

"What is it, Janet?" Phyllida was rather bored, expecting some innocent girlish confession.

"It is Mamma's nephew, Sir Hugh Abingdon! Why, have you not *heard* of him?" she asked as Phyllida looked blank. Janet warmed to the scandal, her voice sinking to a dramatic whisper: "Goodness, he is most *tremendously* dashing and wicked! Of course he is quite old, even though I suppose we are cousins—about twenty-six at *least*—but Mamma and Papa were in a proper taking when he arrived yesterday to ask if he might spend the weekend with us."

"La!" teased Phyllida, amused by Janet's expression. "Whatever has he done?"

"Dreadful things—things you and I aren't even supposed to know about they are so bad. But, well, he is devilish handsome, so I thought I should warn you before you meet."

Phyllida was immediately interested. "I can't believe you unless you tell me more—you're probably making it up, Janet!"

Incensed, Janet spoke more vehemently, "It is WOMEN," she announced, her eyes even wider. "I heard Mamma talking to a friend this morning! Sir Hugh Abingdon flirts shamelessly with young girls, she said, leaving them heartbroken—and all the time he is carrying on notorious affairs with married women not only here in England but all over Europe, for he travels a great deal." Janet edged closer, her voice sinking again: "And there is much, much more! Once he gambled away a fortune in a card game that lasted for four days and nights without pause. Can you imagine such villainy?"

Phyllida's pulse was racing but she managed to ask coolly: "What else has he done? I declare you make him sound *very* dangerous, Janet."

"Oh, there is worse yet." Janet was encouraged at last by her much admired friend's interest in her scandalous relation. "For a vast wager it is rumored that, one night, he drank the Prince Regent himself under the table! Mamma said it was an incredible feat, for the Prince can drink prodigiously and show no sign of drunkenness." She laid her hand on Phyllida's arm: *"Please* be warned, won't you, before we go into the ballroom?"

"I promise, Janet—and I am most grateful."

"You see—he *is* extremely handsome," repeated Janet anxiously.

"I will remember. Shall we go in now? Your mother

13

will think it rude of me to detain you from your birthday party."

Arm in arm the two girls went through the wide hall, brilliant with flowers, to the ballroom. Phyllida could scarce contain her inner excitement. Was she, now, to meet a man of her own mettle? Someone who defied convention and gave not a fig for gossip?

The ballroom was charming and not too large, with a musician's gallery at one end and a supper room opening out through a graceful archway at the other. Although gasoliers were the latest rage, Lady Randall preferred the soft light of candles in the crystal chandeliers. Velvet chairs were arranged in groups round the walls so that mothers and chaperones could sit chatting in comfort instead of having to sit in rows observing the dancers. After all, nothing improper could take place while the young people were actually dancing.

Phyllida saw Sir Hugh Abingdon at once and paused near the doorway to watch him for a few moments.

He was escorting his aunt in a most courtly manner as she introduced him to the older guests, paying flattering attention to each one with exactly the right deference. Phyllida was enchanted—he was not, as she had half expected from Janet's account, an effete fop with a weak, handsome face. No, he was truly a man in every way: taller than average, his body was lean and taut as a bowstring—certainly not portraying overindulgence; his face was slightly saturnine, having high cheekbones and a determined chin redeemed from severity by warm, chestnut brown eyes and thick dark hair gathered back very simply into a wide ribbon bow above the fashionably high collar of his sapphire blue velvet coat. His only signs of opulence were a magnificent amethyst signet ring on his right hand and fine gold-thread embroidery on the collar, cuffs and wide skirts of his coat. Sir Hugh Abingdon was not merely handsome—he was devastating.

At that point Phyllida was noticed by five or six young men, who surged toward her eagerly, requesting a dance. The sudden movement attracted Sir Hugh Abingdon's attention, although he only glimpsed a vision in gold before her hopeful partners obscured her.

"Pray, what is the particular enthusiasm about?" he asked his aunt lightly. Lady Randall glanced toward the door, then looked up at him sharply.

"Now, Hugh, I will *not* have you flirt with Janet's innocent young friends!" she said severely. Then her eyes softened—she was very fond of her dashing young nephew and secretly found it hard to believe that he was really so wicked. "And that girl, Phyllida Chase, is not only my lawyer's daughter but is like to be the toast of Bath this spring. Heaven knows, she has enough suitors already and her poor mother is plagued with the migraine and vapors from worrying about her without having a scandalous creature like *you* adding to their number!" She tapped his arm firmly with her fan.

Sir Hugh laughed, "Dear Aunt Randall, do not take on so! I swear that young maidens scarce out of the schoolroom bore me to distraction. I merely wondered what little honeypot drew such a rush of young men, that is all."

"Well—stay near me, I want to introduce you to Lady Frensham."

"Yes, Aunt," he said meekly, his eyes twinkling.

Miss Smith, creeping into the ballroom, saw that her charge was suitably surrounded by harmless young men, so she gladly joined another chaperone, with whom she often whiled away the hours on duty by exchanging embroidery patterns and snippets of gossip.

Phyllida was whirled on to the floor first by young Lord Swinton, who gazed down at her so ardently her heart sank—he would surely be the next young man to go down on one knee and Mamma would have very serious vapors if she turned down *two* titled husbands within a week. She did her best not to meet his eyes, letting her glance stray round the other dancers.

Suddenly, brown eyes met green across the ballroom,

for Sir Hugh Abingdon had persuaded Lady Randall to take the floor with him. Phyllida felt a fluttering of her heart—a feeling she had begun to despair of, yet now, for a second, it made her quite dizzy. For Sir Hugh the sparkling, vivacious eyes came as a shock. So *this* was the young beauty he had lightly described as a "honeypot"! Vainly he tried to follow his aunt's conversation, for she talked to her partners rather than actually danced with them, but his concentration kept wandering. In spite of his avowal that young girls interested him not at all, this one—this Phyllida Chase—was the most glorious creature he had ever seen and there would be no rest until he met her. Hopefully her voice might prove high and grating, her talk inane—better still, perhaps the teeth behind those enchanting lips would be unsightly through decay—an affliction common amongst the aristocracy, since sweetmeats and pastries were so popular.

But how could such a meeting be achieved? His aunt had most firmly set her face against any such thing. His bad reputation must be a great embarrassment to her on this the evening of her daughter's birthday cotillion. Cousin Janet! Dear, plain Cousin Janet should provide the answer!

"You will not object if I dance with my cousin on her birthday will you, Aunt Randall?" he asked innocently. "I pose no danger to her, since we are related, and it seems only civil to pay her such a harmless attention!"

"Of course I have no objection, you silly boy," exclaimed Her Ladyship indulgently. By asking her permission it seemed as though her nephew had taken her stern warning to heart. "In fact I should be going about my duties as hostess instead of gallivanting round the ballroom with you! The poor old Duke and Duchess look positively hungry, so I shall take them into the buffet for an early supper before all the young people crowd in."

Sir Hugh smiled inwardly—his plan grew better and better.

Janet herself was overcome with blushes when her

16

handsome, wicked cousin bowed before her and requested the honor of a dance. She dismissed her callow, would-be partner without a second thought, for Sir Hugh, secretly, had become her idol—the more so for being far beyond her reach.

He was extremely charming and attentive and only laughed sympathetically when her feet failed to execute an intricate step.

"Pray don't apologize, Cousin—this is your *birthday!* Do you not know that tonight you can do no wrong? Why, if you choose to send a partner sprawling on the floor it will surely be hailed as a great jape. A birthday queen's comment on his dancing." His voice was so affectionate and his smile so warm that, from then on, Janet managed to dance much better. As the music drew toward the end he said:

"I believe—from your mother—that Miss Phyllida Chase is a very old childhood companion of yours. Do you think, on that score, that I may be introduced to her? Oh," he added quickly, "do not think that I find her particularly pretty, for your qualities shine far more brightly—your beauty comes from within, Cousin, and many worthy men will see this before long, I promise you. But if she is a lifelong friend since your childhood, it seems only right that I should pay her my respects— I *am* your eldest cousin, remember."

Janet was too bemused by then to recognize the ruse.

"I have warned her about you," she smiled, with an attempt at coquetry, "so an introduction can do no harm."

When the music stopped, Phyllida sensed that Janet and Sir Hugh were coming toward her. She glanced quickly across to where Miss Smith had been sitting, to find that she was walking away toward the buffet. Nor was Lady Randall anywhere in sight. Her pulse was racing but she deliberately turned to one of her admirers and began teasing him lightly.

"By my faith, Sir Anthony, I cannot believe that you

fell off your horse out hunting last week! Tell me it is a tale put about by friends jealous of your horsemanship."

The youth flushed with pleasure. "I—I *did* catch my boot in the stirrup but, you see, it was like this . . ." The long, dull rigmarole—dull to Phyllida, who took no interest in riding at all—was never to be told, for at that moment Janet caught her arm.

"My dear, my cousin *insists* on meeting you," she giggled, her small, pale eyes darting from side to side like a frantic guinea pig at such daring indiscretion. "So, may I present him? Sir Hugh Abingdon, this is my friend, Miss Phyllida Chase."

Phyllida held out her hand very formally but her smile was bewitching and showed perfect, white teeth. Sir Hugh lost his head a little at finding her even more flawless at close quarters and, deliberately misinterpreting her outstretched hand, took it firmly in his own and drew her into the dance that was just beginning.

Her eyes laughed up at him. "That was extremely wicked of you! I had promised this dance to Jonathan Bowles." Her voice was soft and musical, so he had only one slender branch to cling to before falling headlong in love with her—that her conversation would prove girlish and silly. It didn't. Instead of giggling over petty gossip and frills and furbelows, she asked about his travels and really listened to his replies while dancing like an angel in his arms.

Dear Heaven, this was a folly of the most fatal kind, one part of his mind insisted. For him a serious infatuation was out of the question—a threat to his entire lifestyle; he had skillfully avoided losing his heart to some of the most beautiful women in Europe, so how could he be ensnared by a girl of eighteen? A provincial lawyer's daughter whose horizon stretched no wider than the city of Bath? And yet . . .

As they passed the musicians' gallery Sir Hugh looked up and made an almost imperceptible sign to the leader, who smiled knowingly—he would indeed extend this dance awhile longer.

Phyllida's heart was also in turmoil in spite of her outward calm. It was *unthinkable* that she should be in love with a notorious rake and a wastrel. He was merely dancing with her out of politeness and probably longing for one of his worldly mistresses. Besides, she would certainly never see him again after tonight, so she must curb the wayward heart that already ached to stay in his arms forever.

When the music was approaching the extended finale Sir Hugh made up his mind.

"I must see you again," he said abruptly. There was such a strange note in his voice that Phyllida looked up in concern. Immediately he smiled apologetically, his brown eyes mocking himself. "Forgive me—that was a *most* ungracious way to express myself! The truth is that my Aunt Randall makes me very nervous! She thinks I am a wolf amongst defenseless lambs here tonight and fears me dancing with anyone under eighty! She believes the very worst rumors that have been spread about me."

Phyllida opened her eyes very wide, though they glinted wickedly, "You mean *none* of them is true, Sir Hugh? La! what a disappointment!" She laughed lightly. "I had thought to boast of having danced with the most dangerous man in all Europe . . ."

There were only a few moments left before the music stopped and he would have to relinquish her:

"Please, Miss Chase, I am serious. I cannot ask you to dance again or tongues would wag; but I should very much like to know you better before I have to leave Bath in two days' time. Will you not take tea with me tomorrow? Perhaps at the Cumberland Tea Rooms where we can talk quietly without being disturbed."

Absurdly, she felt somehow betrayed. She had so nearly lost her heart to him, feeling sure that he was strong, noble and not a rake at all. But he was, indeed, out for nothing more than yet another flirtation with a young girl in the shadowy corners of a little-used tearoom.

As they faced each other, clapping automatically at the end of the dance, she looked at him frankly.

"I will take tea with you on one condition—that we meet at the Grand Pump Room Hotel at four o'clock." She saw a flicker of dismay in his eyes so she went on deliberately: "If you are *really* innocent of all the rumors then surely you will not be afraid to meet me publicly, in front of all the *ton?*" It was a challenge.

He smiled. "I am not in the least afraid, I swear! I had thought only to protect *your* reputation from unpleasant gossip. But if such independence amuses you I will certainly be at the Pump Room at four."

He escorted her back to Janet and with a curt "Thank you," he strolled away. Phyllida was suddenly troubled as she watched him go, her defiance crumbling rapidly. What was she to believe? Her heart, that insisted he was good, or Janet's tales of his loose living? And why had she chosen the Grand Pump Room of all places? She had been there for tea once with her mother, and the high-pitched chatter as a hundred or so members of the *ton* devoured cream cakes and gossip had given her quite a headache.

Mentally she defended herself. "I shall see at once from the way people look at him whether he is true or false," she thought.

Hugh, wishing he had had a few more minutes to dissuade her from her foolish plan—which would hurt him not at all but might well damage Phyllida—sighed philosophically. She had bewitched him tonight in her golden, diaphanous gown made even more magical by the light of candles. But in daylight the spell would break —*must* break. Phyllida Chase would appear in her true colors as a very beautiful but very ordinary young lady of Bath, and no memories would linger to haunt him. Yes, the Grand Pump Room would do as well as anywhere else for the purpose.

Phyllida could not sleep that night. Fortunately Miss Smith had not seen her dancing with Sir Hugh Abingdon, so, to her mind, the evening had been most proper—even enjoyable, for she had daringly partaken of a little wine at supper. And the elderly Miss Smith had—with relish—enjoyed every detail that another chaperone had heard about a dastardly villain called Sir Hugh Abingdon, whom they could actually *see in person* in that respectable ballroom. How devilishly handsome he was, to be sure! Oh, the poor, poor ladies whom he had deceived with his wicked wiles! They shivered every time his tall, elegant figure strolled past their chairs. Yet, in the secret places of each spinster's heart lurked a tiny pang of envy—how dangerously exciting it must be to be wooed by such a dashing rogue . . . but such evil thoughts were quickly dismissed.

So, while Miss Smith fell innocently to sleep, encased in iron virtue, Phyllida lay wide-eyed and restless in the dark. *Why* had she insisted on the Grand Pump Room Hotel? As she thought of the cool strength of Sir Hugh's hand on hers, the set of his chin and the vivid intelligence in his dark eyes, to put him to such a frivolous test seemed despicable. And what did the uninformed opinion of the narrow-minded matrons of Bath matter anyway? They would no more know the truth about this brilliant, much-traveled man than his younger cousin Janet.

"Whether he regards me as just another light flirtation or not, I am in love with Sir Hugh Abingdon," said Phyllida aloud, seeking strength and comfort from the sound of her own voice in the haunting silence around her. She had always known that no ordinary man could capture her heart. The young men who courted her so ardently were mere puppets, seeking no adventures more dangerous than the hunting field and sporting the latest fads of Beau Brummell to prove their modernity.

But Sir Hugh . . .

He had thought only of her—trying to protect her

from his reputation by suggesting a quiet, little-used tea-room. Yet she had insisted on a parrot-house of high-pitched gossip—a place where every word between them would have to be spoken loudly if it was to be heard at all—and heard it most certainly would be by occupants of nearby tables and avidly passed on, with embellishments, to others further away.

In dire remorse Phyllida tossed and turned. Having at last met a man who stirred her heart, she had deliberately done her best to ensure that they would never meet again.

Dawn had broken before she fell into an uneasy sleep.

Next morning Mrs. Chase, still pale after her attack of migraine, was wholly taken up with household affairs, for her husband had ordered a dinner party that night for eight of his most prosperous clients, including a duke and duchess high in the royal favor. So she did not notice her daughter's heavy eyelids (which actually enhanced her green eyes) when Phyllida said:

"If I may take Miss Smith for about an hour, I am bidden to tea by a friend of Lady Randall's at the Grand Pump Room Hotel at four o'clock. We shall be back in plenty of time to help with the menu cards and flowers, Mamma." Mrs. Chase agreed abstractedly.

But her brother was more perceptive.

"Well, my sleepy-eyed goddess, what in thunder could have happened at a formal cotillion to shake your poise?" His voice was amused yet affectionate.

Phyllida's troubled eyes met his candidly. "I believe that I have fallen in love, Gareth, and if I have, then I've made the most abominable mess of it!"

At once he was in tune with her mood, for he realized that his sister was deeply troubled.

"Tell me about it."

She did, sparing herself nothing. It was such a relief

to have one person whom she trusted absolutely and who would always be on her side, no matter how foolish she had been. At the end Gareth thought for a few moments, then said:

"I think you have done the right thing, Phyllida. I must confess I have never met Sir Hugh Abingdon since I find social circles so boring compared with the company of artists and writers, but I have heard of him. No, I am sure you are wise to challenge him to the Grand Pump Room because one of two things will happen: either he will funk turning up at all—in which case you will know that the worst rumors are true; or else he will admire your courage at risking your own reputation, and be there. In that case it will prove that he is, at least, gallant and brave—worthy of your feelings, in fact."

"Oh, Gareth—how comforting you are! Yet I am afraid, I must admit . . . I feel," she hesitated. "I feel that he meant it seriously when he suggested a quiet tearoom, that he really *wanted* us to talk quietly and *not* start a passing flirtation. Why did I judge him so cruelly without proof?"

"My dear girl, a man with his reputation will respect you for wanting to learn the truth—to run the gamut of the tongues in Bath—*and* their lifted eyebrows! From what you have told me Sir Hugh is not a man to admire a young girl who cringes in corners to avoid gossip but a girl with spirit who is prepared to defy it as he does."

"I have never felt fear before. Oh, I wish *you* were coming with me instead of Miss Smith!"

Gareth burst out laughing. "Oh, Phyllida! You really *are* in a taking, aren't you? I should have to share your table—be treated as a gooseberry yet on equal terms with him and so spoil any conversation he may wish to have with you. No, Miss Smith can be placed firmly out of earshot and rewarded by a slice of rich fruit cake. My advice —if you heed it—is to go to your tryst looking as beautiful as you can and sail through that sea of ill-natured women

23

with your head held high, smiling regally as you pass. Just remember my sketch of you as an Amazon—they were true fighters and so are you."

Much of her color had returned and her eyes were regaining their brilliance. "I will do my best, Gareth— I promise."

Chapter
Two

Miss Smith was pleased by the prospect of tea at the fashionable Grand Pump Room Hotel and, in honor of the occasion, she added a bunch of glossy cherries to the two artificial roses on her gray bonnet. She even chattered a little in the carriage on the way.

"You say you are to meet a relative of Lady Randall?" she asked Phyllida. "How pleasant that will be. Some titled cousin, I don't doubt."

The unconscious humor of this remark helped Phyllida to control the nervousness that threatened to overwhelm her. Miss Smith's face would be a sight to see when, instead of some noble matron adorned with pearls and escorting a young daughter, Sir Hugh Abingdon waited to greet her!

Only, *would he be there?*

For a moment Phyllida felt herself torn between a longing that he would be and a cowardly hope that he might not. Then she braced herself, remembering Gareth's heartening words and the memory of his sketch of her as an Amazon. She was practically certain that she was in love with Sir Hugh and if it proved true, then this was only a skirmish compared to the battles that lay ahead.

Head high she sailed into the famous hotel, followed a ritual two paces behind by the shadowy Miss Smith. Smiling porters and lackeys bowed her on her way to the

Tea Lounge in mute tribute to her beauty. The cacophony of many female voices, almost drowning the four-piece orchestra, met her at least fifty yards from the ornate glass doorway.

The Tea Lounge was Regency-Oriental in style. Potted palms were mingled amongst the tables in white wrought-iron urns, while giant aspidistras lurked in the corners. Prints of Chinese and Japanese murals hung on the walls and the roof was composed of heavily leaded glass panes almost covered by an artificial vine. The defeated orchestra sat on a small dais surrounded with ferns; although it was only four o'clock the lady cellist was already perspiring heavily in her vain efforts to make her solos audible.

When Phyllida entered there was a momentary pause in conversation as a sea of flowered hats and bonnets turned in her direction, and murmurs of approval could be heard quite distinctly:

"The Chase girl! Such a charming young creature . . ."

"By my faith, she will be the beauty of the season!"

"Such *sensible* parents, m'dear . . ."

"They say she will marry young Lord Swinton during the summer—such a suitable match, don't you agree?"

Phyllida deserved the praises—the last she might hear for a long time. Her gown was of emerald faille, the exact color of her eyes, covered by a matching redingote of heavier ribbed silk adorned by a small ermine collar and exaggerated ermine cuffs. On her golden hair perched a jaunty cap of ermine and, since the early spring weather was still chilly, she carried a small muff of the same fur with a bunch of fresh violets pinned to it.

Her courage held as she moved through the crowded room but—suppose Sir Hugh were not there? What would be said if she settled to a small table accompanied only by her drab chaperone?

Then, in the furthest corner, she saw him rising to

welcome her. He had secured a secluded table for two partly screened by greenery. As she caught sight of him her breath caught in her throat—he seemed even taller and more glamorous than the night before; and Sir Hugh, having quite made up his mind that Phyllida by day would prove to be no more than an ordinarily pretty girl who couldn't possibly obsess him, was stunned as he watched her progress through the crowded lounge. She moved with such graceful poise, knowing that she was the center of interest, and she seemed ten times more beautiful than he remembered.

As he moved forward to take her hand, a muted gasp ran through the assembled ladies and a momentary silence fell as they watched the handsome pair greeting each other. Miss Smith went further than gasping. With a shocked expression she moved to Phyllida's side and spoke harshly.

"We cannot stay, Phyllida—it is—it is *unthinkable* for you to take tea with such a companion! Why, I swear your poor mother would have a heart seizure if she were here—we must leave *immediately*."

Sir Hugh stepped smoothly into the breach with his most charming smile. "Pray do not distress yourself, dear lady. Naturally, I assumed that Miss Chase would be chaperoned—as is only proper—and I have made arrangements that I trust you will approve." His smile and his deep, courteous tone mesmerized Miss Smith and she allowed herself to be placed at a very small table close by that already held a most tempting three-tiered silver cake stand offering hot buttered toast wrapped in a snowy napkin and more rich cream cakes than had ever been set before her in her life. Although managing to keep a severe expression of disapproval, she succumbed to temptation. Surely, nothing scandalous could pass between her charge and Sir Hugh in such a public place?

This slight contretemps banished Phyllida's nervousness. As she took her place opposite Sir Hugh and well-tipped waiters in white gloves hurried to supply their every whim (after all, Sir Hugh *was* highy favored by the Prince), she laughed.

"Goodness, it is all such *fun!* And, I declare, I was frightened to death all the way here!"

"Of the social tongues—or of me?" Sir Hugh asked blandly, still vainly trying to curb his emotions as he noticed her slightly shadowed eyes, which touched his heart with tenderness.

"Both, I believe," Phyllida answered honestly. "I wished I had accepted your invitation to a quiet tearoom after all—and I feared you might not be here. It was so silly of me to offer you such an unwelcome challenge. Oh," she added swiftly, "I would not have blamed you for not coming at all!"

"Surely you were not anxious about *my* reputation?" his eyes teased her gently. "Have you not heard that it is deplorable?"

"Yes, Janet warned me most thoroughly before we met but . . ."

"You do not believe it? Not wholly?" Suddenly his expression was earnest, almost pleading, and Phyllida met his eyes frankly for a moment before she answered slowly:

"No. Oh, I'm sure you have had many adventures," she added, "but my brother tells me that most men in society have and that they are of little consequence."

"Your brother sounds as nice as you, Phyllida—if I may make so bold? 'Miss Chase' sounds so very formal," he said. "Besides, yours is such a charming name. Now, pray tell me about this brother of yours . . ." He wanted to shift the conversation away from themselves, for, if Phyllida continued to look at him with such glowing favor in her lovely eyes, he might throw caution to the winds. As two waiters hovered deferentially, setting the tea service in front of Phyllida and placing covered silver dishes of hot toast and muffins on the table, she spoke willingly of Gareth. Nearby ladies, just out of earshot, asked the waiters in whispers what the outrageous couple were talking about and seemed disappointed at the harmless replies.

While Phyllida poured tea and amusingly sketched Gareth for Sir Hugh, he was only half listening—his common sense was making desperate efforts to reassert itself. For this unique, glorious emotion (like nothing he had experienced in all his twenty-six years) *could not be*. He was not free to marry or take any woman too seriously, and he had never felt the need to explain his inner life or his actions to anyone. Now, watching Phyllida's slim, dexterous hands ministering to his every need—cream? milk? sugar?—he knew an alarming and highly dangerous longing to stop all pretense and tell her everything. To counter this he steadily strove to compare her with all the beautiful women who *were* permissible if he wanted to take advantage of them: Joséphine in France, whose vivid, piquant charm was almost irresistible; the statuesque Orieta in Rome, perfect as a Michelangelo sculpture; lively, laughing Consuela in Madrid, with her burnished black hair and languishing dark eyes ... These and many more he conjured up to help him, but, compared to the glowing English girl facing him, they were as ephemeral as ghosts.

He was in love. And it was a forbidden love.

Phyllida sensed his subtle withdrawal and, although puzzled, did her best to help him. He was in full control of his voice and his conversation (which was witty and filled with delightful anecdotes of his travels), but it was not in his power to hide the expression in his dark eyes, which told her, with every glance, that he loved her. That was enough, and, although she followed his lead in talking of impersonal matters, she loved and admired him all the more. He was indeed honorable, as her heart already knew, and felt the need to clear his name before declaring himself.

So an hour passed in a moment as their voices talked and laughed, yet their eyes spoke a very different language of which they were far more aware. To Phyllida it was delicious, dangerous and full of promise. For Sir Hugh it spelled heartbreak. He must not see her again, although her tender emerald eyes would haunt his dreams for all time.

Miss Smith approached them, a fleck of chocolate from a final, unwise cream-eclair still in one corner of her mouth.

"It is five o'clock," she told Phyllida sternly. "You promised your mother to be back in time to help her with the preparations for her dinner party!"

Guiltily, Phyllida rose. Surely she and Sir Hugh had scarce been together for more than five minutes? Eagerly she turned to him.

"Thank you for a most charming afternoon," she said formally, her smile belying the formality, which was for Miss Smith's benefit. "I hope we may meet again before you leave Bath?" She knew that it was unmaidenly for her to say such a thing, but surely she had not mistaken the message in his eyes?

To her dismay he held out his hand with a remote smile and answered, "My dear Miss Chase—you are free to enjoy life but I have much to do before I leave England for a short visit abroad."

It had the effect of a douche of iced water. Had she imagined it all? Was she only, after all, just one more pretty, insignificant girl with whom he might pass a brief hour of gentle dalliance?

Tears threatened to fill her eyes, and she strode swiftly through the Tea Lounge—curious eyes following her now with condemnation—praying that she might reach the privacy of her carriage before emotion overwhelmed her.

In fact it was to be some time before Phyllida could indulge in the release of tears. The moment they were inside the carriage Miss Smith turned waspishly on her charge.

"Well! I hope you're thoroughly ashamed of yourself,

young lady!" she snapped, a touch of dyspepsia after her rich tea adding venom to her tongue. "I declare, you won't be the beauty of Bath now, but the scandal of it! I vow none of the gracious ladies present this afternoon will invite you to their houses again after such a—a *wanton* display! How could you, a mere girl, agree to meet such a wicked, *wicked* man as Sir Hugh Abingdon? And in public, too?"

"I know nothing of his 'wickedness,' and you yourself enjoyed his hospitality to the full, I noticed," retorted Phyllida caustically. Miss Smith flushed angrily at the taunt, then thought of a proper answer.

"*I* know what is seemly," she replied with hauteur. "I would not sink to making a common scene in public, so I was forced to swallow my wrath for the time being— *and* his cakes, although I swear I shall suffer for that, they were mighty rich. When your parents hear of your escapade, Miss—and they shall, just as soon as I have removed my bonnet and pelisse—they will soon have you off your high horse and soundly rapped for your goings-on!"

Phyllida was shocked by this heartlessness.

"Oh, no, I *pray* you do not trouble Mamma with this matter until after the dinner party!" she pleaded urgently. "You know she has scarce recovered from the migraine and surely your story can wait just a few hours? This evening is most important to my father too, and I would not have them distressed beforehand for the world!"

"You should have thought of that before being so rash," and Miss Smith's thin mouth closed triumphantly like a trap.

With difficulty Phyllida swallowed her pride and her deep anger. "*Please,* Miss Smith! I swear that I have made no future assignations with Sir Hugh, besides he is far too honorable—whatever you may think—to have suggested such a thing!"

The carriage drew up at the door and Phyllida got out quickly. This last statement was all too true and it brought back her wretched heartache. If he had wanted to meet her again so much, why, *why* had he rejected any idea of seeing her even once more?

But there was no time to indulge in melancholy. As she entered the front door, an ominous sound of several feminine voices greeted her from the drawing room. Surely, surely none of the ladies taking tea at the Grand Pump Room had reached here already?

But they had. Her mother had heard Phyllida's carriage arrive and threw open the door, her face anguished.

"Phyllida! Pray step in here immediately; I swear I can scarce *believe* what I have heard!"

There was no escape.

Phyllida, summoning all her pride, went in to confront at least six accusing faces, harsh with condemnation under their highly fashionable bonnets. Mrs. Chase, distressed and angry, said:

"I want the truth, Phyllida. You know that all these kind ladies are my trusted friends of many years and have only spoken out of a deep sense of duty. Did you or did you not take tea alone with Sir Hugh Abingdon this afternoon?"

"Miss Smith accompanied me," Phyllida's voice was defensive.

"Ah! But she did not share your table," Mrs. Claverdon wagged a reproving finger. "That man had had her placed quite out of earshot, I swear."

"Surely a conversation at tea can do no harm?" asked Phyllida coolly, although her heart was filling with dread. These middle-aged members of the *ton*, including Mamma, wielded a terrifying power over young girls, and they were implacable, refusing to hear reason.

"You are being extremely rude to your betters," said Mrs. Chase. "Besides, you deceived *me*." Her voice suddenly threatened tears at the thought. "I declare you led me to believe you would be meeting a relative of dear Lady Randall's this afternoon."

"Sir Hugh Abingdon is her nephew, and I declare that he is a very fine gentleman indeed!"

"La, girl, so he has beguiled you as he has so many other unfortunate, stupid girls!" retorted Lady Smythe acidly—and with reason, since her own daughter had mooned about the house and frequently succumbed to the vapors for a whole week after dancing twice with the wretched reprobate.

Phyllida felt her color rising; she probably *had* allowed herself to be deceived by Sir Hugh's charm and was still smarting under his refusal to fix another meeting, but the upshot of so much disapproval was merely to crystallize her certainty that she loved him.

"I declare his conversation is not only highly proper but most—most intellectual!"

During the frozen silence that greeted this outburst Miss Smith, who had been listening outside the door, went up to her room highly satisfied. Now she could curry favor with Mrs. Chase by, most considerately, not making her own report until after the dinner party. "I would not distress you, dear Mrs. Chase, knowing you have been unwell," she decided she would say—and then she would pour the final venom that should cook Sir Hugh Abingdon's goose for good!

"Go to your room, Phyllida," commanded her mother in a voice shaken with emotion and shame. "You will be the talk of Bath from your foolish actions and have quite broken my heart, I swear."

Phyllida left without another word. Had she stayed to hear more taunts about Sir Hugh she must surely have burst out with the truth of her feelings. Besides, she was on the verge of stormy tears.

The dinner party that night was a success, in spite of a slight air of abstraction in the hostess. John Chase was highly satisfied and a little mellow after liberal glasses of his own excellent claret followed by port. Now he wanted to finish his cigar in peace, relishing the flattering remarks of his prominent clients, and then go to bed.

But his wife would have none of it. Instead of departing upstairs, she hovered about, fidgeting with the ornaments until Mr. Chase realized that he must have been remiss in some way. Then he remembered that she must be fretting about Phyllida, whom, she had declared with apologies, was not herself this evening and so unable to be at dinner.

"Anxious about the gal, eh?" he asked kindly. "Why not send for Pinkerton if she's peaky—ease your mind."

His wife whirled round and her expression made him quail. A scene at this hour would ruin his digestion.

"Phyllida is *not* ill at all! No, things are more serious than that—she has brought shame and dishonor on us all, I swear, by her outrageous behavior this afternoon! Worse still, she is not at all repentant; indeed, she offended some of the most influential members of the *ton* here on her return! Oh, we shall never be able to show our faces in society again!" Her face crumpled and she burst into noisy, childlike sobs as the restraint she had exercised all evening finally broke under the strain.

Mr. Chase, who dreaded women's tears, lumbered to his feet and dabbed ineffectually at her stout, heaving shoulders, suppressing his heavy sighs with difficulty. What a dismal end to a delightful evening.

"Now, now, m'dear, calm yourself I pray. Sit down quietly and tell me all about it. Phyllida is a good girl and I'm sure twas only a peccadillo. After a good sleep you will have forgot it by morning!"

"*Peccadillo!*" Sheer anger stemmed her tears and Mrs. Chase rounded on her husband in a way that positively alarmed him.

Bitterly she poured out every detail of Phyllida's wickedness—embellished by her own imagination now, and added to by Miss Smith's report given as soon as the last guest had left.

Mr. Chase listened, his brow furrowing, until his wife ended with a flourish:

"I declare that, before we know it, Phyllida will elope with that—that wanton wastrel, that dastardly villain! Poor Miss Smith is in a dreadful taking and swears she dare not be responsible for the girl outside these walls! Something must be done—*immediately*."

"Hm. Yes . . ." But what? He could scarcely call young Sir Hugh out to a duel at his age. Fortunately a solution had occurred to Mrs. Chase while she was dressing for dinner.

"We must send her away—out of England altogether." Her tone was harsh. "She refuses all the suitable young men who come begging for her hand. Well, Europe is packed with young princelings—perhaps she will consider *that* rank more worthy of her! At least she will be out of reach of this Sir Hugh Abingdon."

Mr. Chase's heart sank—surely it was too drastic and, besides, he could scarce bear the thought of losing his beloved daughter. Not a man much given to emotions, Phyllida received all the love he was capable of giving.

"But, she cannot be packed off, bag and baggage in five minutes!" he protested. "Where would the poor child go?"

"It is a simple matter—she shall go to her godmother, Tante Emilie, in Paris."

"'Tante Emilie'?" John Chase looked blank.

"Oh, surely you remember my friend Emily Barton? She married the old Comte Du Roy some twenty-odd years ago and put on absurd French airs directly she discovered that he was rich and taking her to a splendid house which was almost untouched by the Revolution. We correspond now and then, and she holds grand salons and thinks she is all the rage! It was her idea that the children should call her Tante Emilie—such foolishness— but she has a good heart and I shall write to her this very night," ended Mrs. Chase defiantly.

Mr. Chase knew that he was beaten, but he put up a last defense.

"Come, Mary, you are too hasty. At least sleep on the matter and I insist on talking to Phyllida myself in the morning. She is no longer a child, you know, and must be consulted first."

" 'Consulted'? A girl with no sense of propriety or decency whatever? I swear that I will not be responsible for her in the future—and Miss Smith refuses absolutely. I am going to write to Emily this minute! The mail packets to France are excellent and all should be settled within the week!" She left the room, determination in every step.

Mr. Chase sighed and sat down by the now dying fire. His earlier pleasure in the evening lay in ashes, too. Helplessness was a stranger to him normally, but he felt it now. All the same, he *would* talk to Phyllida in the morning.

Phyllida had spent a wretched evening alone in her room. And just when she needed her brother's presence so desperately, Gareth was out, attending a party with his friends. Usually her buoyant spirits could overcome anything, but not tonight; wherever her thoughts turned there seemed no gleam of hope anywhere. Sir Hugh cared not a jot for her, that was clear; her freedom, limited enough as it was, would surely be curtailed even more by her mother, and Miss Smith would be intolerable, suspicious of every glance, every shadow.

At last, worn out, she fell into a heavy sleep.

She woke unrested with a sense of dread and depression possessing her. Mamma would have recited her misdeeds to Papa last night, and she wondered what judgment was waiting for her downstairs. She could not enlist Gareth's help so early, since, after a party, he slept late, so she dressed slowly, putting off the evil moment when she must open the dining room door and learn her fate.

Mrs. Chase had risen early, too, tired though she was and with another migraine threatening, for she was determined that her husband should have no chance to sympathize with Phyllida, nor find means of preventing her banishment to Paris. To make doubly sure of this she had indeed written at great length to Emilie Du Roy the night before and sent her maid, posthaste at seven o'clock this morning, to catch the mail.

Mr. Chase had slept not at all, troubled with dyspepsia from the mild excesses at dinner and a mind torn and tormented over the problem of Phyllida. *Must* she go so far away? Had her behavior really been as black as his wife claimed? He could not believe it, since, although she was a trifle headstrong, she was also sensible and a most dutiful daughter. When he reached the dining room his heart sank to find Mrs. Chase already ensconced behind the silver teapot, her face set. He was genuinely fond of his wife, but in that moment he almost disliked her.

Minutes later Phyllida came in looking wan, her green eyes apprehensive. She bade her parents a grave "Good morning" and took her place at the table—waiting.

Her father opened his mouth to speak, but Mrs. Chase was before him.

"Well, Phyllida, I trust you have had time to reflect on your disgraceful behavior?"

"Yes, Mamma." Then a ghost of her normal spirit asserted itself, "Although I swear I had no intention of making you so angry, and I did no harm."

"No *harm!*" Her mother was outraged. Her tone grew sarcastic. "You have not only placed yourself, but most likely your father and myself as well, beyond the pale of respectable society! You should have heeded Miss Smith's orders to return home immediately, as soon as she saw that this—this rake would be receiving you alone!"

Both Mr. Chase and Phyllida started to speak, but Mrs. Chase was in full spate.

"However, we shall have no cause to worry in future. Your father and I must restore our reputations as soon as we can, so we are sending you to France—to Paris—to stay for an indefinite period with Tante Emilie, the Comtesse Du Roy. My letter is already on its way to her and, we hope, you can set off within the week. *That* should put a stop to your wayward pranks! The French aristocracy are extremely strict and you will be well out of the clutches of this odious Sir Hugh Abingdon."

Phyllida gasped. She had expected severe restrictions—even a punishment of some kind—but not this, not banishment from home almost without warning. Her father was gazing at her helplessly, so she knew he had failed to champion her and could not stop the sentence. At last she said, in a small voice:

"But, Mamma, Sir Hugh was the soul of honor and chivalry. He has asked for no further meeting with me, nor will there be one." Then her voice broke, "Must I really be sent so far away, simply for taking tea for scarce an hour with a fine young man in full view of all the members of the *ton?* Oh, please, *please* do not deal so harshly with me. I have never been from home before, and I declare I have never even met Tante Emilie, even if she is my godmother."

"Arrangements are in hand already," said her mother firmly. Then, against her will, her heart melted a little; Phyllida *was* a constant anxiety, especially when she refused one fine suitor after another, but, in trouble, she could be a great comfort. However, she recalled the sour remarks of the ladies yesterday afternoon, and her resolution hardened.

"You cannot stay here in Bath," she said flatly, "and you have no one to blame but yourself. However, Tante Emilie is very much the thing in Paris, entertaining most lavishly and attending many important functions. She also has a son, Henri, who will doubtless escort you to balls until you make friends with other highborn families."

Had she not felt so tired, Phyllida might have felt a spark of excitement at the challenge and adventure of exploring a whole new world—a world Sir Hugh had already sketched vividly for her. And, as Mamma perhaps was unaware, he was just as likely to appear in Paris as in Bath. But that thought could not cheer her, since he would surely avoid her wherever their paths might cross. So all her reactions were against such ruthless uprooting.

"Mamma—I speak French poorly, and I declare undertaking the journey alone will be alarming." Suddenly she had a comforting idea. "If I *have* to go, at least will you send Gareth to accompany me? He longs to travel, I know and—and a brother's protection will reassure me."

" 'Gareth'?" Mrs. Chase was indignant. "I swear he is as wild as you? Indeed, I lay much of the blame for your wayward behavior at his door! Fortunately, I believe he will outgrow his tiresome ideas of becoming a painter and settle down well in Papa's firm as his brothers have. No, Miss Smith will be your companion and most vigilant chaperone!"

" 'Miss Smith'?" Phyllida was aghast. The thought of that narrowminded woman being at her side as she tried to enter a new life was the last straw. Vainly she protested, "Oh, Mamma, I *beg* you do not send her! Send anyone else—one of your maids, a new chaperone if needs be, but I pray you not to inflict Miss Smith on me. Besides, she heartily dislikes all foreigners—as she has often told me; being forced to leave home is punishment enough, but with her as my only companion it will be intolerable!"

At last Mr. Chase found a chance to speak, "Mary, surely you are being too stern? Since your heart is set on this plan, I trust you can find someone more congenial to Phyllida?"

"There will be no time," snapped his wife. "Besides, Miss Smith is thoroughly trustworthy, as she has proved, and will send regular reports to me on Phyllida's actions in Paris."

Phyllida stood up, her breakfast untouched. "So I am to be not only an exile but also a prisoner?" she said bitterly, going to the door. As she opened it she turned and looked back at her mother. "I wish I had *truly* done something to deserve it!"

"Well, I hope you are now satisfied," said Mr. Chase coldly when Phyllida had left them. "I shall send this Comtesse of yours a handsome sum so that my dear daughter shall be provided with every fal-lal she fancies." And he, too, went out.

In her heart Mrs. Chase was not a little shocked at herself. But she had made her decision, and now she must inform Miss Smith of the news.

Later, Phyllida told Gareth all that had happened, adding an earnest plea:

"I implore you to seek out Sir Hugh—he has only one more day in Bath; *please,* Gareth, tell him of my plight and see what he says? If he suggests a meeting I will go gladly—anywhere—for nothing can increase Mamma's cruel punishment now and . . ."

Her brother, deeply shocked by the news, looked at her in surprise. "Are you serious? Do you care for a man you scarcely know so deeply that you would have me chase after him? Where is your pride, Phyllida?"

She looked at him frankly, "I have none where he is concerned—I want with all my heart to see him once more."

"Very well, then." Gareth was very disturbed by the whole business and, in an effort at cheerfulness, he said, "I will try to do something outrageous myself so that Mamma may banish us together. I shall miss you sorely but I swear I will visit you at the first opportunity. Paris!" he grinned. " 'Tis ironic that you are being forced to go where I would go so willingly!"

"I know. But hurry, Gareth, I pray. It is almost noon and—and even if he does not want to meet me now, he travels widely and perhaps he will soon be in Paris. You should find him at Lady Randall's house, I believe."

Gareth wondered, as he made his way to Lady Randall's, what kind of man had had such an effect on his independent sister. He was not left long in doubt.

Fortunately Lady Randall and her daughter were out shopping. The butler showed him into the morning room, where Sir Hugh was pacing the floor lost in thought. As soon as he heard the name Chase he looked up and, for a moment, his fine dark eyes glowed, for he had thought of little but Phyllida since yesterday.

"I am mighty glad to meet you, Mr. Chase; your charming sister praises you highly." And he held out his hand.

Gareth liked him at once and his handshake was warm. Now he understood Phyllida's feelings and, if Sir Hugh Abingdon gave him any encouragement, he determined to help her. He came straight to the point while Sir Hugh listened quietly. When Gareth had finished, he said:

"I declare this is sad news for Miss Chase, but I feared something of the sort when she chose The Grand Pump Room, although I did not expect such severe measures. However, I believe she will come to like Paris, for it is a splendid city and extremely gay." His tone was detached, impersonal and Gareth knew that no further meeting would be suggested. However, at least Sir Hugh might send some encouraging message.

"In truth, Sir, I wish I were going in her place! But may I at least convey your good wishes for her journey— I swear I have never seen her in such low spirits."

These words struck Sir Hugh to the heart—the idea of radiant Phyllida cowed and frightened was unthinkable. But still, outwardly, he maintained a formal attitude. How well he had been trained, he thought bitterly—so well that, after six years of leading his mysterious, secret life, by now he could hide any sign of inner emotion.

"By all means, Mr. Chase. Pray give her my good wishes for this new life—I am only sorry that she is to be sent against her will. And reassure her that Paris will prove much to her liking."

And with that Gareth had to be content. The two

men again exchanged a firm handshake—which amounted to a dismissal on Sir Hugh's part—and Gareth retraced his steps homeward with a heavy heart, believing the man did not return Phyllida's feelings at all.

Miss Smith was in a bad humor throughout the packing and preparations for the dreaded journey, even though, as a final persuasion, Mrs. Chase had recklessly doubled her salary from 35 pounds a year to 70 pounds—an unprecedented amount for a lowborn chaperone. But life among the dreaded foreigners (whom, she was convinced, were both dishonest and spoke gibberish), as well as responsibility for Phyllida, overwhelmed her.

Phyllida, after Gareth's report of his interview with Sir Hugh, was apathetic and scarcely spoke, so Mrs. Chase, with the help of two maids, supervised her packing. It seemed the girl was to be gone for a very long time, since, once the portmanteaus and valises were finally locked, her bedroom was bare.

Her father and Gareth were to see her onto the steamer at Dover, traveling by coach and spending a night at an inn on the way. Even Gareth could not rouse her into lively conversation and, on a misty April morning with a steady drizzle falling, Phyllida, with tears in her eyes, embraced her dear father and brother and swiftly embarked for the unknown.

As the boat disappeared into the mist the two men strained their eyes to catch the very last whiff of smoke from the funnel. They had never been close until now, but Phyllida's departure formed a new bond between them. For both of them the loss seemed irreparable.

In spite of the weather, Phyllida stood at the rail straining her eyes for a last glimpse of England. Where, oh *where* was her dearest Hugh at this moment?

Chapter
Three

Although the Channel was choppy, Miss Smith, mindful of her big salary and the new pelisse embroidered with jet beads that Mrs. Chase had given her, for a time stayed grimly on deck while Phyllida watched England receding. Then seasickness overwhelmed her and, gripping Phyllida's arm, she said:

"We must adjourn to the Ladies' Lounge below; it is not seemly for ladies to remain out here."

Phyllida turned to protest. The motion of the sturdy little boat bothered her not at all and, in spite of her sense of desolation, she found being on the sea an exhilarating experience. But when she saw her chaperone's pinched, green face she followed without arguing. After all, Miss Smith was her only companion on this strange voyage into an unknown world, and illness always touched Phyllida's heart.

The companionway down into the body of the ship was narrow, so Phyllida urged Miss Smith to go first while she took a last look out over the sea. Suddenly she gasped. In the prow, staring toward France, stood a tall, lean figure in an elegant, caped traveling coat with a tall beaver hat pulled well forward. Surely, *surely* it was Hugh! Instantly her spirits rose and her heart beat faster. Was his presence accidental or was he secretly accompanying her? Making sure that she had a safe journey?

"Phyllida!" The querulous wail from below quickly reminded Phyllida of her duty and she descended, hating the heat and the smell of oil that rose to greet her, though the rhythmic beat of the engines—unnoticed on deck—merely echoed her own heart.

The Ladies' Lounge was already filled with sufferers, some prone on couches and others huddled in chairs while stewards in crisp white jackets hurried among them providing small tin basins, smelling bottles and glasses of water. Miss Smith subsided into the nearest chair and closed her eyes stoically; it was not her place to be sick in public. Phyllida did her best, dabbing the suffering forehead with eau de cologne sprinkled on her own handkerchief and sending a steward for water; but she knew that if she stayed longer in this airless atmosphere she, too, would feel ill. So, when Miss Smith appeared to be asleep, she hurried up on deck and into the blessed fresh air.

Would he still be there? One glance told her that the prow was deserted. Her search was fruitless. The elegant figure had vanished as though it had stepped off into thin air.

I am bound to see him when we land, she thought hopefully—every passenger would have to file down the gangway and he could not remain hidden then.

But it was not to be. As the mainland of France grew so near that it was possible to distinguish the houses and other buildings, a young ship's officer approached her and, with a small bow, asked:

"Miss Chase?"

"Why, yes," Phyllida was surprised.

"The captain sends his compliments, Miss, and asks that you and your companion come to his cabin."

"But why? Surely we are close to land. Besides Miss Smith is unwell and resting below in the lounge."

The young man smiled. "Perhaps I may escort you there first and then I will find the poor lady and bring her to join you. You are a very important passenger, Miss."

44

His smile changed to an engaging grin. "To be met like royalty, I believe."

Tante Emilie! Phyllida remembered her mother reading aloud a long letter from the Comtesse to which she had been too angry and heartsore to listen properly, but there *had* been mention of being met.

She was ushered into a small but cheerful cabin high on the bridge. It was empty and the officer explained that the captain was supervising the boat's safe landing, after which he departed to find Miss Smith.

Her spirits rising, Phyllida watched curiously through the large porthole as the boat was edged expertly into her berth by the teeming quayside. High-pitched excited voices jabbered in the now sunlit morning as blue-bloused porters and men with carriages or flies for hire jostled for position as the gangway went down. Beyond them coachmen in livery and groups of people meeting families or friends waited with more dignity. Everywhere there were large notices in French to guide passengers into the customs shed and the place to collect luggage.

As Miss Smith was brought in, a little unsteady, Phyllida turned a glowing face to her.

"Oh, look! Is it not wonderful? We truly are in France! I declare I can't understand one single word they are shouting down there but it is so exciting."

Miss Smith sat down heavily without attempting to look out.

"Mind you don't allow one of them to snatch your reticule, now—we're among thieves, Phyllida."

Phyllida's green eyes were dancing with suppressed laughter as the burly captain came in accompanied by a figure so grand in dark blue livery covered with gold braid that she wondered if she ought to drop a small curtsy. Instead, he swept off his cocked hat, bowed low from the waist and said:

"Welcome, Mam'selle. Zis way please," and, with scarce time to thank the captain, she and Miss Smith were borne grandly away through the people still waiting to go down the gangway as their escort merely brushed them aside. He led the ladies across the now hysterical quayside by the same maneuver, which caused many curious glances, and beyond to where a splendid coach was waiting, its glossy dark blue doors emblazoned with an enormous coat of arms.

As he moved to hand them in, Phyllida said, "But where is our luggage? We cannot leave without it."

"All is well, Mam'selle," he bowed again. "Pierre, fetch!"

Miss Smith was agitated. "What did I tell you, Phyllida? Thieves, that's what they all are. I swear we shan't see a single valise, much less the portmanteaus with all your beautiful gowns!"

"*Restez,* Madame," said the splendid footman (as he turned out to be). "*Tout va bien.*"

"Gibberish as well," snorted Miss Smith crossly as Phyllida persuaded her to lie back on the beautifully upholstered seat of the coach. "We should never have left England, I declare."

Phyllida felt her temper rising. "Really, Miss Smith—do at least *try* to enjoy being here now we are no longer at sea! I swear my Tante Emilie has been to great pains to make us welcome, sending this grand coach and men to look after us! The head footman, who has been so thoughtful and courteous, evidently understands some English. He will be extremely offended if you keep referring to the French as thieves!"

"Truth is truth," retorted Miss Smith primly, her thin lips pursed with righteousness, "and you are getting above yourself, Miss, criticizing your elders! I know what I know and hope I may be proved wrong—but I doubt it." She settled back more comfortably, closing her eyes. Phyllida looked at the thin, bigoted face and disliked her companion more than ever, but she made a firm resolution. She would *not* allow the tiresome woman to spoil one jot of this new adventure. With youthful resilence she pushed

46

homesickness and a lingering anger against her mother to the very back of her mind. She was going to enjoy every minute of this new country—and of the Paris that Sir Hugh had painted so vividly for her. Hugh! Her mouth curved in a tender smile. He *was* here, she felt sure of it, and if not he would be before long.

Suddenly the coachman whipped up the four handsome grays, the footmen sprang to their places behind, and, at a spanking pace, they bowled away through the narrow streets of Boulogne and out onto the highway to Paris.

Phyllida sat well forward, eager to see everything: the narrow, crooked houses, peasants in clogs, loose blouses, and baggy trousers, beating their donkeys out of the way of the grand equipage; the women, in wide, heavy skirts, their hair closely coiffed in white linen kerchiefs, carrying huge baskets of fruit and vegetables. Oh, it was all so different and exciting, even the air itself.

When they were out in the countryside, the highway often edged by avenues of swaying poplar trees, Phyllida fell to dreaming: How childish, how stupid she had been to allow Hugh's seeming indifference to hurt her! Why, he was only protecting her from more gossip in Bath, knowing that in Paris they could so soon be reunited. How chivalrous he was, how thoughtful for her welfare!

The country was flat and not very interesting and the midday sun made her sleepy, so, content and happy in her new faith in Hugh, Phyllida curled up as far from Miss Smith as possible and dozed.

Because they would not reach Paris before evening, after nearly three hours of fast driving the coach drew in to a wayside inn with extensive stables at the side. Again, the polite footman handed them out and led them into the low, white building. The long room was spotlessly clean, the floor spread with fresh rushes that smelled sweetly of spring. Small tables were covered with red and white checked cloths and each held a carafe of red wine that winked and glowed in the sunlight reflected from burnished copper pans hanging on the walls.

Madame herself came forward and dropped a low curtsy before smilingly indicating the best table. In rapid French the footman ordered *café au lait* and brioches before hurrying off to join his companions in the stable.

Miss Smith looked round with hauteur and sniffed. *"Wine* on the tables—and at this hour! Let's hope our driver does not partake or we shall never reach Paris alive! I must say this is *not* the kind of place we are used to, at all—make sure your cup is clean before you touch it, Phyllida."

Phyllida couldn't contain a ripple of laughter. "I think it's a glorious place—just like a farm Gareth and I used to visit with Papa when we were little."

Miss Smith continued to glare, but even she could find no fault with the delicious coffee accompanied by a foaming jug of hot milk and brioches fresh from the oven.

Soon they were on the road again, the gray horses replaced by a team of gleaming bays. To Phyllida's disappointment they did not drive through Paris, as Tante Emilie's mansion was in the Bois du Boulogne. It was too dark to see very much, but as they rounded the last curve in a wide driveway Phyllida drew in her breath with delight. The old, turreted house was ablaze with light like a castle in fairyland. As they drew up, the double doors were thrown wide by flunkies, and in the center stood a diminutive figure waving her small hands in excited welcome.

"Phyllida! *chérie*—come in, come in," cried Tante Emilie, in her fluting voice, excited as a child. But as Phyllida reached the top step, the glowing little face gave a comical grimace. "La, child, you are a giant—come down a little so that I may embrace you, I pray."

As Phyllida bent down, laughing, Tante Emilie kissed her ardently on both cheeks, then looked at her closely with deep approval. "Why did not your mother tell me that my goddaughter is now a great beauty? I expected a timid little English miss, dull as a mouse—but the *Bon Dieu* has sent me one to set all Paris by the ears! Come in, *chérie,* come in—you must meet my old Pierre, and my most beautiful son, Henri." She spoke rapidly, as one more used to speaking French, and her hands, never still, were even more eloquent than words. Now they waved and hurried Phyllida through into the Grand Salon, which was quite dazzling, since everything—even the furniture—was gilded, and the great chandeliers were reflected again and again in large, ornate mirrors bordered by gilt scrolls and cherubs.

In front of the marble fireplace stood two men, waiting a little uncertainly. However, like a puppet mistress, Tante Emilie gaily waved them into life. She made a strange contrast, indeed, to her solemn family. The old Comte, very tall, very bent, very elegant in a black velvet coat with diamond buttons, leaned heavily on a gold-topped cane, his white hair escaping from its ribbon into small wisps round his tired, gentle face. Phyllida liked him immediately.

"My dear child, you are most welcome," he said in a deep, soft voice. "And how pretty you are," he added smiling. Phyllida wondered if she should kiss him on the cheek, but Tante Emilie whirled her round excitedly to meet her "most beautiful son." Phyllida was too deeply shocked to remember her manners for a moment. Henri could not have been more than twenty but his face was the color of parchment, his pale blue eyes heavy-lidded and mouth solemn. He was dressed in a somber fashion—dark gray coat and breeches with no ornaments at all and a severe, starched white stock at the neck. He bowed gravely over her hand, making no attempt to kiss it, and said in a reedy voice, "I am pleased to meet you," with no enthusiasm at all.

Goodness, she thought, *what* a dull stick! and, with a

49

pang, she remembered Gareth and wished with all her heart that he was here. If Henri was destined to be her partner at balls in Paris, they would not be amusing at all.

"Now sit—sit," urged Tante Emilie gaily, regardless of the fact that Phyllida still wore her traveling bonnet and redingote. "In your honor we shall take a glass of wine, then your maid will have unpacked enough for you to dress for dinner."

"She is not my maid, Tante Emilie—she is my chaperone," said Phyllida anxiously, dreading Miss Smith's wrath at being treated like a servant. Tante Emilie burst into silvery laughter.

"La! Your mother sends you with a *chaperone* when, from now on, that role will be my pleasure? No, no, she will do very well here as your personal maid. I will arrange all, all."

"I—I don't think our luggage can have arrived yet," ventured Phyllida. "It was not on the coach with us."

Tante Emilie stared at her, round-eyed with amazement. "Not *arrived?* My dear child, it was installed in your suite at least one hour before you came!"

Phyllida wickedly longed to ask "By broomstick?" for the Comtesse seemed to possess magical powers, but she decided to rest a little and enjoy this extraordinary household to the full. Only the furniture had not been made for relaxation—rather for a museum: The handsome gold-velvet-covered seats were like boards, while the back of her chair was so upright and seemed so fragile she dared not lean back against it.

Wine was brought on a silver salver, glowing ruby in the crystal glasses. The two men raised theirs in a toast to the visitor and, before she had drained hers (for wine had not yet been allowed to her at home in Bath), Tante Emilie sprang up and held out her hand.

"Come—let me show you your suite. Tomorrow I shall inspect your wardrobe." She cast her blue eyes upward. "The English have taste—yes—but no chic! Fortunately, the materials will be excellent and my couturier will soon put matters right for you. In Paris chic is all!"

Tante Emilie swiftly dismissed Miss Smith's indignant protests at being classed as a ladies' maid, "But, *ma chère* Miss Smith, here in France the ladies' maid is considered most important! Do you not want Miss Chase to shine?" Her puckish eyes grew very serious. "It is on you—and you alone—that her success will depend! Think of the pride you will achieve! Why, every aristocrat in Paris will be trying to bribe you away from us if dear Phyllida is a success." She glanced at the gowns already hanging in the wardrobe and sniffed. "She will need much help, but it can be achieved." She took our Phyllida's finest ball gown. "This will do very well tonight, since we are holding an intimate dinner. Tomorrow the couturier will make all *comme il faut.*"

During dinner, a delicious but prolonged affair— Phyllida made her first grave mistake. Lulled by more wine and the effects of her journey she felt comfortable and relaxed as a kitten. Quite forgetting that her mother had written at length to her godmother about her misdeeds, she asked, with a tender smile that conveyed her deep interest,

"Pray, Tante Emilie, do you know a charming Englishman called Sir Hugh Abingdon? I swear I saw him on the boat today and he spends much time in Paris, I believe."

Instantly the atmosphere became electric. All animation vanished from the Comtesse's small face, leaving it sharp, middle-aged and extremely angry.

"Phyllida! C'est impensable, ce question! You will never, never mention that wicked name in my house! Oh," she tossed her head, "he is accepted in some very undesirable circles, I admit, but by the beau monde *non, non, non!"*

"He is a *roué* and a sinner," said Henri in his cold, clipped voice, passing an unshakable judgment.

Phyllida was too stunned to reply. Here, in France, she had expected to find quite a different attitude toward the dashing young baronet. Tante Emilie went on more calmly,

"The French are very strict, my child; young girls are carefully guarded and then a suitable marriage is arranged so that they become united with a good family of our own class. You will soon learn but, I implore you, do not ask improper questions! Your place is to remain obedient, demure and mindful of your manners. And now you will be tired after the long journey, so I will escort you upstairs. From tomorrow I shall ring for Miss Smith to fetch you at ten o'clock each evening if we are dining *en famille* and not attending a function."

Phyllida bade a subdued good-night to the Comte and Henri before following the small, erect figure with a meekness she was far from feeling. Miss Smith was not in the suite but, when Tante Emilie would have rung for her, Phyllida pleaded,

"No, please—not tonight. The poor soul felt very ill on our crossing and I can manage easily by myself. I always do at home."

Tante Emilie's eyebrows raised in horror. "You mean you have no *maid?*" She shrugged with pitying resignation at the modern ways of her native country. "As a girl I always had one. To do one's own *toilette* was unthinkable."

Phyllida smiled, "I find mine very simple."

"*Mon Dieu!* you have much to learn, Phyllida—and you will oblige me by learning our ways as quickly as you can. It will be wiser if you speak little in public—your smile will be enough. To make a *faux pas* would be most embarrassing." She obviously regarded the tall beauty as an embarrassment already, but did her best to resume a kindly, affectionate attitude. She fluttered once round the vast bedroom, occasionally moving something a fraction of an inch with a "tst, tst!" Then she held up her bird-like arms,

"Come, kiss me my child, for you truly *are* welcome —and rest well, for tomorrow we go to my couturier."

Left alone, Phyllida made no attempt to undress but sat by the ornate dressing table. Decked with so many pink muslin frills and ribbons, it resembled a cloud rather than a piece of furniture. Abstractedly she stared into the triple gilt mirror.

"It isn't to be a wonderful adventure at all. This is a prison," she murmured morosely, her spirits quite dashed. Homesickness washed over her like a heavy, gray tide. At least in Bath she could rely on Gareth's support at all times, and Papa adored her, but here, in this luxurious house, Tante Emilie ruled absolutely—even the splendid old Comte obeyed her every whim, every glance. As for Henri,

"He is a *hateful* young man!" said Phyllida vehemently as her green eyes filled with mournful, rebellious tears.

With heedless hands she tore off her finest gown, and, convinced that she would not sleep a wink for misery, sank instantly into sleep as soon as she climbed into the four-poster bed.

Next morning, after a *café complet* served in her rooms, Phyllida put on her smartest *tailleur* of royal blue velvet with a matching bonnet. She felt refreshed, and much of her natural optimism had revived. It could not do otherwise when she looked through the tall windows and saw, above the treetops of the Bois, Paris itself glinting most invitingly in the April sun.

Tante Emilie, too, had recovered herself and, with much gaiety and waving of hands on her part, they entered her private carriage to drive into the city.

"Is it not beautiful, our city?" she inquired needlessly for the tenth time in as many minutes. Phyllida's expression was the answer. She was sitting well forward, as she had in the coach from Boulogne, drinking in each passing sight with delight.

"Monsieur Chassonne will be entranced by your beauty, *chérie,* and will swiftly arrange all so that you will have both chic and distinction! I shall insist that he prepare the *grande toilette* for you within two days, for my dear old Pierre and I plan your debut for that evening. Oh, pray do not thank me," she added gaily as Phyllida glanced round with some curiosity. "It suits us well—it will be the grand opening of L'Opéra in Paris, which signals our summer season. Everyone will attend! We do not bother with the *music,*" she shrugged cheerfully, "so boring and the poor singers so fat. No, there are many intervals in which we promenade, and young debutantes are presented for the first time! We shall give a small dinner first—not more than twenty, I think—with sons and daughters of a suitable age to amuse you and Henri. Yes, that number will be comfortable in the four boxes that Pierre takes every year at the Opera House."

Now Phyllida stared at her godmother in admiration. Then, with a rueful little laugh she said frankly, "Tante Emilie, I declare you *must* have magic powers. Why, Mamma has the vapors if we have twelve guests for dinner and you speak of twenty with their families as a 'small' dinner!"

"Not magic, my dear—merely a great, great deal of money and position," replied the astonishing Comtesse, but her eyes twinkled with amusement. "It is my intention that you, too, shall attain such a position in life. It makes everything most enjoyable. Ah—look, we are turning into the Champs Elysées; a truly terrible place during the Revolution but now it is once more the height of chic!"

Slightly bemused, Phyllida turned back to the carriage window, her eyes widening in delight at the broad, straight street stretching as far as she could see. Bordered at intervals with slender, well-pruned trees it presented a spectacle of color and elegance. On either side, beyond wide pavements, were the gaily decked shops of modistes, milliners, shoemakers and many more, interspersed with open-air cafés with people laughing and talking at small tables protected by cheerful striped awnings.

"Oh, Tante Emilie, may I walk here sometimes? I swear it is the most wonderful place I have ever seen!"

"Suitably accompanied, it will be quite *comme il faut*," said her godmother benignly. "I never promenade myself—so wearing—but," her voice sharpened, "never, never must you sit in one of those dreadful cafés. It is the height of vulgarity to display oneself to passers-by. Henri had a penchant for such things, but, when it was reported to me, I instantly put a stop to such disgraceful behavior."

"But why? They seem such happy, harmless places."

"My dear Phyllida, Henri is the Viscomte Du Roy! Only the hoi polloi expose themselves thus."

To her surprise Phyllida felt a sudden sympathy for Henri. Perhaps there was more to him than met the eye. Gareth would never have allowed Mamma to browbeat him into such spineless submission, of course, but an only son, heir to a great fortune, might easily have been overruled by a fiery mother like the Comtesse.

The *haute couture* house of Monsieur Chassonne proved to be a tall, white building with no outward sign that it was a business at all, save for a doorman in a long brown frock coat with a tall, cockaded hat which he swept off as the Comtesse alighted from the carriage. Inside, all sounds were muffled by heavy rose velvet curtains and deep pile carpets stretching to every corner and up the beautiful, curved staircase, down which tiptoed an elegant old man dressed entirely in palest dove gray to match his luxuriant silver hair.

"This," said Tante Emilie in a suitably muted tone, "is Monsieur himself."

Phyllida was secretly amused at such a refined old man—or any man at all, for that matter—being a dressmaker; but the hushed atmosphere impressed her, and she was dutifully subdued. Tante Emilie graciously accepted a chair, but Phyllida was left standing as Monsieur walked slowly all round her, silently viewing her from all angles. The establishment had the unreality of a dream—no gowns to be seen, no display of rich materials such as she was used to at home and, above all, no people anywhere.

At last Monsieur seemed satisfied. He and Tante Emilie began to talk very rapidly in French, smiling, frowning, gesticulating dramatically with their hands while Phyllida stood apparently forgotten. Suddenly they stopped and, with a slight inclination of his head toward Phyllida and a low bow over the Comtesse's hand, Monsieur tiptoed back up the stairs and out of sight. A big woman in a plain black working dress came through a side door, took Phyllida's measurements silently, and also vanished.

Tante Emilie rose, evidently well satisfied, and moved to the door. Once again in the carriage Phyllida's curiosity exploded.

"Tante Emilie, I declare I have never been in such an extraordinary place in my life! Why, we have been shown nothing, offered no materials to choose from, I—"

Tante Emilie's tinkling laugh held a reproachful note. "How ignorant you are, *ma chère!* Nobody chooses with Monsieur Chassonne. If he approves of you, and, fortunately, he admires you, he *creates* for you and all is perfection!"

"But suppose he chooses a color one doesn't like?" protested Phyllida obstinately. "I have always made my own choice before."

"Monsieur *never* makes a mistake," declared Tante Emilie with a touch of impatience. "You do not understand what an honor he has bestowed on you, Phyllida. When you see the many exquisite creations he plans for you, you will be quite overcome, I swear."

"But—but almost all the gowns I have brought with me are new already."

Her godmother slapped her wrist lightly with a delicate kid-gloved hand. "Now do not be difficult, my child, or I declare I shall be very out of patience with you."

They continued the journey home in silence.

Phyllida found Miss Smith grim-faced when she went upstairs.

"I'm very put about, Phyllida," she announced as soon as the girl opened the door. "I have never in my life been so insulted—being treated as a servant is *not* my station in life, and I intend to inform the Comtesse at the first opportunity."

"Oh, Miss Smith, do not be so distressed, I implore you." The lovely green eyes turned on her with the nearest approach to affection that her chaperone had ever seen. "I confess I am as homesick and unhappy as you. I know I have been a burden to you in the past but now . . . well, nothing is as I expected either and my godmother appears to rule this whole place with a rod of iron; I hoped so much to become fond of her, but she seems to regard us all as puppets." Swiftly Phyllida related the events of the morning and the short, stern lectures she had already received (omitting any mention of Sir Hugh Abingdon). "So, you see, I have no one to talk to now except you and, if you will pose as my ladies' maid for a while, at least we shall both have a chance to discuss things. Oh," she added hastily, "you know that I shall demand no duties from you; but—well—if Tante Emilie packs us off back to England in disgrace, Papa and Mamma will be in a great taking. If you will help me, we may grow more used to this strange new life."

Bright spots of color came into Miss Smith's thin cheeks. No one had ever appealed to her for help before and, in her meager heart, she felt triumph that it should be this proud, wayward beauty who had proved so troublesome in Bath.

"Very well," she said at last. "But it must not go on in this manner for very long or, I declare, I shall send in my notice to your mamma."

"Not long, I swear." Phyllida felt her old dislike of

the woman flooding back. "Because already the Comtesse has referred many times to a 'suitably arranged marriage' for me, which is outrageous! I will marry *no one* except of my own choosing; and, if she persists, we shall both return to England immediately."

"Very well," repeated Miss Smith stolidly. In her mind she wondered if an "arranged marriage" might not serve admirably to quell the rebellious girl.

She went out and Phyllida felt desolate. Why, *why* had she felt the need to confess so much into such deaf ears? She drifted over to one of the big windows.

"Oh, Hugh, if you *are* in Paris, *please* rescue me!" Her young voice drifted away into the clear, impersonal blue sky.

Chapter
Four

The following morning Phyllida had a message asking her to attend the Comtesse in her boudoir immediately. With a touch of apprehension she followed the maid. Why was the summons so urgent?

She arrived to find Tante Emilie in a splendid mood. Looking like a child in a pale pink negligee, reclining on a magnificent chaise longue covered in gold brocade, she held out both hands as Phyllida entered.

"Ah, *chérie*, you are fortunate indeed! Henri himself wishes to show you Paris! Naturally, Miss Smith will accompany you, but you will find him the most informed and amusing companion, I assure you. You young people must become friends, I insist, since you are both so beautiful and he has the *intelligence formidable*. Are you not delighted?"

"Oh—of course, Tante Emilie, I—I think Henri is very nice."

"Nice"?" The Comtesse gave a peal of tinkling laughter. "My son is *magnifique*—you will see! Then, tonight, we attend a musical soiree given by the Viscomtesse de Fernand—such charm but so old and, now, so poor—her husband was careless enough to be headed in the Revolution. But she is much respected, and one of your English gowns will do very well, since she is not chic. Now go—go, my child, and enjoy your glorious day!"

Phyllida readied herself without enthusiasm. The thought of being shown Paris by the straitlaced Henri was only one step better than not seeing it at all, she felt. They should no doubt visit monuments and old churches instead of the teeming life she had glimpsed yesterday. Miss Smith, however, seemed pleased for the first time since their arrival.

"It is a great honor to be escorted by the Viscomte," she said. "And he is so correct!"

But Henri proved a pleasant surprise to Phyllida. They drove in his mother's carriage beyond the Bois until they reached a turning down to the River Seine. There, with a gentle smile, he said, "I understand that you enjoy walking, Mam'selle, so I think this will be a good place to start the tour." He ignored Miss Smith, so she had no choice but to follow, although her buttoned boots were a trifle tight.

He ordered the driver to meet them at the top of the Champs Elysées in two hours' time.

Phyllida's spirits rose, and, when they reached the embankment bordering the famous river, her eyes sparkled with pleasure. It was wide and beautiful, busy with barges and small sailing boats, while, at intervals along the embankment, artists in smocks and berets were painting the scene. To her surprise Henri appeared to know most of them, and they accepted her jovially, asking for her opinion of their work in progress. Luckily, Gareth's teaching helped her here, so that her comments were received with astonished respect—and Henri became a great deal more friendly.

"Are you, perchance, an artist yourself, Phyllida?" he asked. It was the first time he had used her Christian name.

"No—but my brother is a fine painter and has taught me much." She looked round her and sighed, "How happy he would be here, I declare."

Henri said, "Come, we will visit a sight even more beautiful."

They turned up a steep street and she looked at him curiously. "You love Paris very much, I think?"

"No," he said quickly, his face closed and serious again. "But *natural* beauty, yes, it is a gift from God."

Phyllida hastily withdrew to formality, any hope that they might at least be friends quite dashed. Then they turned a corner and she gasped aloud. They were in a wide place, tree-lined and surrounded by old houses, but the entire center space was a dazzling mass of living color —color putting the rainbow to shame in its infinite, subtle variety.

"It is the Flower Market," Henri announced unnecessarily. "The most perfect blooms are brought fresh each morning from many miles around to supply the great houses and restaurants."

Indeed, top servants now in shirt-sleeves and baize aprons, were bargaining as they amassed whole cartloads of brilliant fragrance for their employers. Here and there young men in tall hats selected dewy gardenias or deep red roses to present to a beloved; betrothed couples, arm in arm, wandered among the stalls while the girl chose a single bloom here, a charming nosegay there, for which their lovers paid the full price without a murmur.

"Oh, may I buy some?" cried Phyllida, her eyes glowing.

"Most certainly," he said gravely. "Only pray allow me to present them to you. It is not *comme il faut* for a lady to pay."

That restricted her choice—although she knew he was rich. She had longed to fill her arms with as many blazing colors as she could carry; now, instead, she selected a pretty nosegay.

"Oh, I *wish* I could paint!" she cried.

Henri frowned. "Artists live most improper lives," he said curtly. "Except, of course, monks who paint to the glory of God."

Phyllida stared at him. "Yet you appeared to know most of the artists we passed just now!"

"I admire *skill,* of course—but I would not visit one of them nor become intimate; creativity is a gift one must appreciate."

Oh, dear, thought Phyllida, I fear I cannot truly like such a priggish bore after all.

When they left the Flower Market, Henri showed them a beautiful old church—the first Roman Catholic one that Phyllida had ever entered. The thin, fluttering candles in front of the many-colored, gentle figures of the Virgin and a calm figure of Christ in a plain, brown robe surrounded by small lambs enchanted her. She loved the strange, musty smell of incense, too, and wanted to see everything. But Miss Smith stepped up beside her shoulder to whisper,

"This is popish heresy—I beg you to keep your eyes closed against it! We must not offend the Viscomte, of course, but you *must* make an excuse to leave immediately."

Phyllida was angry and about to protest when Henri, who had genuflected deeply in front of the far High Altar, rose up and said,

"Oh, you are not of the Faith; I understand, so it would be sacrilege to show you further," and turned to leave. Miss Smith bridled at this insulting remark and would have given him a piece of her mind about *true* faith, but held her tongue, since Henri was not attempting to lead Phyllida further into temptation.

Silently, the three arrived at the top of the Champs Elysées and found the carriage waiting.

"You have promenaded far enough," announced Henri.

"Oh, *no!* Tante Emilie promised that I might walk down this exciting, delightful street—I declare I am not in the least tired!" Sharp disappointment edged her voice with temper. Henri merely opened the carriage door.

"Maman is expecting you for *déjeuner*," he said. "Kindly inform her that I shall be at home to escort you to the soiree." And he handed the two women in with authority. Phyllida's temper flared,

"While you, I suppose, will be carousing in one of those cafés she has forbidden you!" She caught the inside of the door and slammed it shut so violently that Henri was left with his hand extended, an expression of astonishment upon his face.

All the way back to the Bois Phyllida riled against the impossible, odious behavior of the young man, her green eyes flashing with frustration. At last Miss Smith interrupted primly,

"Pray remember you are a *lady*, Phyllida!"

On their return Tante Emilie was hovering expectantly in the salon doorway.

"Ah, *chérie!* But Henri is not with you?"

"No," said Phyllida shortly. "He will be here this evening."

Tante Emilie's face fell for a moment, then she recovered her animation. "La! He has so many friends, that one—tell me, Phyllida, is he not a most charming companion?" She drew the girl eagerly into the great room where the Comte sat close to the fire, a rug over his knees. Then, catching sight of the nosegay Phyllida carried, she clapped her hands in delight. "*And* he presented you with flowers—the dear boy, he would not do that unless he liked you *very* much, he is too sincere!"

Phyllida, unable to stand much more of this blind, maternal worship, had an inspiration. Holding out the nosegay, she said,

"In truth, they are for *you*, Tante Emilie. Henri bade me choose them in that market, then he bought them. I trust I have chosen flowers that you like?"

Tante Emilie took the small bunch crossly and laid them carelessly aside on a small table, then returned to her probing. "No doubt to thank me for giving him an opportunity to know you better. Now, tell me all—*all*. You have been gone two hours, so I swear you two must now be fast friends!"

"Why?" The gentle voice of the Comte surprised both women and they turned to him. His eyes were twinkling as they met Phyllida's. "I find Henri very worthy —but so solemn for one so young." He smiled. "Now, when I was his age—ah! what pranks I got up to; and pretty girls were like wine—of which I partook freely— I . . ."

"Pierre, please," snapped his wife, "Phyllida has no wish to hear of your scandalous behavior, for, I declare, *I* do not believe a word of it! You sit there dreaming, that is all."

"Oh, but I do," and Phyllida drew up a small chair and sat beside the old man, who beamed and patted her hand. "Pray tell me, Comte, was Paris very gay before the Revolution?"

"Gay, I assure you, in a way the world has forgotten now. Most young noblemen were popular at the Court in Versailles and, of course, Le Petit Trianon where the glorious Marie Antoinette gave such fetes and romps as you cannot imagine!" His eyes were young and excited by all the memories. "You, my beautiful child, would have been an immediate success, I promise you—and it would have been a point of honor, and pleasure, to protect you from His Majesty's advances. Then duels would have been fought between your rival suitors, each attempting to steal a handkerchief or bibelot from you to flaunt as a sign of your favor!"

Phyllida's lips were slightly parted, her eyes shining as he conjured such a brilliant picture before her fertile imagination.

"Please continue," she begged when he paused. "Tell me of your own adventures."

Tante Emilie's voice broke the spell. "You are being extremely selfish, Phyllida, exhausting an old man so. Pierre is not supposed to sustain any excitement whatsoever! Come, you must discard your walking attire and prepare for *déjeuner*." She went to the door and opened it purposefully. Reluctantly, Phyllida stood up but, as she turned to go, the Comte said very quietly,

"Have patience with my poor Henri, I beg. In spite of his serious manner I love the boy, and I fear your godmother is seeking a wife for him, which I know will distress him. This makes him more withdrawn."

" 'A wife'?" exclaimed Phyllida, shocked.

"Go quickly or she will be yet more angry," he said, and closed his eyes.

Phyllida went quickly up to her rooms, her mind in a whirl. Behind her she could hear Emilie already reprimanding poor Pierre. *A wife for Henri!* Could it possibly be—yet surely not, it was so ludicrous—that she herself was being considered? Was that what lay behind Tante Emilie's insistence that the two young people must become fast friends? Such a plan might explain the Comtesse's remark in the carriage that she intended Phyllida to attain a position in life as rich, noble and powerful as her own?

Miss Smith was waiting for her with dire warnings about the dangers of being, as she insisted, "lured into popish ways."

"Do not worry," Phyllida assured her vehemently. "I intend to avoid the company of the young Viscomte as much as possible from now on! I declare it was heartless of him to refuse to accompany me on a promenade through the Champs Elysées!"

Hastily, Miss Smith took a different tack, for to criticize a wealthy young aristocrat for such a frivolous reason was tantamount to sacrilege of a different sort.

"I think, perhaps, he was being highly considerate for *me* on that occasion. He must have noticed that I was limping a little, since my boots were highly uncomfortable! A fact that escaped you, Phyllida, in your thought only of your own pleasure!" Her voice was accusing. Instantly Phyllida was contrite,

"Oh, poor Miss Smith—I confess that the sights we

saw had quite bedazzled me. Pray forgive me, and I will ask Tante Emilie if we may go to her own bootmaker and order new ones to be made."

Mollified, Miss Smith withdrew. Like Mrs. Chase, she had to admit reluctantly that the girl had a good heart and, since her boots were old, it would be a great luxury to have a new pair.

Phyllida descended to the dining room slowly, her thoughts still occupied by the possible horrific schemes that might lie in Tante Emilie's mind. From now on, she vowed silently, I shall be cool to Henri; and, surely, she cannot force the matter if both of us are unwilling.

That evening, at the singularly boring musical soiree, it appeared that Henri shared her thoughts, for, without appearing impolite, he also took evasive action—even insisting that his mother should sit between them while they listened to the seemingly endless recital of trios and quartets of indifferent music, during which many of the older guests fell into peaceful slumber.

On the morning before the Grand Night at L'Opéra, during which Phyllida was to be presented officially to the *ton* of Paris, four exquisite boxes in rose and silver wrappings arrived from Monsieur Chassonne's establishment. Tante Emilie, still *en négligé,* twittered excitedly behind the footman carrying them into Phyllida's private sitting room.

"La, *la! Les créations!*" she exclaimed, sounding like a child on Christmas morning. Phyllida, too, was excited— but slightly apprehensive. Whatever they turned out to be she would be forced to wear them, and she prayed that they might not prove to be in his beloved pink and silver shades, which she disliked.

Mrs. Smith was summoned to the ritual unpacking and came, for once, with good grace. Assuming that it was expected of her, she set to and began unwrapping the packages with true British vigor, ripping the paper if a silver knot proved troublesome. In a moment Tante Emilie was on her like a virago, snatching the precious box from her, and screaming, *"Non, non, non!* you clumsy creature! Such things must be handled with respect and reverence— even the wrappings are a work of art!"

Miss Smith sulked but Phyllida, curious, drew closer. At last the first box lid was lifted, the rose tissue gently laid back and, with an awed "Aaah!" the Comtesse unveiled the first gown.

"Hold it up, *chérie,"* she commanded Phyllida, who did so in some trepidation, then moved to the tall cheval glass and held it against her.

It was perfect—perfect as she had never dreamed a gown could be.

Of pure white sarcenet, a silk so fine and soft that to touch it was a sensuous joy, it fell from the high waistline to the ground in lines that would reveal Phyllida's slenderness. The top was cut daringly low in front and wide enough to allow a glimpse of shoulders, but trimmed with a wide lace fichu that also edged the short, elbow-length sleeves. The simplicity was breathtaking. In the box Monsieur had included soft kid slippers of palest gold, long white gloves, a white lace fan and a small evening reticule that could be attached to the wrist by a slender gold chain.

"Well," said Tante Emilie at last, impatient that the girl did not respond instantly wtih Gallic emotion—cries of delight, even tears of gratitude. But, when Phyllida turned to her at length, the burning glow in her huge green eyes said more than any words could express. Tenderly she spread the gown over a chaise longue, then embraced her tiny godmother with almost overwhelming fervor.

"Eh bien!—let us open the next one."

"No—please," pleaded Phyllida. "I declare I should be overcome by still more perfection! May we not open each one on the day when I am to wear it?"

The Comtesse found such restraint hard to understand—a French girl would have been hysterical with excited eagerness to examine them all but, to her credit, she smiled and patted Phyllida's arm. "Very well, we shall do as you wish, *ma chère.*"

The Paris Opera House glittered with chandeliers, gold cupids, mirrors and men and women dressed with a magnificence Phyllida had never even imagined before. Priceless jewels gleamed and winked in the strong lights, adorning every neck, wrist and ear of the older women of society and the men almost equaled them in their embroidered velvet coats, diamond buttons and opulent rings—some fops wore one on every finger.

Tante Emilie sailed from the carriage on Henri's arm, while the Comte escorted Phyllida—a perfect foil in his elegant black velvet, white lace ruffles and gold-topped cane. The Comtesse had lent her a luxurious white fur wrap.

"I shall not *give* it to you, *chérie,* although you may wear it whenever you wish. No, it is *de regueur* in France for an affianced girl to receive furs only from her future husband—and you will not have long to wait, I assure you!"

These words woke Phyllida's fears anew, but the Comte restored her equilibrium—at least long enough to allow her to revel in this most special evening.

As they descended from the carriage and he held out his arm in a most courtly manner he smiled into her eyes.

"Hold your head high, little one, and walk with pride. You resemble the mythical Snow Queen and are quite the most beautiful young woman I have ever had the honor to take on my arm."

Their entrance certainly caused a stir. Heads turned, conversation paused, then rippled round the foyer in excited undertones. Could this vision in white and gold possibly be *English?* The expected goddaughter whom the Comtesse Du Roy had warned them might well prove to be frumpish and stupid? Why, she had chic and Parisian *savoir faire* that put their own carefully trained daughters to shame, and hopeful mothers lamented in whispers to each other that the sooner she was safely married the better!

Seemingly unaware of the stir she caused, Phyllida's only sign of nervousness was a tightening grip of her fingers on the Comte's arm; he bowed and smiled benignly on all the groups they passed, but when they reached the crimson-carpeted stairs that led to his boxes, he said softly, "Nervousness in a young girl is quite proper—but you have no need of it, my child. You must have encountered jealousy long since among the so-worthy mothers in Bath? In one moment you will be seated, where your knees may stop trembling, and you can gaze calmly round on the whole panorama of the society you are about to enter."

He drew Phyllida to the place of honor in front of the stage box, seating himself at her side as a final accolade of the Du Roy's approval. Tante Emilie and Henri, perforce, took gilt chairs a little behind them. Furious, Emilie whispered to her husband,

"Why do you prevent Henri from taking his rightful place as her official escort? Really, Pierre, you are outrageous! We discussed it most carefully but I declare you never listen to a word I say!"

Coolly he answered, "The child is still a little nervous and I wish to sustain her for the ordeal of the promenades; Henri is a good boy but hardly reassuring."

His wife flounced back. At least Henri should take Phyllida on *his* arm during the promenades to establish his prior claim.

Opera glasses of mother-of-pearl were supplied to all the guests of the Comte, and he handed a pair to Phyllida.

"See, with a slight adjustment you can look more closely at the magnificent emeralds worn by the Duchesse de Longville in the center box. She inherited them from her great-grandmother, Catherine the Great, Empress of Russia."

"But surely it is very rude to stare?"

The old man chuckled. "Dear child, how charmingly naive you are! At least a hundred pairs of glasses have been focused on you ever since we took our places! *Non, non*—the opera tonight is purely a social occasion—to see and be seen. Good music will come later in the season, so pray look at whom you like."

Phyllida found this highly diverting and, after looking at the famous emeralds, she shifted her gaze at random, since she knew none of the brilliant company as yet. Once she caught a brief, angry exchange between husband and wife obviously in undertones; another glance showed a secret, loving look between a very proper young couple. Then her heart stopped and she laid the glasses aside with an unsteady hand.

She had not noticed the couple entering the box opposite. A tall, dark, debonair young man was helping a most vivacious woman remove her sable wrap, letting his fingertips rest teasingly on her bare shoulders for a moment. She looked up and laughed into his eyes before settling herself in the gilt armchair.

The man was Hugh! With a truly dazzling young woman of utmost chic. Two aigrettes joined by a diamond clasp ornamented her crisp, black hair. Two ropes of flawless pearls matched the white neck and bosom rising from a daringly lowcut lilac satin gown; yet she needed no flashing jewels, her face was so lively and her dark eyes sparkled so brightly there was no need of more.

Tante Emilie bent forward and, in a satisfied, vicious whisper said, "I hope you notice your 'charming' Englishman, Sir Hugh Abingdon, in the box opposite!"

Phyllida summoned up all her self-control to keep her voice steady as she attempted to say lightly over her shoulder,

"Why, I declare it is! Who is the lady with him?"

"Lady Jacqueline Camden, the French wife of your ambassador in Paris." Then she added spitefully, "I am mightily glad that *we* do not move in diplomatic circles, for I swear that young woman's behavior is a public scandal!"

Phyllida could think of several retorts to the effect that perhaps ambassadors' wives were forced to entertain visiting diplomats—if Hugh *was* one—but she could trust her voice no longer. Another glance showed Hugh so absorbed in his companion that he was, in effect, sitting with his back to the fashionable audience while Lady Jacqueline wielded her fan like a coquette and flirted up at him quite shamelessly.

With the instinct of a lover, Hugh had seen Phyllida the moment he entered the box, and his heart almost failed him. For a blind moment he cursed the fate that had brought him to Paris on vital matters, knowing that there was a risk he might meet her; but he had never dreamed that he might have to cut her so cruelly. With a heavy heart he renewed his attentions to the charming, shallow Lady Jacqueline Camden.

Fortunately at that moment the lights went down and the orchestra struck up the overture. In the still-glowing darkness, lit only by the stage footlights, Hugh stole a quick look across the audience toward Phyllida, who stared at his box, although she could no longer see him in the shadows. It was for the best, he sighed. Phyllida was so young and would soon forget him in the heady delight of becoming the toast of Paris, besieged by suitors. He hoped that soon (or so he persuaded himself) she would fall in love with a worthy, handsome young aristocrat, and tea at the Grand Pump Room in Bath would not even be a memory.

During the first act of the opera Phyllida felt free to indulge her bitter sadness, although she checked her tears, for the Comte's box was plainly visible to the audience.

"So I *was* just one of his little flirtations," she thought with a terrible sense of loss. "How bored he must have been in Bath. Oh, how could I have been so foolish! No wonder he sent no message—made no attempt to call on me here, in Paris. I *must* forget him and I *will*. It is too degrading to watch his shameless behavior with that Frenchwoman in such a public place!"

The Comte, who was enjoying the music, bent to point out something to her on the stage and broke her miserable reverie.

By intermission she was calm, cool and remote, obediently taking Henri's stiff arm for the promenade. If they met Hugh, she determined to cut him entirely. But there was no chance, since everyone, it seemed, converged on Tante Emilie, demanding to be introduced to her enchanting young guest. The air was full of elegant compliments, both in French and English, and a shower of invitations were promised.

In her frozen state Phyllida scarcely noticed that her godmother made it plain through playful hints (mostly in French) that Henri had already found favor with the beautiful Miss Chase.

But Henri, who understood it all perfectly, merely grew more pale and stiff. He did not care a jot for society and its foolish follies, but he was still young enough to be hurt by the knowledge that they thought him a prig, a bore and more than something of a joke. He had already agreed, reluctantly, to act as Phyllida's escort and partner for a short time until she made other friends; but after that, he vowed, he would leave Paris, pretend illness—anything to escape his mother's machinations.

So it was a very quiet foursome who left the Opera House at midnight to return home and partake of a small cold collation. With two hour-long intervals for the famous parades, it was an exhausting evening and few people—apart from young couples—held parties afterward. Most families wished to have privacy to discuss the gowns, jewels and, above all, the young ladies who had been presented to society for the first time.

Only the old Comte was perfectly contented and appeared to have noticed nothing emotional in either of the young people. He loved music and, during the drive, made knowledgeable remarks about the singers. Tante Emilie sat tight-lipped, waiting for her moment later on when she certainly meant to scold Phyllida for smiling so little and making no effort to please the august people to whom she had been introduced—and after presenting her with such a perfect *toilette* to set off her beauty, too! As to Henri! Even his adoring mother knew in her secret heart that he was unpopular amongst the *ton* and he had done nothing to improve that situation tonight, even while escorting the girl whom everyone had acclaimed. In fact her only comfort was the assurance of so many desirable invitations to arrive in the near future.

Both Phyllida and Henri betook themselves to their rooms when they reached the house, although Tante Emilie said she would be down in five minutes and would give orders for the excellent wine to be opened for their simple meal.

Phyllida was alone with the Comte in the salon.

"My poor child," he said gently. "I fear you did not enjoy the evening."

"Oh, it was—superb," Phyllida assured him hastily. "I just developed a stupid headache, probably because I was so nervous."

He shook his head, "I may seem so but I am not blind, my dear. I think you care a great deal for that Englishman you mentioned after your arrival; it must have been painful indeed to see him with a notorious coquette like Lady Camden. But, you know, at heart she is a harmless creature and extremely fond of her elderly husband. It seems to be her duty to entertain young visiting diplomats and I assure you she flirts outrageously with them all—and there it ceases."

"It was not her behavior so much." Phyllida could contain her heartbreak no longer. "It must have been obvious to all that audience that he is *enslaved* by her!" Her eyes glistened with barely controlled tears. The old man smiled.

"How difficult it is to be young," he murmured. "I

have quite a different explanation to suggest to you, Phyllida. I saw them enter that box and he noticed you immediately." Phyllida gave a small gasp. "Oh, he most certainly did—so much so that he kept well behind the lady while his eyes rested on you entirely. It was only when *you* saw them that he began that charade. Further, he kept his back half turned to us throughout the evening, like a man resisting temptation."

Phyllida smiled tremulously. "Do you *truly* believe so?"

"Oh, I believe nothing. I merely observe the world these days and draw my own conclusions—not always correct, I fear."

In a burst of affection Phyllida forgot all his grandeur and spontaneously embraced him, kissing his parchment cheek with deep gratitude. At which point Tante Emilie entered and was far from pleased.

"So—now, at last, you deign to show a little life, child! You made no effort in that direction during the parades, I fear."

Henri did not reappear, so the three of them went in to be served with delicious fresh salmon in aspic, elaborately decorated, followed by tender slices of capon masked by a mushroom sauce made with thick cream, and chilled white wine from the Comte's vineyards. To her godmother's disgust Phyllida ate heartily, including two of the hothouse peaches served for dessert.

"Pierre, what did you say to the child?" his wife demanded crisply when Phyllida had gone up to her rooms.

"Why, nothing of great interest," he raised his white eyebrows quizzically. "When you came in she was thanking me very prettily for a charming evening. She is extremely well-mannered."

As promised, the desired invitations flowed in during the next few days. Scarcely an hour passed without a smart equipage arriving at the door and a lackey handing an embossed envelope to the Du Roys' butler.

The Comtesse's ill-temper was quite restored. Phyllida's beauty had won the day and her quietness had obviously been attributed to a most becoming awe and shyness in face of the great French aristocracy. She sought out her son.

"Henri! We are bidden to no less than six grand balls, three *fêtes-champêtres* (which may still prove a little chilly) and nine dinner parties. What ails you?" her loving voice edged with a rare impatience until a most welcome thought struck her. "Can it be that already you are jealous? That, already, you are in love with Phyllida?"

He was staring out of the window and did not turn. "No, Maman, pray believe me, I would not disappoint you if it could be avoided. But I am not in love with the charming girl—in spite of her beauty—I have never enjoyed the life of society and I have not changed."

Deeply shocked at her son's words—although she knew them to be true—Emilie tried tenderness.

"My dear son—my only child—*what* ails you? You are so pale I sometimes fear that you have a malaise and need a physic."

Henri could smile most charmingly and he did so now. "*Chère* Maman, I am very healthy, I assure you, and I will honor my promise to escort Phyllida as you wish."

"But surely you find her *très charmante?*" insisted Emilie.

"Naturally. What man could fail to admire her?"

Emilie bustled away suddenly well satisfied. She had a great gift for turning the most innocent phrases round to suit her own purposes. Now she convinced herself that her mother's heart fully understood her quiet, reserved son. Poor dear Henri was *nervous*—after all, at twenty, he was little more than a baby! And, until the coming of Phyllida, she and the Comte had entertained few young people, so of *course* he would not admit to warm feelings for the lovely creature, for fear of appearing foolish! He had been the same ever since he could walk and talk, carefully practicing his steps and words by himself in a corner of the nursery.

The fact that the two young people had known each other scarcely more than a week worried her not at all. Wise women such as she could guide and make decisions for them.

All that night Henri paced his room wondering how to deal with the great problem that tormented him increasingly and which he dared to discuss with nobody lest it reach his father's ears. Phyllida, lying awake in another wing of the house, tried vainly to believe the old Comte's explanation of Hugh's behavior without great success. The vivid face of Lady Camden teased behind her eyelids whenever she closed them, and, hard as she tried to believe otherwise, Phyllida knew that Hugh had never looked at *her* in that caressing way. Oh, his eyes had glowed quietly over the tea table at the Grand Pump Room Hotel and she had mistaken that expression for unspoken love because she wanted it to be. But the ardor he had shown tonight was tantamount to an embrace!

Happily unaware of all this—since her own emotions were never of such depth—the little Comtesse Du Roy sat at the escritoire in her boudoir the following morning and began a long, carefully worded letter.

Chapter
Five

Phyllida was too young and high-spirited to let the shadow in her heart spoil her delight in the lavish entertainments which they attended nearly every evening. She had never imagined such gaiety set in surroundings of luxury on which no expense had been spared. A surprising number of grand houses, not in the very center of the city, appeared to have escaped the ravages of the Revolution, and more and more *émigré* aristocrats had already returned to their beloved Paris.

Monsieur Chassonne's creations proved as exquisite, in different ways, as the original white one, and more seemed to be delivered every day. He knew, apparently by instinct, her favorite colors—using gold, silvery green, pale turquoise, the yellow of primroses and a daring bronze shot silk which highlighted her golden hair. Henri dutifully fulfilled his promise to his mother, but, to their mutual relief, he was rarely called on to dance, as Phyllida was swiftly surrounded by handsome, eager partners. Yet always, secretly, she hoped that Hugh might appear.

The valse was sweeping Paris and the romantic, lilting tunes were enchanting, and Phyllida's natural gift for dancing enchanted her admirers still more. But Tante Emilie was ever watchful, drawing the girl back to her side —and, inevitably, Henri's—promptly after each dance so that no light dalliance was possible. She insisted, too, that supper must always be taken in their company.

"You must take French lessons, Phyllida," she decreed one morning. "Since I expect you to become affianced to a Frenchman it is only proper."

"I shall enjoy learning the language—it is beautiful," agreed Phyllida, but then she protested, "although I have no intention of marrying a Frenchman at present, I assure you!"

Tante Emilie smiled wisely. "We shall see!"

The lessons, taught amusingly by a small, white-haired man who had spent many years in England, went well, "You have the natural ear," he informed his pupil proudly. "We shall make a Frenchwoman of you in no time, I believe."

"I am glad—though I have no thought of becoming a Frenchwoman at any time," laughed his pupil, "but French is often used by English people who have traveled much in Europe."

Then Phyllida received a puzzling letter from her mother which she read several times: *". . . Your father and I are delighted that you seem to have found great happiness in Paris; it has particularly pleased Papa, since he did not altogether approve at first of your being sent there. Now our minds are at rest, and we look forward to a very pleasant visit quite shortly."*

"Are my parents coming to spend time here in the near future?" she asked Tante Emilie.

The small hands waved merrily in the air.

"Tiens! But your *chère* Maman never could keep a secret! Between us we prepare many delightful surprises for you, *ma petite,* but much, much must be arranged first. Your papa is a most diligent and careful lawyer, I understand, and is not to be hurried."

Since Tante Emilie had suddenly become extremely French, Phyllida took this to mean that Papa could not leave his busy practice in Bath without considerable warning. Indeed, what else could it mean?

A week later a short, angry note from Gareth enlightened her:

> *My dear Amazon,*
>   *I cannot believe my ears—unless you have run mad. Scarce six weeks after leaving home, tearful and carrying on about that charming rascal, Abingdon, Mamma and Papa speak of nothing but plans for you to marry a* French*man! Quite soon, too, I gather. What, pray, is the matter with you? Or have you been tortured, bludgeoned, handcuffed, drugged—or the whole lot of them? And why not one word to me? I confess I am disgusted with you. Gareth.*

Phyllida stared at the furious scrawl, her cheeks flaming. Then, brushing Miss Smith out of her way, she marched downstairs and found all the Du Roys in the salon, where Henri was taking his leave before going out for the day. In a harsh voice that startled them all, Phyllida commanded,

"Wait!" Then she thrust the letter at Tante Emilie. "I demand an explanation immediately!" The Comtesse read the few lines, then handed the paper to her husband.

"I am deeply shocked by such unwise behavior," she began, but Phyllida interrupted her,

"I want a full explanation *now!*"

The Comtesse rallied as best she could, "My dear child this is most unfortunate, I meant—"

"Tell me what my brother means!"

Tante Emilie held out her hand to Henri and then to Phyllida, who both ignored it. The old Comte sighed quietly.

"This should have been disclosed at a grand family dinner—not in this unmannerly way. But, yes, it is true—I have been delicately negotiating with your father and mother for two weeks and we are all delighted that you and Henri are to be officially betrothed! Is it not splendid?"

She smiled hopefully but hurried on, "Your father is being most generous, Phyllida, with an excellent dowry and a house in Bath so that you may both enjoy English society as well. It will all prove most happy, you will see—these arranged matters always do."

The two young people stood like petrified statues and glancing anxiously from one to the other, the old Comte could not decide which of them was more appalled. Phyllida broke the silence.

"It is abominable," she said in a low, firm voice. "I shall arrange to return home at once."

"I cannot possible agree either," said Henri stiffly.

Tante Emilie gave a small trill of indulgent laughter.

"Oh, my children, my children—how typical is your reaction! Then, in no time, you will become like turtle doves, for it is always the case."

Phyllida looked down at her, her green eyes blazing with scornful dislike. Without a word she turned and left the room, closely followed by Henri.

The Comte held out a comforting hand to his poor little wife—she was so headstrong and often foolish, as now, but he was very fond of her.

"You have made a grave mistake, my dear. I have always felt so, as you know, in this matter. But they will become calmer, you will see."

To his surprise she rounded on him, her face like a virago.

"This marriage *shall be!*" she cried. "Do you not see it is all for my precious Henri?"

As Phyllida reached the stairs, Henri said in a low, urgent voice,

"I must talk to you, Phyllida. Please come to my study." His tone was so desperate that much to her surprise Phyllida obeyed and followed him.

The room was small and bare of ornament but Henri closed the door firmly and motioned her to a leather chair.

"First you must be assured that I guessed nothing of this—nothing—and under no circumstances can I marry you. Oh, I am not offering you an insult, you are very, very beautiful but . . . I think I must confide in you." He looked deeply distressed.

Phyllida, determined that she would be on her way to England within hours, felt curious.

"Pray do—if you are sure. We have both had a great shock, you know, and you might regret it."

He shook his head. "Never. I need to talk and, since we are both in this terrible situation 'arranged' by Maman, it may help us if you know my true mind."

As he deliberately stripped off his cold, stiff self-defense, Phyllida felt unexpected sympathy growing for what was, after all, a very young and suddenly likable person.

"Tell me," she said gently.

"Ever since I was fourteen I have known—quite positively—that I have a vocation to enter a monastery." He looked at her anxiously for ridicule but Phyllida, although completely astounded, managed to keep a quiet, receptive expression. Reassured by this Henri opened floodgates of silent agony too long held in check. "I have dared to tell nobody—except my confessor, a priest most saintly who has a small church in a village ten miles outside Paris; each week I ride out there, while Maman believes I am riding in the Bois." He hesitated before rushing on. "My great sin, my weakness, has always been fear of her—and deep love and respect for my father, whom I dread to disappoint, for I am his only heir."

"Oh, my poor, poor Henri," exclaimed Phyllida with almost maternal warmth. "Having lived in this house for some weeks, how well I understand both those problems!"

By instinct they had both kept their voices low and Tante Emilie, listening briefly outside the door, departed well satisfied. They were already behaving like turtle doves now that they were alone, and she felt triumphant.

Her son would not only marry shortly, but marry a great social asset. No longer would he be spurned and laughed at.

"Had I only had brothers and sisters," continued Henri, "all would have been straightforward, but being an only child put the pressure of duty on me at a very early age. Maman has always been ambitious for our family and impressed on me my destiny for as long as I can remember." He gave a rueful, boyish grin which quite transformed his severe features. "Even in petticoats my nurses and the servants had to call me 'Le petit Viscomte.' It made me feel isolated from other children."

"Did your father allow it?" asked Phyllida, astonished.

"No one can defy Maman for very long but, while he was still an active man, he took me out riding. He also taught me to love and appreciate beauty in painting, music and literature. Reading became my passion and my refuge, and through books I discovered mysticism and true religion. It gave me a secret defense against Maman, and to need such a thing against a mother is a sin for which I shall have to do penance all my life."

"Oh, no," cried Phyllida in protest. "She should do the penance! And now that I understand, I admire you so much for making a stand for your beliefs—cutting yourself off from society and dressing differently from all other young men."

Henri smiled sadly. "It was cowardice—a way to make sure that no girl would want to marry me, but I should have known Maman better!"

"But surely now, now when we are both defying her together, you have your chance to go away? To join a monastery."

"I cannot bear to hurt my dear father. He is an old man now and has such great hopes of me even still. Often we talk together after dinner, and he explains all his plans for the future of our large country estate and the vineyards. He is trusting me to carry out his wishes for our tenants' welfare and care of the land. He has little left in life, Phyllida, except these hopes; and, through my deep faith, I know that he will pass into a great joy when he dies and understand all things. I have thought that, if I could wait until that time, I need not break his heart."

"I believe he would understand you now, Henri. He has seen very clearly into my heart already. But you must not stay here now, for, if I do not accept her offer, your mother will choose another girl."

They sat silent for a while, Phyllida feeling strangely responsible for this sad, earnest young man.

"Will you come with me to England?" she asked at last.

"It is a Protestant country, and I must enter a Catholic community either in this country or Italy."

With a sudden thrill of adventure, Phyllida made up her mind.

"Listen, Henri, my brother Gareth will help us. I know he will. Now that I think about it I am very, very angry with my parents for allowing all this to be arranged without even *consulting* me! It is outrageous!" Her eyes sparkled with hurt fury, for now the full cruelty of their parents' actions came home to her as the first shock was passing. "No, I will write to Gareth immediately—in here if I may? Then you must take the letter to the mail collecting post yourself, for we dare not trust the servants. I hope there may be a packet boat to England this evening and that this will reach him swiftly."

Henri pulled out the chair at his bureau for her and placed paper, ink and a fresh quill pen ready.

Phyllida wrote quite a short letter—a single impassioned plea for help. As she sealed the envelope and handed it to Henri, he said,

"You are extremely good and unselfish, Phyllida! And you will wait and help me through your brother instead of hurrying to England as you have every right to do?"

"Of *course* I shan't leave you immediately," said Phyllida, "although I must confess that if Gareth suggests no plan I doubt I can endure it here for many days. But now we can talk often together, and I vow I will help you to find a solution over your father."

When Phyllida went up to her rooms she found Miss Smith in a thorough taking. Indeed, her pinched face was mottled with rage as the torrent of reproof poured out.

"What is this disgraceful story that I hear from the servants, Phyllida? That you are going to marry that— that *papist* and become one yourself, I suppose? Well! Your parents need not expect me to stay and endure such downright blasphemy another day. I shall leave at once without waiting to give notice. You have always been an ungrateful, downright nuisance, my girl, and here I have been subjected to infamous insults. I have been treated as your ladies' maid, forced to take meals with the upper servants, if you please! Well, I declare I have put up with it only for your poor mother's sake, knowing what a willful daughter you have always been to her and hoping you might mend your ways. But now I swear I have finished with you. My parents may have been poor, God rest their dear souls, but my father was a proud, God-fearing vicar. Why, he must be turning in his grave to know that I am now in contact with a headstrong young heretic!" She was forced to pause for breath, drawing the air in in angry rasps.

Since listening to Henri, Phyllida felt strangely calm and grown-up—no longer a girl but a young woman very much in control of her own life and that of others.

"Miss Smith, pray be calm and listen to me. I am truly sorry that you heard this story from others, but I was informed myself only an hour ago. Now do not take on so, for I promise there is no need. Neither the Viscomte nor I have the slightest intention of becoming betrothed, much less married, and we have told Tante Emilie so." Phyllida smiled very sweetly. "She refuses to accept that, of course, because she always has her own way and these arranged marriages are quite the thing in France. But I am *not* French and I am quite as proud as you are. I have already written to England conveying my absolute refusal, and I intend that you and I should leave here forever in a very few days."

Miss Smith was in a quandary. She had expressed her feelings most freely, yet now she was forced to admire the girl. She could never bring herself to apologize but she showed that she was mollified.

"Well, Phyllida, I'm thankful to hear that you have so much sense," she admitted grudgingly.

"But please, please do not cause a stir with the Comtesse, I beg you. And you know I trust you not to repeat what I have said to any of the servants." Miss Smith bridled indignantly at the very suggestion. "Henri and I have discussed the matter, and we mean to keep things outwardly as pleasant as we can until I leave. Will you help us—just for a short while?"

"Oh—very well. I trust I have never failed to do my duty," said the good lady piously. "But I shall certainly give notice to Mrs. Chase when we return!" Her honor was restored.

Downstairs Phyllida found it hard to maintain her new-found calm. Tante Emilie had kindly decided to overlook the earlier outburst. Always able to believe whatever suited her, she decided the young people's reaction had simply been shock. Hadn't she heard the young couple cooing most affectionately in Henri's study immediately after?

Unfortunately there was no social engagement that evening, so they were forced to dine *en famille*. The Comte said little, but eyed Phyllida and Henri anxiously from time to time. The Comtesse showed no restraint whatever—her lifelong ambition to "settle" her son suitably was achieved and so she prattled exultantly.

"Ah, *mes chères enfants,* all is now so happy, *n'est-ce pas?* I have so many, many delicious plans you will be quite enchanted, I swear!" She fluttered her hands merrily. "Yours shall be the grandest wedding of the year. The ceremony must be in Notre Dame, I insist, for I have already sent a note to our local curé informing him that he must begin to prepare you immediately to enter the Catholic Faith, Phyllida. It takes some months to complete this preparation, but if you are under instruction I am sure you will be given dispensation to have a full wedding Mass. Then we must decide where you shall live." She paused long enough to enjoy a mouthful of delicious veal in cream sauce.

Throughout this stream of plans, Phyllida had kept her eyes on her plate in what, she hoped, might be taken for becoming modesty, since she was determined to remain calm, although inside she was seething. Now the Comte intervened in his gentle voice.

"Emilie, *ma chère,* I think you overwhelm these poor children. There is no need to look so far ahead when they are scarce used to their—er—surprising new situation."

"Oh, Pierre, you believe that all can be achieved *pouf!* like that," retorted his wife irritably. "I want our lovebirds to know there is nothing for them to concern themselves with except each other. All, all will be quietly arranged for them."

Without glancing at him Phyllida sensed how Henri must be recoiling inwardly from the dreaded phrase that had ruled his life until now.

I *will* rescue him, she vowed more strongly than ever in her mind. She realized with gratitude that the Comte sensed their mutual reluctance over the whole business, but nothing could stem Tante Emilie's enthusiasm.

"As I was saying—since Henri is heir to all the property, why should they not live here, in this most beautiful house? We can prepare the South Wing so that they may be quite alone whenever they wish, yet I can assist Phyllida with her first entertaining." She clapped her small hands in anticipation. "Oh, but what grand balls and fetes we shall hold for all the *ton! Tout le monde* will wish to celebrate the marriage of our beautiful young couple!"

Satisfied that she had explained all her superb plans so far, the Comtesse settled down to enjoy her dinner, for, despite her diminutive size, she was quite a gourmet and her chef was the finest in Paris.

After dinner—finished almost in silence—she was delighted that, instead of withdrawing to his own quarters as usual, Henri escorted Phyllida into *le petit salon,* which led off the grand one. Happily, Emilie settled to her tapestry frame, saying to her husband,

"You see, Pierre? Already they wish to be alone, those two!"

The Comte was deeply unhappy. Indeed, he had made a poor dinner, since he was so aware of the undercurrents running between his dear son and the beautiful girl for whom he felt great affection.

"I tell you, all is far from well, Emilie," he said. "If you are wise—which you seldom are, my dear," he gave her his tender smile, which she ignored, "if you are wise, I repeat, you will not continue to rush things so. Give them time . . ."

But his wife was not listening. She had resolved to drive down to Monsieur Chassonne tomorrow morning to discuss the wedding gown. Of course the ceremony could not take place until late summer but she saw no reason to consult Phyllida on the matter. Monsieur would need time—much time—to create a work of genius, and it was necessary that the gown should be a revelation of expensive perfection to all Paris.

Meantime, Phyllida rested her rosy hand on Henri's pale one, clenched in mute rebellion.

"Henri, please, *please* trust me," she begged, keeping her voice low. "I have learned one thing tonight which must surely help you. Your father is as set against this absurd marriage as we are. Forgive me, I pray, but I dare to think that I understand him better even than you do —oh, not with your depth, since I am not his daughter. But..." she hesitated a moment, "I truly believe that he will accept your decision to become a monk with far less pain than you imagine."

"But—how could he?" Henri's eyes, no longer veiled as before, pleaded for proof—this vital proof that might govern his whole life from now on.

"Because he loves you," said Phyllida simply. "He *knows* you have avoided becoming like so many vain young men of your own class, and he is so sensitive he must have realized that you have a vocation. What else could explain it?"

Henri thought for some while as, unconsciously, he enclosed her warm hand between his cold ones as if they were a salvation.

"I think," Phyllida ventured at last, "that if Gareth does as I desperately hope he will and engineers an escape for us, you should take it thankfully. After all, surely you cannot be accepted as a novitiate in a monastery without trial?"

"That is true," he agreed eagerly. "One must stay there for some months before even being asked to make a decision."

"Splendid. Then, if we go, you could leave a letter for your father telling him that you are seeing whether you are sure. You will be able to return and talk to him after that."

Phyllida was quite alarmed at the emotional affection in his eyes. How dreadful if he should, after all, fall in love with her!

In fact her nerves were much on edge during the next two days. She knew it was too soon to hope for a reply from Gareth, but Tante Emilie drew her web closer all the time, calling her "dear daughter," giving her beautiful pieces of valuable jewelry from her own collection and always hinting at new "arrangements."

A ball and then a soiree were welcome diversions,

and Phyllida flirted gaily with bejeweled young dandies as a positive nervous relief.

On the third morning, as she was sipping her *café au lait,* Phyllida heard the sound of a carriage drawing up, and a flurry of voices in the hall. Then one young voice rose unmistakably. Still in her negligee, Phyllida flew on winged feet to the top of the staircase, her eyes brimming with thankful tears.

"Gareth!" She cried, "Oh, Gareth, you are truly here!"

The next moment she was down and embracing him, caring nothing that his traveling coat was stained and dusty from the night's voyage and a nonstop drive from the port in a hired carriage. He was rescue—salvation—strength, and she knew then how close she had been to the breaking point.

Laughing, he held her away, looking down at her smiling yet tearstained face with his warm, gray green eyes.

"Well, well—my poor little Amazon, you *have* landed in a pretty plight, haven't you?"

"But not any longer—not now that you are here," she said. And hugged him again.

"Phyllida!" The voice was shrill with disapproval. *"What* are you doing with this strange young man and you *en négligé!"*

Phyllida turned a radiant face to the stairs. "Oh, Tante Emilie, it is my brother—my dear brother Gareth come from England!" she cried.

"Hm! The young man who writes the so ill-mannered letter I imagine!"

Gareth looked up with his most disarming smile, "Dear Tante Emilie—for I believe I, too, may call you that? I much regret such a hasty note. I confess I was dumbfounded at the news, knowing nothing about it. But Phyllida wrote to me afterward, explaining everything, and I could not wait to come here and meet you and be with her."

Slightly calmer, the Comtesse said, "Very well. I will receive you when I have made my *toilette*. You, too, Phyllida will dress at once!"

"Indeed, yes," Phyllida replied eagerly. Then, to her brother, "Go in through that door and wash up and I will order coffee for you—I shall be with you in scarce five minutes!"

She dressed like lightning, her heart light as a bird. She had never dreamed that Gareth would come himself —but now she would be free and away in no time at all. She even forgot Henri for the moment.

Gareth had divested himself of his coat, washed, and was looking unbelievably dear and English as he sat in front of a well-laden tray. "Now, Phyllida—tell me all of it, for I confess it is hard to believe you are not exaggerating! You do, you know. How *can* that little woman have arranged all this without either your knowledge or consent? I've never heard of such a thing in my life!"

"Nor had I," said his sister with feeling. "But it happens in France all the time. Listen, and I'll tell you from the beginning . . ."

Hungry though he was, Gareth forgot his breakfast as he listened in horrified amazement. Phyllida spared herself nothing—her dislike of Henri until these past few days, the incident at the opera when she had seen Hugh ("Yet truly, Gareth, I *still* love him! I fear I always will"). She related the old Comte's kindness and his helplessness against his dominating wife, until she came to Tante Emilie's declaration of the betrothal. "And, worst of all," she cried passionately, "Mamma and Papa seem to have agreed without even *asking* me! That's when I wrote to you."

"By Gad, you've convinced me. Now I'll tell you what steps I have taken. I confronted Papa with the whole thing and found he was most unhappy about it all —but Mamma refused to listen, declaring that it was an ideal match for you. She then showed him letters from Tante Emilie which, I must admit, painted a lyrical picture of you and this Henri—loathsome phrases like 'turtle doves,' 'cooing in corners' and 'they cannot bear to be apart,' which made me feel rather ill they were so unlike you! However, Papa signed the massive legal documents that began to arrive, wanting your welfare—yet he was mighty glad when I went to his office to see him privately and told him you were desperately wretched and that I was coming over here at once. He sent you a message, assuring you that he will never press a marriage you are against and, if he withdraws his consent, it cannot take place."

Phyllida sighed with relief and smiled. "Poor Papa—he is as much under Mamma's thumb as the old Comte is out here. All the same, I cannot trust Tante Emilie for one moment—and I have promised that we will rescue Henri as well. We *must* go, Gareth. I promise she will stop at nothing to get Henri married. But . . . I confess I don't wish to go home—not yet. Mamma is far too anxious to be rid of me, and she and the Comtesse seem to be hand in glove. What *shall* I do?" Her green eyes were beautiful in their pleading.

Gareth grinned and patted her hand. "That's my Amazon again! I swear I thought I had lost you altogether. Now, since I am here and you know you are in no danger, I think you should try and dissuade the small virago once more, for she sounds a dangerous enemy. But, if she insists, I have enlisted the help of someone most influential—in other words, he has money and I have none!" he grimaced cheerfully. "In three nights from now a splendid traveling coach will pick us up secretly—that will give us many hours start—and a refuge has been arranged. You can bring this Henri along if you must."

"I must," insisted Phyllida, but her eyes were sparkling again. "Oh, Gareth, how wonderful you are! Who is this 'someone' with a coach ready to save strangers?"

"That I cannot tell you," he said firmly. "Now—I

will suggest that I spend a morning out with my future brother-in-law so that I may get to know him, while you tackle his fearsome mother."

"Must you leave the house?"

Gareth burst out laughing.

"My dear girl—she cannot *eat* you—you are far too large a mouthful! You must not become nervous now all is fixed!"

Tante Emilie swept down in a dauntingly chic morning gown, having quite decided to dislike and berate the ill-mannered young Englishman. But she had reckoned without Gareth's charm. Tongue in cheek he gradually beguiled her, and she was all smiles when he asked her permission to spend the morning walking with her son. "After all, this is my very first visit to this glorious city and it will be a splendid chance for Henri and me to become friends."

The Comtesse rose to the bait instantly—any suggestion of friendship toward Henri always pleased her. "I will go and inform him to prepare immediately," she said and left the room. Gareth looked at his sister with renewed sympathy.

"Poor young devil—he *is* on leading-strings, isn't he? I see exactly what you have had to face. Gad, what a woman!"

When the two young men had set off, Phyllida braced herself for the ordeal. Cutting across the Comtesse's endless chatter about future plans, she said as steadily as she could manage,

"Tante Emilie—I know that my first protest against this marriage was unseemly and made in a state of considerable shock. But I need to talk to you most urgently."

"Ah! You wish to apologize at last, *chérie,* now that you have seen how well things arrange themselves."

Phyllida stood up, using her slender height to add force to her words, "I fear not. I wish to inform you

92

again, most seriously, that I cannot—indeed, will not—marry Henri."

The small face contorted into formidable anger. "How *dare* you utter such outrageous words to me? *Now*, when all the documents have been signed as gladly by your father as by me—*now*, when you and Henri have been as close as turtle doves during this past week and your so-charming brother has arrived to make friends with him . . ."

"I dare because it is the truth," said Phyllida, her spirit rising to its height. "We have *not* been like turtle doves, I assure you. No, we have been talking quietly together and made friends at last, since you have placed us in this dilemma without even consulting us. But I will never take such marriage vows—indeed, I cannot, since my heart is already given elsewhere and Henri will understand this." She relaxed her hard tone into one of beseeching. "You have been so good to me during my time here, surely, surely you will not insist on an unwilling wife for your son? Have you no heart after all, Tante Emilie? I declare it is hard to believe."

The Comtesse was momentarily speechless in her blind fury at this obstinate, ignorant girl. At last the words came out in a stream—mostly French—which battered against Phyllida's mind like giant hailstones. Finally she said, in vicious triumph,

"You are merely hysterical, you proud, ungrateful girl! And besides, you are too late! Your father's signature is on all the papers of consent and, from your poor, dear Mamma I have letters not only loving but in total agreement with the arrangements. I suggest you go to your room at once and I will send my own maid with a posset to soothe the nerves." More indulgently she added, "Young girls are often thus during a betrothal and you will much regret such foolishness by the time your affianced and your brother return for lunch. For myself, I shall forget this unpleasant little scene," she waved her

93

hands magnanimously, "for you are now bound to my son and *nothing can alter it!*"

Phyllida went to her room gladly but, when the posset came, she thanked the maid and promptly threw it away as soon as the woman had gone. When they all assembled for the midday meal the slightest shake of her head—so slight it was noticed by no one else—conveyed Phyllida's failure to Gareth. Later, they strolled in the gardens together, where, after a short interval, Henri joined them. From the windows they appeared to be three, happy young people, and the Comtesse smiled with satisfaction. Had she heard their conversation she would have been extremely shocked, for, with Henri's help, they were examining all the doors leading out of the house which might be approached by a coach without notice. When a side door close to the drive had been chosen, Gareth left the others.

"I must send messages and make the final arrangements," he said with a touch of youthful importance. In truth, he was as excited as the others by the daring plan. Phyllida had made certain that there were no engagements on the third night from then. On such evenings after a family dinner, it was usual to retire soon after ten o'clock. The Comte and Comtesse had adjoining suites in the West Wing, facing a quiet rose garden, so they would hear nothing.

"Good—then we'll leave at midnight," said Gareth, adding with an infectious grin, "Besides, midnight sounds so charmingly melodramatic!"

When he had gone Henri laughed, the first time Phyllida had heard him do so. "Oh, but your brother is splendid!" he declared. "He does not blame me in the least for not wanting to face Maman's wrath, so I shall leave a letter for Papa and promise to return in a few months to discuss matters with him."

After that, they all three behaved with charm and correctness. Gareth accompanied the family to a ball and a fete and was bewitched, as an artist, by the graceful elegance of the scenes. Only Miss Smith presented a problem, for Phyllida dared not leave her behind. At last it was decided that Miss Smith should be given a scant hour's warning in which to pack—too little opportunity for her to give the secret away if she wished to.

The governess grumbled bitterly but was glad to be going away from the Comtesse. Besides, Phyllida was so gay and excited as she packed only the clothes she had brought from England, leaving all the "creations" and gifts of jewelry behind, that Miss Smith felt sure they must be returning to England.

Just before midnight the three conspirators met silently by the side door. Then they went out into the clear, starlit night and, in five minutes, saw the welcome shadow of a grand coach waiting. A tall, caped figure advanced to meet them and help with the valises. With her heart beating in her throat, Phyllida recognized him instantly. With a cry of delight she said,

"Hugh—oh, *Hugh!* But I can't believe it! *You* are the rescuer!" Love tinged her voice with shining gold, and he answered, husky with emotion,

"My dearest girl—you did not think I would leave you to such a fearsome charade, did you?" And, as the coachman handled the luggage, Hugh took Phyllida's hands in his, and they gazed at each other in the moonlight as if such hunger could never be satisfied.

Suddenly, Miss Smith saw his face. With a single gasp of horror, she promptly swooned away on the gravel walk. Gareth and Henri lifted her between them and placed her firmly inside the coach, then they were all inside, Phyllida still clinging to one of Hugh's hands. The coachman flicked the horses and they were away—to what far destination no longer mattered, they were free at last from Tante Emilie and her "arrangements."

Phyllida's heart was full. Hugh had come, his dear presence was close at her side, and the incident at the opera was forgotten forever.

Chapter
Six

Miss Smith recovered, moaning, but by that time the coach was traveling at great speed.

"Oh—is that wicked, wicked man still with us?" she cried.

Phyllida laughed joyously. "I declare, I don't know what you can be thinking of! Of course there is no wicked man here—just my brother, the Viscomte and our most gallant rescuer, Sir Hugh Abingdon, to whom we owe everything."

"That name! Phyllida, I swear your parents will never forgive you—never! I shall leave immediately . . ."

Hugh's deep voice came to her through the darkness. "I fear that will not be possible. Pray use your smelling bottle to revive you, for this coach will not stop until we have crossed the mountains out of France. We should reach our final destination at about noon tomorrow and then, I give you my word as a *gentleman*," he stressed the word slightly with a smile in his voice which delighted the others, "tomorrow I will personally arrange a voyage back to England if you wish."

Grumbling to herself, Miss Smith fumbled in her reticule and perforce took his advice, adding, "And not a moment too soon!"

Hugh placed a warm fur rug over her knees and

said, "I advise you to sleep now, Miss Smith—after all, it will pass the time more easily for you."

In a short time when gentle snores told the others that she had, indeed, taken Hugh's advice, Henri leaned forward, his young voice eager,

"Dare I hope, Sir Hugh, that our destination is in Italy?"

"This journey is to be a surprise," said Hugh firmly. "This adventure is the first I have enjoyed for many years and I don't intend to spoil that pleasure. Follow my suggestion to Miss Smith and sleep." There was a youthful zest in his voice which thrilled Phyllida. Had he, by a miracle, forsaken his wild life for her sake? She turned further toward him.

"Oh, Hugh—please tell me how all this came about?" The excitement, the strange unreality surrounding this dramatic flight by starlight had overcome all pretentious barriers of formality and stiff propriety. Only he, in all the world, could have rescued her in such a splendid, dashing manner. "And the coach!" she went on, "it is the height of luxury . . ." She ran her hand over the thick velvet upholstery.

"So it should be," he replied with a touch of dryness. "The Prince Regent maintains it in Europe solely for his rare private visits."

"And he lent it to you?" She was incredulous.

"You ask too many questions so late at night," he teased her. "There is no need for such haste, for we shall have several days together now—so come, let me wrap my cloak around you, for the air will grow cold as we reach the mountains, and then sleep. Oh, do not protest," he insisted as he sensed her slight body tensing in the dark so close to his side. "You have been under a tremendous strain, poor little one, and I mean to be your physician tonight and I order you to rest!" His voice was very tender and she meekly let him enfold her in the cape. She *was* sleepy, it was true, but fear caught at her heart and she stiffened once more.

"Hugh? I am afraid to sleep. Suppose when I wake that you and the coach should vanish as if you were only a dream?"

Gently he stroked back a strand of shining fair hair that had fallen over her forehead, then eased her position until her head rested against his shoulder. "There! Now I am your prisoner, for I cannot move without disturbing you!"

She gave a sleepy, rueful little laugh, "I must still hold your hand to make doubly sure! But please—promise to wake me when we reach the mountains, for I have never seen any before and would die sooner than miss such a sight."

"I promise. Besides, I am selfish enough to want to show you that glorious spectacle."

Satisfied, she fell almost instantly into sleep like a contented kitten, her slim hand slowly slackening its grip on his.

But Hugh, the only wakeful member of the party now, sat staring into the darkness, his fine-drawn face bleak and anxious.

Dear God, how deeply he loved the beautiful girl in his arms—and her feelings for him were unmistakable. But—was he doing her harm to remain with her once they reached what, to him, was the most romantic city on earth? Scarce four days ago a dejected Gareth had come to him with the news of Phyllida's betrothal. Hugh was in Bath, staying with the Prince Regent, who had returned there to have treatment for a gouty foot that plagued him. His Highness was in a vile temper and Sir Hugh was one of his few favorites who could still amuse and beguile him.

It was, however, a far from easy task as other courtiers, hurrying away in umbrage after some unnecessarily biting taunts, assured him. But Hugh, by gaming with the Prince—and allowing him to win—could always bring a smile when the Prince asked for tales of his recent conquests in Europe.

"Pray, how is the naughty, enchanting Jacqueline Camden in Paris? It must be three years at least since I have seen her," he sighed and shifted his heavy body impatiently as the bandaged foot on a velvet footstool shot a protesting pang of pain up his leg as he took another sip of claret.

"A little naughtier—a little more attractive," said Hugh lightly. "I escorted her to L'Opéra and had a devil of a job persuading her to return to the embassy before her husband grew suspicious!"

"Ah, husbands," the Prince sighed deeply. His own marriage was another thorn in his side, for he could not abide his wife. Indeed, her only virtue was a willingness —in exchange for luxurious private apartments and a full, royal retinue at all his residences—to turn an indifferent eye on the Regent's affairs.

Sir Hugh was waiting for a judicious moment to make his request—permission to use the royal coach, stabled in France—to achieve a mythical romantic conquest that would involve travel.

Not for the world would he betray the true depths of his love for Phyllida, for nothing would bore and irritate the Prince more. Although, at the end of the evening, he intended to hint—with suitable mystery— that this time his heart might be a little more involved than usual, that he might vanish from the Prince's coterie of amusing dilletantes for a time. With the Prince in his present frame of mind it would not do for his more or less official Court Jester to suggest that he intended to vanish forever from Court circles. The Regent favored him for his gay disregard of morality.

"Tell me—have you visited the luscious Orieta in Rome lately?" The august fat fingers selected a hot-house peach from a dish close at hand, and bit into it with relish. "She is a trifle dull, don't you agree?" he chuckled. "But succulent as a peach in small servings!"

Hugh laughed. "If it were possible she is even more luscious now since she has put on weight but, being

Italian, it suits her very well. But I must confess I do not tend to linger in her company! True, her gossip about Roman society has bite but little wit."

The Prince took another bite from the peach as if to underline this remark. Hugh felt repelled as juice trickled unheeded from the prominent lips. Tactfully, he dipped a silk napkin in a bowl of rosewater and handed it with a smile.

"I see that you are wearing a particularly fine cravat, Sire," he said. "No doubt a new design from Beau Brummell? It would be a pity to stain it."

The Prince looked first annoyed, then grateful. Dear God, thought Hugh, I must seize a chance to make my request soon. For he and Gareth intended to catch the midnight packet to France.

"I have a respectful request, Sire," he said, keeping amusement in his voice. "I have met a new enchantress who needs rescuing. She lives in France and I have promised an assignation with her tomorrow evening. Would you graciously consider allowing me to use your coach for the purpose?"

The dull eyes lit up. "Rescue from a husband, eh? For that, my dear Sir Hugh, you may claim every royal facility at your disposal on the Continent! Is she very beautiful—and young?" He licked his lips.

"Would I favor her otherwise?" asked Hugh. "One day I will make sure that she shall be presented to you."

"Ah! A fresh beauty! That will be a treat indeed. Though, mind you, do not enter an idyll, for you are due to meet the glorious Sultana in Turkey scarce a fortnight from now! When last I saw her, five—perhaps six years ago, she seemed the most desirable creature on earth! I shall expect a full description of her—and much news— in truth, I am handing you a rare dish, Sir Hugh, and wish I could return to sample it myself. But I doubt you will achieve much satisfaction—those Eastern potentates guard their women wisely—but selfishly, to my mind."

Hugh rose. "Thank you, Sire, for the use of your

coach. Now your physician is waiting, so I will take my leave."

"Come again soon—with news of your new conquest."

Hugh closed the door behind him with a determined click.

Every word of this distasteful interview stood out clearly in his mind as Hugh now glanced tenderly at the sleeping girl, and a heavy sigh escaped him. How he cursed the youthful craving for adventure that had lured him into this position so long ago, when he was scarcely twenty. But he was a born royalist, anxious only to have the chance to serve his prince, and the prospect of unlimited travel, of coming in contact with famous beauties all over Europe had fired his blood. That his own reputation must, inevitably, suffer seemed a mere trifle—indeed it would be exciting to pose as a rake, shocking staid English society, which he found boring. He had been very naive for his age, having been brought up most strictly on a remote, country estate, and had no idea that his handsome looks and manly bearing would have such an effect on women—women carefully selected by His Highness.

The air grew chilly, and, drawing up the blind closest to his seat so as not to wake the others, Hugh saw the splendid peaks lying rosy though still snow-capped, in the first May dawn.

"Are you awake, Phyllida?" he whispered and she started into full consciousness.

"I am indeed—in fact I doubt if I really slept, it was such a miracle to know you were beside me. Have we reached the mountains?"

"Look," he said, and she leaned across him to stare with awe out at the magnificent panorama stretching as far as the eye could see. In a whisper she urged,

"I know it's selfish of me, but *please* don't wake the others just yet. This is a sight to be enjoyed in silence, and Gareth would speak of color, Henri of God, and Miss Smith . . ."

"Most certainly *not* Miss Smith," agreed Hugh, smiling as he wrapped her more closely in his cape.

The coach was moving slowly now, laboring up the steep, winding track which at times had a sheer drop on one side and a wall of rock on the other. Bound together in a sense of closeness and perfect silence, the lovers watched the changing vistas of splendor as the dawn light steadily grew stronger. At last they reached the pass and began to descend into a wide, green valley where cattle grazed and a small church with a bronzed green dome dominated a village of white, pink and pale yellow houses. In the distance a sheet of water gleamed.

"We are in Italy." Hugh broke the precious silence with a note of relief in his voice. "In a short while we shall stop at a small hotel—or *albergo,* as it is called here —for breakfast."

"Is that our final destination?" asked Phyllida.

"No. That lies two or three hours' distance away— and, no," he laughed down into her inquiring eyes. "I am *not* going to tell you where it is until we arrive! It gives me rare pleasure to surprise you, Phyllida—most of my companions during recent years have been too sophisticated for surprise." The shadow that fell across his face was echoed in her heart and she was torn with jealousy. How many women, far more beautiful than she, had shared the enchantment of dawn in the mountains with him? She withdrew a little and he made no effort to hold her.

Soon they drew up in the courtyard of a pink building with *Albergo Frascati* printed in bold black letters over the entrance.

The two young men woke instantly, well rested and enthusiastic, but Miss Smith roused crossly, her mouth pursed, her face wan.

"A *most* unpleasant journey," she said haughtily,

although her regular snores had never ceased for a moment. After washing in fresh warm water, brought by a smiling girl in embroidered petticoats and a huge apron, they all assembled in the small dining room. Miss Smith sipped gingerly at her coffee while the others ate voraciously, enjoying the fresh rolls, homemade preserves and fruit from the garden. Phyllida resolutely put her jealousy away—after all, Hugh was with *her* and she resolved to put all thoughts of yesterday and tomorrow aside and try to live each moment as it came.

The rest of the drive was enthralling, passing the shores of Lake Como, which had Gareth in ecstasies; then there were small walled towns of ancient stone perched on hillsides, olive groves, farms and villages. Soon they were trotting through the beautiful towns of Verona and Padua, with its colonnades, both so beloved by Shakespeare. At last, in the distance, appeared what looked like an ocean, calm and quiet in the morning sun. Round it were buildings—many with great, golden domes and minarets and, even at a distance, the rich music of bronze-tongued bells rose into the still, blue air.

"Surely—I declare!—it must be Venice, Sir Hugh," said Henri, his pale hands clasped fervently together in his excitement.

Hugh laughed. "At last I can keep my secret no longer—it is indeed and, after two more bends in the road we shall arrive at the quayside and embark for the *palazzo* of our host, who lives on the Grand Canal." Seeing their surprise, he explained, "There are no roads and no traffic in the city—instead, canals link every street and one travels everywhere by boat, arriving at a private jetty belonging to each grand house—the quietness is a great experience, I promise you."

"Not a voyage—not after all these dreadful hours," groaned Miss Smith. "I swear I cannot agree."

"Then I fear you will be stranded," said Hugh lightly. "Why not wait until you see the beautiful gondolas which will have been sent to welcome us?"

As they alighted at the quay Phyllida clutched Hugh's arm in delighted amazement. As the coach drew up, two gondoliers in splendid livery with cockaded hats bowed low and escorted them to two long, narrow boats with high, cleft prows painted gold. The seats, each capable of holding no more than two people, were lavishly upholstered and scattered with velvet cushions. The gondoliers led the way down steps and then handed each of them in with grave courtesy. Miss Smith stumbled a little but the water was so still the boat scarcely moved at her clumsy descent.

Their luggage was quickly unloaded and placed in the other gondola. Then the chief gondolier stepped up into the prow, raised a tall, white pole and propelled them smoothly out into midstream, uttering the high, harsh cry used by all gondoliers to warn other boats coming from side canals of their approach.

"Oh, Hugh—it is more like a dream than reality! And the soft coloring of the buildings! All muted and mossy and—and so *very* beautiful."

He smiled. "I had no intention of disappointing you."

Soon they emerged into the Grand Canal, wide and colorful as a painting, bordered by magnificent *palazzi* mostly built from pale golden stone, yet each one quite different. Some were high and turreted, others had long terraces filled with exotic plants and shrubs, and each jetty sported freshly painted mooring bollards striped in red, white and blue, while banners fluttered to proclaim which noble family resided there. Along with the many gondolas there were flatboats selling fruit and others with fish just caught. The only sounds were human voices calling their wares or bartering with servants who had summoned them.

"I should like to stay here forever and never wake up," breathed Phyllida.

"I intend to!" said Gareth firmly. "And by Gad, how I shall paint!"

Their host came out onto the jetty to welcome them

—a thin, spare man with silver curls and bright, searching blue eyes.

He embraced Hugh with warm affection, kissing him on both cheeks, "My dear Hugh—it has been too long! Now introduce me to my other guests . . ."

"Phyllida, this is my dear friend, Signor Piero Roberti —Piero, allow me to present Miss Phyllida Chase." The elderly man took both her hands and gazed at her face, then he smiled, "My dear child—how Botticelli would have loved you!"

"Piero is probably the greatest art connoisseur in Europe," explained Hugh before drawing Miss Smith forward.

"And this is her chaperone, Miss Smith—she has found the journey a sore trial, I fear."

"My poor lady—you are safe now. Leonora," he called over his shoulder and an elderly servant appeared. "Pray take this lady straight to her room—she suffers from exhaustion and needs attention!" Miss Smith, slightly overcome by such manners and so much grandeur, allowed herself to be led away. Hugh then introduced the two young men, explaining each one briefly.

"Ah, Gareth—for there can be no formality between artists—you and I will have much to talk about I know. And Viscomte, you shall be speeded on your way to the Monastery of Santa Dominica up in the hills as soon as you are rested. Now come in, all of you, for you are so very welcome."

They passed through the wide, stone-flagged hall in bewilderment at the wealth of rich hangings and paintings on the walls. Gareth would have paused at each one but Signor Roberti smilingly drew him on, "No, no, my boy —each piece in my great collection must be savored slowly and in peace. We shall have much time together, I hope, and it will give me pleasure to be your guide. Now you must see your rooms and after washing and refreshing yourselves we will take luncheon on the terrace—from there you can watch all the pageant of Venice passing by."

Only Hugh remained at his side and followed his friend into a book-lined study. There, Piero studied his face anxiously.

"How does it go, my son—you look very drawn, and that is unlike you."

Hugh relaxed. How good it was to be with someone who knew all his secrets and, indeed, often helped in his missions,

"For me, it goes badly—the Prince refuses to release me, even after so many years of service. He has 'presented' me with twelve days of freedom," his smile was bitter. "So it is impossible to ask the lovely Phyllida to be my wife."

Piero poured a glass of wine for him, then listened quietly while Hugh sketched in the story. At the end he shook his head,

"Strange that such a selfish, self-indulgent prince should have exquisite taste in art. I must think over your problem carefully, Hugh. It is indeed fortunate that I know the Prince so well. He has visited me many times during his search for treasures to ornament his pavilion in Brighton. I cannot believe there is no solution. It was clear to me from the moment I met her that the lovely Phyllida is an ideal choice for you."

At the mention of her name Hugh got up and began to pace the small room restlessly, "What plagues me, Piero, is that I may only hurt her grievously by remaining here. It was difficult enough during the journey not to declare my love—but here, in this wonderful city, where she will respond to every perfect sight I show her and feel the absurd romanticism in the very air, *shall* I continue to keep my control? Yet, if I do not, she will be distressed and puzzled—she is so open and honest herself."

"You most certainly *must* stay while you can!" Piero's voice was quite peremptory. "It will bring a far greater knowledge of each other, and when, as I feel sure you will, you finally gain your release from service, she will marvel at your courage and restraint."

"You will never know what it cost me to see her at

the Paris Opera—and have to pay exaggerated attention to the flighty Lady Camden! Oh, Phyllida looked a vision that night, Piero—more perfect than even your Botticelli could have painted!"

"Take heart, my dear Hugh. Meantime, this visit to Constantinople is of very great importance, for your country as much as your Prince. I have many details to give you."

"And I am instructed to see the Contessa Orieta during this precious time here. Yet I will *not* waste many hours traveling to Rome and back!"

"Calm yourself. I shall arrange that she comes here—oh, not to my house of course, for that could be embarrassing," a smile twitched his lips. "She is very—demanding—our *bella* Orieta! But so useful. Now, leave your burden with me and let us go to luncheon in a spirit of fiesta!"

And, since Miss Smith had taken gladly to her bed, that is precisely what the meal became. The terrace itself was a revelation to the visitors—the walls charmingly decorated with mosaic frescoes, framed by ornamental vines, small orange trees in tubs standing sentinel, already bearing globes of fruit amongst their glossy leaves, while the exotic colors of carefully nurtured hibiscus flowers twined round the pilasters of the low parapet looking out over the canal.

The young visitors might have been overawed—especially by the long table set with heavy old silver and priceless crystal—had not Piero been a perfect host, used to entertaining everyone from Crowned Heads, great art lovers like himself, to aspiring, penniless young painters whom he occasionally subsidized once he was convinced of their talent. Now, he sat Phyllida on his right and gave her almost his entire attention. He wanted to know more of this beautiful creature who had won the heart of one of his dearest young friends.

They were soon delighted with each other. Their conversations were accompanied by the musical voices of gondoliers, singing Venetian airs—not all the same but blending harmoniously through the musical Italian language and the gift of a natural ear to capture a hint of melody.

"Ours is the language of music," Piero told her as she paused to listen. "And, for myself, I think also of love —although the French claim that distinction."

"Oh, the French," said Phyllida with a slight shudder. "I heard that too, in England—but the reality does not even *permit* love!"

He rested a long, beautiful hand on hers. "That has been a nightmare you must forget, Phyllida." He glanced compassionately at Henri, who ate silently, his face transfigured by the certainty that tomorrow he might be, at last, on his way to a monastery. Piero went on, "To attempt to shackle the two of you together is monstrous! How could anyone be so blind?"

"Tante Emilie—no, she is *not* my aunt, simply my godmother—thought of nothing but heirs and estates. She never considered human beings at all!" Her green eyes blazed with anger at the memory of her situation, which she still could not believe was completely behind her now.

"Venice will lay all the bad dreams to rest, my dear," Piero assured her. "Now, pray tell me about your life until now."

Phyllida laughed ruefully, "Alas, it has been most dull —spent mostly in Bath! No, *your* life, Signor Roberti, that is what I long to hear about. Oh, please do no think me rude—I mean how you came to love art so much and the grand visitors you must have entertained—it is such a new, exciting life for me!"

Under her spell from then on, the fine old man obeyed—and gradually Gareth, Hugh and even Henri were listening, fascinated.

It was well after four o'clock when the meal was finished and the last dregs of coffee drunk and Hugh said,

"Phyllida, you must rest, I insist. You have been awake since dawn and your first night in Venice is something we must celebrate in style. I know Piero will agree with me."

Much later that evening—for Signor Roberti did not dine until ten o'clock—Phyllida wished, wistfully, that she had not been so anxious to leave her Paris gowns behind, especially the white one. Outside her low windows, Venice gleamed and sparkled with a million points of light, all reflected in the still, black waters. There was soft singing, the languorous sound of lutes and guitars floating in the air, and she longed to appear like a princess in honor of it all. But when she looked at her own gowns, unpacked and beautifully pressed by some unseen maid, she wondered why Tante Emilie had treated them with such scorn! Why, they were beautiful, and, with a tender smile, she chose to wear the one of pale gold in which she had first danced with Hugh. Would he remember? Would it break down the subtle barrier which he seemed still to hold between them?

Surely it was strange that he had not kissed her once during the long night drive when in every way he had been so tender, so close. Her musings were interrupted by Maria, a smiling little maid who could speak no English. She seemed horrified that Phyllida had dressed already without help. But in sign language, which made them both laugh, she conveyed the message that she would dress Phyllida's hair. This she did, brushing it with firm, soothing strokes and uttering little birdlike cries of admiration amongst which *"Che bellezza!"* occurred most often. Then, instead of doing her hair in a chignon, she made two thick plaits and wound them round Phyllida's head like a coronet, asking anxiously,

"Va bene, Signorina?"

Phyllida studied the effect with surprise—then pleasure. It emphasized the delicate, cameo lines of her face. She nodded, smiling—she really must learn a few words of Italian, especially "thank you." Beaming, Maria held the door open for her.

Everything about the *palazzo* was perfection, from the wide, curving staircase to the dark splendor of the great dining room. As she entered, Hugh's smile told her that he had remembered their dance, and her heart sang. She dared not ask him how long he would stay, but surely, surely, even if they spent only a few days in this wonderful place, he would say the words she ached to hear.

Dinner was superb but lasted no more than an hour, for Piero had a surprise for them. He led them to the jetty where the gondola was waiting, illuminated by lanterns fore and aft. The gondolier wore national dress—long, crisp white trousers, striped jersey and a wide-brimmed straw hat decorated with gay ribbons. As he pushed off to join the many other gondolas filled with happy people in evening dress and, occasionally, two lovers entwined, he began to serenade them in a pleasant, tenor voice. The songs were lilting, haunting, capturing the magic of the moonlit night and rainbow reflections of lanterns on the dark water. Piero had seated Hugh and Phyllida side by side but, though she yearned just for the touch of his hand to complete her delight, he made no move, although he often pointed out famous buildings as they passed.

"I shall take you exploring on foot tomorrow," he promised. "It is a selfish pleasure of those who already love Venice to show it to someone one . . ." he hesitated, "someone one is fond of." His voice was warm but glancing at his clear-cut profile beside her, Phyllida felt a flick of sadness which she tried hard to banish. Perhaps, she thought desperately, he wants to know me better—to wait until we are quite alone . . . he is very strong. . . .

The next day Hugh and Phyllida strolled leisurely along the sides of many canals, often turning into narrow alleys for him to show her some church or building he especially admired. And, in one of these alleys filled with small shops, which he translated as "The Way of the Scent Makers," he bought her a bottle of rare, exotic perfume. "It would be most risqué in Bath," he laughed, "but here,

it suits the whole atmosphere—I know you will like it."
He asked for her handkerchief and sprinkled a few drops
on it. "Is it not the very essence of Venice?"

"Oh, Hugh—it is delightful. Thank you," she cried.
Then her strong, rebellious spirit rose and the sour pangs
of jealousy wracked her again. How did he *know*? For he
had chosen unerringly. To how many other women had he
given this same gift while taking them on his "Grand
Tour." Watching her with his sensitive dark eyes Hugh
read her mind from the sudden flash of her emerald eyes,
and the longing to take her in his arms then and there, to
put duty aside no matter what the cost was almost overwhelming. So, both fighting their private battles, they
walked in silence to the famous Piazza San Marco. They
passed the pale gold Palace of the Doges and the tall
Campanile crowded by the golden lion of Venice, gleaming in the sun, toward the great basilica at the top, with
the four splendid bronze horses, green now from years of
sun and weather, seeming to strain at the reins to leap to
the four corners of the world.

Jealousy had no place here. Phyllida recognized how
base and destructive an emotion it was. Spellbound by
beauty, she slipped her arm through Hugh's and he smiled
down at her gratefully. She was so dear, so precious. He
knew he had hurt her many times—and would be forced
to hurt her more, but today was their own.

They entered the sudden darkness of the basilica itself and he guided her round the many works of art, the
side chapels and the magnificent high altar all pervaded
by the scent of incense and musk and lighted by ranks of
candles in front of shrines.

"It is magnificent but, in this city of sunlight, why
must it be so dark?" she commented honestly.

Hugh chuckled with pleasure. "My own feelings exactly! But few people—if any—are frank enough to say
so. Come, we will take a light lunch in the piazza, where
you shall have all the sunlight you want. After that it will
be the time of siesta, for the heat grows intense. Shops

close until evening, houses are shuttered and most people sleep but—if you are not exhausted, my Phyllida, I thought we might hire a boat and sail out into the lagoon. There is always a slight breeze there, although the water is like silk, and we can see Venice for the shimmering dream she is."

Her heart rose absurdly at this almost unconscious use of the possessive little word "my," and she turned a glowing face toward his.

"I am certainly not exhausted! And—you are the perfect guide, Hugh."

They went down to the main quay facing the lagoon where there were many gondolas and flat-bottomed sailboats plying for hire. Hugh placed her on a wooden seat. "Wait here while I choose a boat," he laughed. "One has to bargain for a sensible price—when they see what they call 'an English Milord' coming they assume we are made of gold!"

At last he struck a bargain with a cheerful little man who owned a wide, comfortable craft with a brown sail who handed Phyllida aboard with the smiling grace of a courtier. "Oh, *bella, bella principessa!*" he declared admiringly.

Hugh settled her comfortably and they sailed slowly out into the bay, the brown sail flapping gently whenever the slight breeze slackened altogether. Silence and peace enveloped them and, as Phyllida no longer expected a declaration of love from Hugh, at least not yet, she drank in the spectacle of Venice, shimmering indeed under the hot sun and listened to his beloved voice as he pointed out special places of interest.

She was content—but how long would this dream last?

Back at the *palazzo* Miss Smith was waiting for her in her room, her face stern.

"I understand you have been out all day long with that—that *man*," she said crossly. "I declare you are quite shameless, Phyllida, but this state of affairs must not continue! Indeed it will not. I am writing to your poor mother, as if she has not had enough to bear! And I swear that your father will come posthaste to put a stop to this folly and take us both back to the safety of Bath. Of course your reputation will be quite ruined, but you have only your willful ways to thank!"

As soon as she had gone Phyllida sped downstairs to find Piero Roberti and Gareth just returned from visiting an art gallery.

She told them of Miss Smith's harsh words, ending, "Oh please, please can you not prevent her sending such a letter? I—I am so very happy and I fear it may not last long." Piero gave her a piercing glance from his kind eyes; had Hugh told her or was it the intuition of a girl in love that had warned her? He smiled and his eyes twinkled.

"My dear, Hugh warned me that this foolish woman would do such a thing. I gather she even wished to leave while the coach was traveling at speed!" He shook his head pityingly. "Poor creature, there is nothing so ironclad as thwarted British virtue! But do not worry, child—all is arranged. Letters have to be taken by boat from here, carried by one of my servants and no letter addressed to Mrs. Chase, unless written by you and handed to me, will leave at all, I promise you."

"Oh, *why* . . ." Phyllida began stormily, but she caught the wild question back in time. What was the use of asking the question that no one would answer: *Why* was Hugh, with his courtesy and brilliance, considered so undesirable? And why, *why* must she love him to distraction?

Chapter
Seven

Late that evening, when all the household had gone to bed, Piero Roberti and Sir Hugh Abingdon lingered on the terrace. The end of May was a perfect time in Venice, the air warm and balmy with the scent of thousands of flowers and shrubs, but yet not hot enough for the smell of stagnant water to rise from the canals. Piero sat slowly smoking a cigar, in no hurry to force the confidence that Hugh so obviously was deciding to impart. At last Hugh spoke, his voice rough,

"It is no use—I am not strong enough, I longed, above all else, to spend these few days alone with Phyllida, but it is beyond my powers. If only she were not so open, so honest, so lacking in all guile . . ."

"Then you would not love her so dearly," Piero's voice was gentle in the darkness. "I have known you now for almost six years—and sometimes wondered how long it would be before you gave your heart, for you are of that rare breed who does not love more than once. I have often prayed that it might not happen until your missions for the Prince were completed. But one cannot choose these things and it has happened now, when for once I agree with that self-indulgent future king, for you must go to Constantinople; but after that he *must* release you—and I shall do my best to help you insist that he does."

Hugh rose and moved to lean on the balustrade, gazing down at the Grand Canal where lights still shone. "My release will not wipe out the past," he said moodily. "Most people in England outside the inner Court circle regard me with the same revulsion as does the tiresome Miss Smith. I am branded a rake, a loose-liver, a man not welcome in any respectable house that contains daughters. I know Phyllida will understand—or would if I ever tell her. But I have decided that it is unthinkable to ask her to share that stigma. Can you imagine," he went on passionately, "that pure, glorious girl having to be ashamed of her husband? For, believe me, I have lived such a life too long now for opinion to change just because I marry. She would have to face whispers behind fans, scorn for herself as well as me, lying gossip and odious laughter if I even performed a common courtesy such as handing a pretty woman out of her carriage. Dear God, why did I never guess the price for my life would be so high? No, she must go free as I meant her to do when she first traveled to France . . ."

Piero joined him, his heart aching for the boy but his voice still calm, "You cannot 'set someone free' just to appease your conscience, Hugh. At least, not a girl like Phyllida. She loves as whole-heartedly as you do." He sighed. "I understand you wish to be with her, but not alone. Very well, we shall accept invitations and I, too, will plan a splendid party. During the day I shall suggest expeditions either with myself as guide, or ask you to take Gareth to various exhibitions or to meet artists. She will enjoy that. And there is always the so-boring Miss Smith! My housekeeper tells me she is up and about but in a vile temper—oh, I shall intercept any letters to Mrs. Chase, by the way."

"What a true friend you are, Piero!" Hugh turned to bid good-night and, in the reflected lights from a passing gondola, Piero noticed with sadness the grim set of his fine jaw, the darkness in his chestnut brown eyes, usually so alive.

Early the next morning Henri left for the monastery on the mainland and the three of them gathered on the jetty to wish him farewell. His earnest gratitude was quite embarrassing, but when he came to Phyllida he raised both her slim hands and kissed them fervently.

"No words can express what I owe you—but I shall remember you all my days and pray that you may find happiness." Then, in a lower voice with a shy smile, he added, "Dare I believe you have already found it? He has a great heart and all of it, I think, is yours."

Phyllida managed to return his smile, although such gentle faith in something she knew was already flawed in some mysterious way, made her long to cry.

When his gondola was out of sight they turned back into the *palazzo* and Hugh said, with a wry smile, "I must see Miss Smith. I gave her my word as a gentleman that I would arrange a voyage back to England if she wished. Would you ask a servant to bring her to your study, Piero —if I may borrow it for ten minutes?"

He waited for the elderly termagant with some trepidation—knowing he must not lose his temper. But it was likely to prove difficult, since she held such a low opinion of him and would not hesitate to express it with downright rudeness. In five minutes she stalked in, her mouth thin and compressed and spots of high color on her bony cheeks that indicated an unpleasant scene to come. Without waiting for Hugh to speak, she snapped,

"Well, at least you have the grace to send for me— though I declare I don't know how you dare confront me! Taking poor, innocent Phyllida out alone for a whole day unchaperoned—I suppose you are cad enough to take advantage of an old woman's exhaustion!"

"Miss Smith, I have not asked you here to discuss my action, but to fulfill a promise. If you wish I will gladly arrange your journey back to England immediately."

"Ha! And leave you to work your wicked wiles on a defenseless girl, I suppose! I admit she is tiresomely head-

117

strong and willful, but I *trust* she is still innocent?" It was an outrageous insult and Hugh held his temper in check with difficulty.

"I assure you, Miss Smith, Miss Chase's innocence is sacred to me. I have no 'designs' on her whatsoever—she is merely a charming child, eager to explore the many beauties of this city and it has been a pleasure to show her some of them. I do *not* seduce young girls scarcely out of the schoolroom, whatever you choose to believe. Now, about your journey . . ."

Miss Smith tossed her head, "You would pack me off alone, would you? You are wrong, Sir Hugh. Either Phyllida accompanies me, as she most certainly should, or I remain at my arduous post until her parents send me instructions. Oh, yes, I have written exposing your villainy to the full, I declare."

"I see. You would prefer her to have remained in Paris to marry the Viscomte against her will, I suppose. And against his will, too." She gasped in disbelief. "He left this morning to enter a Catholic monastery," he went on silkily. "I understand you dislike all Catholics—but Phyllida would have soon become one, for he is most devout. You cannot arrange people all you own way, Miss Smith, so—you still wish to stay?"

"Most certainly—unpleasant though it will be." And she marched out with the air of a martyr, nobly sacrificing herself for purity's sake.

At first Hugh was angry but soon—as usually happened—the humor of it struck him and he began to laugh. He was still laughing when Phyllida and Piero came in to hear how he had fared.

"Gad, I have never met a woman so straitlaced," he exclaimed. "I wonder that she manages to breathe inside that iron encasement! No," he answered their inquiring looks, "she refuses to budge. Poor Phyllida, you are her cross and bear it she will, protecting you from imagined dangers. Yet she does not care for you very much, I fear. How did your mamma endure her in the house?"

"Oh, she was useful, I suppose," said Phyllida vaguely, then, with a rush of honesty, she went on in a bleak little voice that touched both men deeply. "Mamma has never tried to understand either Gareth or me—she couldn't impose a chaperone on him but she could, and did, set a dragon to guard against—and report—my slightest indiscretion. Miss Smith used to be our governess and might have made us hate learning, except for Gareth's determination! It was he who taught me how to love art and books—and life. I *wish* I had been born a man, too."

"Thank God you weren't!" Hugh cried, his eyes glowing with love, which lit her heart for a moment until he remembered himself and added, "Think how you would have deprived the young men who adore you and the fortunate one who will win you as his wife."

Piero broke into the pregnant silence in his most practical tones,

"We cannot debate your sex, Phyllida, since you are every inch a beautiful young woman, whether you like it or not. Meantime, my gondola is waiting, for I wish to show you certain things that even Hugh may never have discovered. Gareth is absorbed on the terrace, sketching the Grand Canal, using colors available here which he had never known of in England. I believe he has real talent. So—shall we go?"

That evening Piero escorted them all to a ball given by the Duchessa de' Meccini. A flunky in tight-waisted brown livery frogged with gold led them up two shallow, curved staircases and ushered them onto a vast, flat roof garden edged with slender trees and fragrant rose bushes. A parquet dance floor had been laid out open to the stars and musicians were arranging their music in a vine-covered bower. Round the edge of the dance floor small tables of wrought iron were placed, decorated with flowers and surrounded with comfortable chairs. Phyllida looked round her in delight and Piero chuckled at her side. "My friends, you will find, are always artistic and never dull.

Ah, Duchessa," he kissed the hand of a charming woman who had come to welcome them. She was neither young nor beautiful, but her dark eyes sparkled as brightly as the diamonds in her hair and her smile was ravishing. She welcomed Hugh with a laughing reproof,

"Hugh, you are so wicked! Here, in Venice, yet you have not called on me." Then she turned to Phyllida, who had just been introduced, and looked at her with warm approval. "Ah, but now I see the reason I shall have to forgive you. How lovely you are, my dear—and far too young to be monopolized by the naughty, handsome Hugh! Come and let me present you to my younger guests."

It was a perfectly planned assembly, numbering not more than sixty in all. "Crowds are so wearing, I find," explained the Duchessa. "I prefer a gathering of intelligent friends, some my own age and others younger, for they are so full of life!"

Phyllida, who had been rather subdued all day, responded to this unique party with all her being, and so did Gareth. To her delight, her young Italian partners all danced well, and their admiring compliments, even if spoken in Italian, made her feel quite light-headed. If Hugh didn't want her, she thought defiantly, the world was full of men who did.

Her light-headedness was partly due to the occasional intervals when everyone sat at the tables and footmen carried round large silver trays of delicacies—much prized giant prawns from the bay cooked crisply on a bed of savory rice; rich lasagna in cheese sauce; portions of tender spring chicken stuffed with chestnuts; herbs and a hint of garlic served with green salad; even baby octopus which, to her surprise, was delicious. And all accompanied by goblets of iced champagne, which she was not used to.

But at last she came face to face with Hugh himself. In fact he materialized beside her at the end of an interval and said,

"So—you have won many hearts, Phyllida, and I am

glad. But now I *demand* one dance—if only as an echo from the past!"

She looked up at his dark, masterful face and her good resolutions melted away. With his fine head etched against the stars, his long, strong hands held out to her, she knew that he held her heart forever. Like a sleep-walker she rose and drifted into his arms as if she had no will of her own—as, indeed, she hadn't.

Hugh knew that if he looked down into her shining green eyes on this magic night he would be lost, so he held her close as they moved silently, gracefully round the floor.

Watching them with great pleasure, the Duchessa said to Piero,

"Separately they are splendid—together a work of art! Surely Hugh has met his match at last?"

"One cannot be sure, Felicia—Hugh's fatal fascination for women is that he treats each one as though she were the center of his universe," he smiled. "I wish I had been born with such a gift. Now, when will you show me the icon you have acquired from Russia? I fear you will soon have a collection to rival my own and that will never do!"

"Come—you shall see it now, for it is perfect by candlelight and I have danced quite enough."

When the music ended Phyllida clung to Hugh a moment longer—they had never been so close and the strong rhythm of his heart against her breast thrilled through her whole being. But he released her gently with a smile, "Young Count Antonio has been waiting for this moment so impatiently that, if I hold you a moment longer I fear he will challenge me to a duel, and I am sorely out of practice!"

Several days passed in the same way with Hugh and Phyllida together and yet not really so. Each evening, as he had promised, Piero took them to magnificent parties or, on one occasion, a private concert held in a vast, mirrored ballroom. And Phyllida's admirers not only grew in number, but three or four fell in love with her, sending flowers, small gifts and poems so lyrical that she blushed when Piero translated them for her.

"But he cannot love me so much—he scarcely knows me!" she protested on one occasion.

"My dear, the Italians thrive on passion," Piero's eyes twinkled merrily. "Indeed, they are wretched when they are *not* deeply in love!"

"But I cannot return such feelings and—and I hate to break any hearts!"

Piero laughed outright. "For most young men, having a broken heart is a matter for pride—they are so dramatic, you have no idea! It gives them scope for more poetry and to go romantically dressed in black or somber colors so that all their friends will sympathize—usually with quantities of wine until they *all* feel equally maudlin!"

Phyllida had to laugh at such a picture, "How disappointed they must be if the girl accepts them!"

"Oh, they rarely do—the girls here know what is expected of them—besides, they usually know quite early in life who is destined to be their husband and grow up already familiar with him and, if possible, loving him."

"You mean that marriages are arranged as they are in France?"

"My dear, in Italy it is managed with far more finesse and consideration. But it is desirable that certain families —or fortunes—should be joined, and our girls are very practical."

"So all this young heartbreak is just a game!" Phyllida's eyes darkened, thinking how vastly different it would be for her since Hugh did not mean either to woo her truly, much less marry her.

Quite often her admirers serenaded her from a gondola drawn up beneath the terrace where she and the others were dining before setting off for the evening's entertainment. Taught by Piero and watched with amusement, she fulfilled her role perfectly, appearing briefly by

the balustrade and either flirting demurely over her fa
once or twice, picking a hibiscus flower and tossing it down
with a charming smile to the singer. One night she said,

"I declare, Italians must be the most romantic people
in the world!"

"Of *course* we are!" Piero sounded quite indignant.
"How else should we produce so much great art and
literature? Unhappiness produces true creative work—
happiness, nothing, because there is no yearning of soul."

Hugh was miserably aware that his time was running
out—three more days would stretch it to the maximum.
Besides, letters of further instruction from England and
messages delivered by Piero made him realize that his visit
to Constantinople might last some time—even two or
three months, and the thought of charming a luscious
Eastern beauty filled him with loathing.

Piero announced that two evenings later he was giving a party himself—quite different from the ones they had
been attending. Instead of using his *palazzo* he was having
about twenty guests taken across the lagoon to one of the
most distant islands, Torcello.

"It is extremely beautiful," he told Phyllida. "And
almost deserted, unlike the closer islands of the lacemak-
ers and glassblowers. There is an exquisite half-ruined
church, golden sand where the sea ripples with phos-
phorescence and an open cloister where we shall take supper alfresco by moonlight."

Her eyes shone. "It sounds like a dream," she exclaimed.

"Of course. It is meant to be one!"

The evening before this party Phyllida and Hugh had
their nearest approach to a quarrel. In a way it was a relief to her to give voice to some of her feelings for once,
instead of holding them so fiercely in check.

It happened because, that morning when she came
down, Piero said,

"I am afraid Hugh has already gone out—he did not
say where—and I too am forced to go to a meeting of art

collectors. Might it not be a kind gesture if you offered to show Miss Smith some of the sights of Venice?" he chuckled ruefully. "I know it is not to your taste, my dear, but I fear she is quite upsetting my delightful housekeeper with her endless complaints! And she cannot understand why she has had no answer from her letter to your mother! not knowing it was consumed to ashes almost as soon as written."

"Oh—may I not join Gareth instead?" pleaded Phyllida. "I swear that Miss Smith could make even Venice seem ugly."

"Gareth was out shortly after dawn with his paints and sketching pad—he says he has found some backwater with intricate shadows in the early light. There is no stopping the boy, now he has been given his head, from painting to his heart's content."

Phyllida still looked stubborn, so Piero in a voice gentle but for once stern said, "Be generous, my child. Life has endowed you with so much and that poor, frustrated creature with so little. You need not show her the things that especially delight you and she cannot, for instance, spoil the cheerful open market along the main quayside. Besides, although diplomacy may be irksome at the time, you may be glad of this act of kindness in the future."

Phyllida looked startled, "You are warning me, I believe. Are you saying that I shall soon have to rely on her company again?" She was deeply disturbed—was this time of mixed pain and pleasure, of at least having Hugh near if not close coming to an end?

"I am saying nothing—simply that you should take Miss Smith out this morning. Now I must leave or I shall be late and there are rumors of some Leonardo da Vinci drawings coming on to the market which I must not miss."

She could not lose an elusive sense of foreboding as she went slowly upstairs, and Miss Smith did nothing to lighten her mood.

"I see," said that lady with heavy sarcasm. "The at-

124

tentive *gentlemen* are not attending you this morning, so you turn to me, Phyllida," she sniffed. "I declare, I find this place most unhealthy—all that stagnant water everywhere, I swear I have seen refuse floating on it several times! Why they cannot cover it over and have civilized carriages seems ridiculous. It is my duty to escort you, of course, but I will not set foot in a boat."

This restored Phyllida's humor and, in spite of her irritation, she saw Miss Smith for the first time as an object of pity, as Piero had said.

"We need not go by gondola at all," she promised. "There are wide promenades beside the canals—we can pass many noble mansions and *palazzi* which will interest you and then explore the famous market." Her generous heart excelled itself in trying to override her conscience about this difficult companion. "I should like to buy you a present there—a memento, perhaps, of Italy."

So they set forth. Miss Smith determinedly drab in her old gray alpaca, which she refused to relinquish, and Phyllida, used to the growing heat of the sun, in a cool sprigged muslin and wide-brimmed hat trimmed with green ribbons which Piero had insisted on buying for her. They walked in silence, Phyllida looking straight ahead with her proud chin held high in an effort to subdue the amorous glances and coarse compliments which were part of life to all Italian men, however humble. They would shock Miss Smith to the core.

So they reached the market and Phyllida was secretly relieved. It was one thing to walk beside the canals with strong, elegant Hugh on one side of her and the eminent Signor Roberti on the other. But alone, with only dowdy Miss Smith accompanying her, she had flinched once or twice at the raucous voices. Now, in the market, many stalls were run by stout countrywomen in their black cotton skirts and tattered shawls; children darted about, too —thin, brown-faced and beautiful as painted seraphim their liquid dark eyes were everywhere, seeing what they might steal.

Miss Smith caused merry laughter as she held her nose passing the fish stalls but, when they came to the section with finely tooled leather purses, lace handkerchiefs, silk cravats and fragile animals of blown glass, her eyes brightened. She wanted an impressive gift for a friend in Bath, but after looking round she said,

"Well, I declare! It's not like Brighton—I haven't seen a single article marked 'A Present from Venice'— what can they be thinking of?"

Suppressing her laughter Phyllida tried to explain, "They don't have foreign visitors here—at least, only very rich ones who never buy souvenirs. Pray choose one of these charming purses—or look, that glass dolphin is very pretty."

Miss Smith was about to refuse when abruptly she gave a loud squeal instead and her face contorted with rage. "Somebody *pinched* me. I declare, these people are savages!"

"Oh, poor Miss Smith—did it hurt? Where did it happen?"

Miss Smith flushed with embarrassed indignation. "Don't ask indelicate questions, Phyllida! Now, I won't stay in this wicked crowd another minute!" And she stalked off in the direction of the Piazza San Marco. Phyllida followed with a sinking heart—that was one of the special places she treasured and she had planned to turn back after the market and take coffee in a small café on the way home.

She need not have worried, Miss Smith was too busy making sure that no man approached her to take any notice of the beauty spread out before her.

"That unpleasantness has quite upset my nerves—I swear I am about to have an attack of the vapors," she said rather querulously. "I must sit down—and how I shall find courage to walk back to the *palazzo* I *don't* know!"

With a sigh, Phyllida led her to one of the outdoor cafés, so gay under their awnings. Then abruptly she stood still, her heart pounding. There was Hugh! Not only at the same café, but at the very table where they had lunched together on the first day before sailing on the lagoon. He had his back toward her and was bending fo ward most attentively to listen to the voluptuous creature facing him. She was obviously an Italian, with black hair coiffed elaborately round a chic little straw hat that tilted forward to shade her enormous, liquid eyes; the sensuous mouth was full-lipped and red, while her perfectly cut white gown did little to disguise the generous lines of her bosom tapering to a well-corseted small waist. As Phyllida watched, paralyzed with shock, Hugh reached out and took one of the plump, beringed hands in his.

Suddenly dreading that he might sense her horrified stare and turn and see her, Phyllida pulled herself together with some difficulty. Wheeling round sharply on Miss Smith, she said in a small, tight voice,

"I had quite forgot—it is not permitted for women unaccompanied by a man to sit out here. If you can withstand the vapors for just a few moments, I know a quiet indoor café where we shall be welcome."

Miss Smith had not only withstood the imaginary vapors but they had vanished in triumph. She, too, had seen Sir Hugh and his companion and her vitriolic tongue spared Phyllida nothing.

"Now, at last, you have proof before your very eyes of what I have been telling you! Oh, he may squire you about in a fairly correct way—he could scarce dare to do otherwise—but you see how he indulges his wicked ways! I declare that woman is no better than she should be—and him making outrageous advances *in public!* I swear, Sir Hugh is a devil incarnate and the sooner we return to your parents in England the better. *They* won't permit you to get into his evil clutches again, I can tell you!"

Phyllida herself felt a little faint for the first time in her life. The sunlit piazza swam before her eyes and the great bronze horses on the basilica swayed to life, threatening to leap down and crush her under their pawing hooves. But she refused to give way—it would pass quickly if she concentrated on her one haven—the cool, spacious bedroom at the *palazzo,* filled with fresh flowers every day, where she could be alone. The thought of taking coffee with Miss Smith, who would not cease her joyous diatribe, was anathema.

"I think we will go home," she said—her voice sounding far away in her ears—"I have always been escorted by Signore Roberti and Sir Hugh until now but, after your unfortunate experience in the market, I think perhaps it is unwise for two women to venture out alone." The piazza steadied and the horses stood immobile at last. "We need not walk back through the market," she added hastily. "I know of quiet paths beside smaller canals and we can reach the *palazzo* within ten minutes."

"I am delighted to see that, at last, you have been shocked back to your senses, Phyllida," replied Miss Smith, folding her tight lips into an unbearably smug expression. "I am confident that I shall hear from your mother today and then we can leave these nasty, foreign parts without delay."

Knowing that she was being unkind, yet perversely glad that Miss Smith should suffer too, Phyllida set out at a brisk pace that suited both her stormy mood and her long, supple legs. She knew that her chaperone dared not lag behind for fear of being lost in an unfamiliar city. It was a cruel thing to do, for, even with her new Paris boots, Miss Smith's feet always troubled her, but Phyllida's one burning wish was to hasten away as fast as she could from the odious scene she had witnessed.

How *could* Hugh accompany her so willingly, dance with her so closely, and yet feel forced to break away to resume an immoral life? Yet how willingly she herself would have gone into his embrace! But then the vision of the woman with him today rose before her eyes—experienced, older, shameless in her appearance. Could that *really* be what he preferred?

When, at last, safely in her bedroom, she tossed her

hat and reticule on the bed and sank down beside one of the low, wide windows, resting her arms along the cool sill, she was desolate far beyond tears. These golden days in Venice had been so wonderful yet such an enigma, with Hugh so attentive and considerate at times, his eyes glowing with love and his face so fine and true. Then, when an obvious chance came for him to take her in his arms and declare his feelings, he went out of his way to avoid it. *Why?*

How *could* he be a rake at heart, needing the company of fast women like the one today—and the one at the Paris Opera—yet showing no sign of dissipation and possessing such warm sensitivity and intelligence?

Wearily, she rested her now throbbing head on her arms, trying in vain to understand how she could love this mysterious man with her whole being, and trying not to look ahead into a future which held no hope. She felt like two people: one who trusted him in spite of everything and would love him forever, and one who was shocked and baffled by his uncharacteristic actions.

A maid came to tell her that Signor Roberti had returned and hoped she would join him on the terrace for lunch.

"Oh, no, tell him—please make my apologies, Maria. I have been walking in the sun and have a slight headache; I think I will rest quietly until this evening."

When Piero received her message, he looked troubled. Hugh had assured him that he would take Orieta straight to the elegant, secluded Hotel d'Oro, where there could be no risk of their being seen. There was a pleasant, shady garden there where they could discuss the news she brought him and then take lunch. But Orieta was extremely willful, and if she had a fancy to flaunt herself a little (for she adored attention), then Hugh would have no chance of preventing her.

Thoughtfully, Piero selected some tempting delicacies on a plate, called for a small silver salver and added a glass of chilled white wine, a napkin in which he placed a glowing hibiscus flower; and a few minutes later, he knocked gently on Phyllida's door and went straight in without waiting for an answer.

"Oh!" She looked up, startled.

Piero placed the salver on a small table, drew up two chairs before saying,

"My dear, I know that you are not unwell—but, I think, distressed by something—am I not right? Now, come and sit here. Gazing out of the window will solve nothing, but talking can be a great relief."

His voice was so gentle and affectionate that she could not disobey him without positive rudeness. Besides, suddenly she longed to confide in someone, since Gareth was totally absorbed in his new freedom to paint. Slowly she sat in the chair he indicated.

"I fear you will think me foolish," she began abruptly.

"My dear Phyllida, I have never belittled any human action so far in my life. There is always a reason, especially with a girl of your great intelligence."

Gratefully, she poured out her heart, ending with, "I *know* Hugh is so fine, just as I know how deeply I shall always love him. But why will he say nothing? For, when he looks at me, I know he cares! What shall I do?"

Piero was inwardly distressed, knowing the whole truth and yet honor bound not to disclose it. In that moment he hated the Prince Regent as much as he was capable of hating any person.

He took time to select his words, while Phyllida gazed at him with fervent hope that he might help her.

"I have known Hugh for many years," Piero began, "and in all that time I have never known him to be anything but the very soul of honor. Your love is not misplaced, my child, but—I think you may have to wait awhile for things to come right. You are very young, you know, and Hugh much regrets his reputation. He respects you too much to inflict that on you."

Phyllida's eyes glowed like green fire, "If *that* is all, I do not care one fig for his past! I—I suppose he has to see these women from time to time out of kindness. But tonight, I shall challenge him when he returns. I *cannot* endure this uncertainty another day!"

Chapter Eight

On Piero's advice, Phyllida eventually ate the delicious food he had brought and drank the glass of wine. But later, as she dressed for the evening, her despairing anger grew again. She took particular care to look her very best, choosing a shot copper silk and carrying a charming fan of small, gold feathers. Maria dressed her hair high on her head, entwining three or four golden flowers in the shining strands.

Downstairs, she found Hugh alone in the great salon, his back toward the door as he gazed out of the window. Before her resolve could weaken, Phyllida said,

"Do you take all your 'ladies' to the same table in the piazza?"

He turned, smiling, "My dear Phyllida, I had no idea you were there today. Why did you not join us?"

"*Join* you?" She was shocked by such a brazen suggestion. "I am not in the habit of intruding on such *intimate* meetings! Besides, you were paying very affectionate attention to that—that woman."

Hugh burst out laughing, "My dear child—I have known the Contessa Orieta for many years, and Italians enjoy extravagant attentions, as you must have realized by now—to them it is a game."

Phyllida actually stamped her foot in fury at Hugh calling her a child. "I am *not* a 'child' and it never seems to occur to you that *I* might enjoy such attentions sometime!"

He came toward her. "Oh, Phyllida, now you *are* being childish. One treats an English girl with respect—and I must point out that, although I brought you here and much enjoy your company, you do not own me, you know. There is no reason why I should not meet old friends—or treat them coldly just because I have made a new one."

He spoke gently but with sudden firmness and the fight in her collapsed. In that moment she was aware of the age gap between them and ashamed of herself in face of his great dignity.

"I—I am sorry," she said reluctantly. "You make my behavior seem very young and foolish."

She did, indeed, look very young, but utterly charming with her proud eyes cast down, waiting for a further rebuke.

"You are not foolish but outspoken and honest and I would have you no other way." He reached out and tilted up her chin so that she was forced to look at him. "Surely you would despise me if I treated you like a French coquette—oh, yes, I saw you at the opera—or an Italian lady hungry for admiration however insincere. If I did, you would have good reason to believe all the rumors surrounding me. Now, let us be friends again, I pray, and enjoy the evening." He was sorely tempted to add that they had only two more left to them, but that would be cheating—especially as he knew, with a heavy heart, that he must dash all her hopes and hurt her deeply before he left.

Phyllida responded with a tremulous smile. "I will try—and try not to be absurdly jealous when, as you say, I have no right at all."

Oh, my dear, dear love you have every right in the world, he thought unhappily, but his smile remained warm and he placed her arm in his to lead her in to dinner.

That evening proved as exciting and sumptuous as all the others and, to her surprise, Gareth sought her out and even danced with her.

"How goes it, little Amazon?" he asked cheerfully. "I have tried not to intrude on your idyll." Then he chuckled, "No, that is scarcely true—this place is like rare wine to me, Phyllida. After being forced to paint in my beastly attic in Bath under Mamma's fierce disapproval, can you imagine what it has meant to meet Signore Roberti and be given fine paints and the freedom of this perfect city? Will you look at my efforts when you have time? I believe they *do* have promise, though I have so very much to learn—it will take me a lifetime but what a challenge! I mean to stay here, you know, or at least in Italy. That is, if you are happy, too. You are, aren't you?" his voice was suddenly concerned and Phyllida loved him too much to disillusion him. She knew she might not achieve it herself but Gareth richly deserved his new freedom and happiness.

"Tonight I am truly happy," she replied with a radiant smile. Just then an eager young marchese came forward to claim her. Gareth winked at her wickedly.

"Breaking hearts as usual, I see," he grinned. "It seems to be your hobby!" And he relinquished her.

Hugh did not dance with her at all that night. He could not trust himself to hold her lovely body in his arms after her unconscious revelation of her feelings toward him. It had been overt in her eyes and manner ever since he had rescued her in Paris, and he had been indiscreet in his willing response during their coach drive that night. Besides, the news Orieta had brought him increased his fears for the future. It seemed that, however unwillingly, he would have to woo the Turkish sultana to great effect if his delicate mission to that country was to succeed. Indeed, he did not dance at all but spent his time talking in fluent Italian to the most interesting older members of the party. Seeing this, Phyllida was disappointed but not

135

hurt; there would be many other enchanted evenings, she thought, and his words about not neglecting old friends still rang in her ears.

Piero watched them both with approval, although his heart was filled with dread. Would even he, with all his love for human nature and its dilemmas, be able to comfort this glowing girl the day after tomorrow?

On the following day—his last—Hugh devoted all his time to Phyllida, escorting her alone to see some of his most treasured places.

He showed her the large murals of plunging, stout Uccello horses in a small, baroque black and white church tucked away in a corner between two minor canals.

"Oh, they are wonderful," she cried, "like plump rocking horses in the nursery! How did they ever have the speed to fight in battles?"

"By being matched against each other—as you can see," he laughed. Next, he took her to a small gallery where a collection of Fra Angelico's religious paintings had been lent from Florence. The figures themselves were primitive, but the use of lavish gold leaf surrounding them and the still vivid colors of angels' robes, jeweled halos and the wounds of martyrs such as Saint Sebastian, transfixed by arrows, made them thrillingly alive.

All the morning he had been resisting a temptation, but it was crumbling fast. For he longed to give Phyllida a present—nothing as compromising as a ring or one of the popular, heavy gold love knots enclosing two jeweled hearts. Besides, they would not suit her. No, a delicate necklace, perhaps, or a single jeweled pendant on a long gold chain.

He found that he was guiding her down some steps and into the street of the goldsmiths, bordered on one side by a canal.

Here they could see the craftsmen at work with their fine tools, and Phyllida's eyes opened wide with pleasure.

"I have been admiring the beautiful jewelry worn

here—I never saw anything so fine in England; Mamma's rings and brooches are all so heavy."

"Come and talk to my friend Gioffredo; he uses the same workroom that his father and grandfather used before him. It is an art and a skill that takes much learning."

A tall man, much the same age as Hugh, looked up from his bench and his rugged face broke into a broad smile of welcome.

"Sir Hugh—you are back then? It has been too long since we met and I was able to make a gift for you." Fortunately he spoke in Italian so that Phyllida was not, again, reminded of Hugh's past. Besides, after returning the smile, she was eagerly looking at some finished pieces waiting on a side table to be packaged in elegant boxes for delivery.

"You wish a worthy gift, now, for your glorious companion?" asked Gioffredo hopefully. "It will be hard to do her justice but—I have one or two special pieces set aside, made for my own pleasure, which I will gladly show you if you wish."

"Gioffredo, you are a wicked tempter," laughed Hugh, "but, yes, you have read my mind. Not a ring, though," he added quickly. "Perhaps a pendant of unique simplicity—she is very young."

"I understand perfectly," the goldsmith's blue eyes twinkled with amusement. "A token, but not so extravagant as a betrothal gift. One moment . . ."

He darted to the back of the small room, returning with a small, glass-lidded case, which he set down.

"Signorina?" He smiled and explained, with eloquent gestures, that he wished to show her more of his craftsmanship.

Phyllida joined him gladly and, together, she and Hugh looked down at five perfect pendants, each one a single stone, polished and set either in plain gold or fine filligree work. Hugh asked if he might raise the lid—though in his eyes one stood out far beyond the others, but he wanted Phyllida to examine them all. She laughed up at him,

"You are cruel, Hugh, showing me such workmanship that I shall never be content again, I declare. They must be very expensive." Slowly, reverently, she lifted out one after the other, holding the stones up to the sunlight as a child would to see it reflecting through the clear gems —agate, sapphire, amber, emerald and, lastly, a single drop of cloudy green jade a little larger than the others and shaped like a teardrop. With pure artistry Gioffredo had not encased it in any setting, for it needed none. A plain gold ring at the top held it suspended by a long, slender chain. Phyllida returned to it a second time and Hugh was delighted—it would have been his own choice for her.

Taking it from her hands, he removed her hat, then carefully placed it round her neck—standing back to judge the effect. It was two shades lighter than her eyes, but the same tone, and Gioffredo beamed.

"Tell the signorina that I must have made it especially for her, guessing she would come. For her, it is perfection."

Phyllida looked up in astonishment. "You mean—it is *for me?* Oh, Hugh, how can I accept such a present— it is far too valuable and—"

"It is a memento of our night drive from Paris—and of many perfect hours here, in Venice. Don't refuse it, Phyllida, I did not bring you here just to tempt you. Take it as a token of our deep friendship, I pray."

Phyllida blushed with confusion and pleasure. It was unseemly to accept anything more valuable than flowers from a man, she knew, but—Hugh was no ordinary man.

"Thank you," she said, much moved. "I shall treasure it always," and to Gioffredo she held out her hand, which he grasped. *"Che bellezza!"* she told him, wishing she could praise him more fluently, but it seemed to satisfy him completely.

She walked beside Hugh in silence for several minutes, restraining herself with great difficulty from asking the question that had sprung unbidden into her mind: Was it a farewell gift? If their time together was nearly over would it help her to know? But when he said "a memento" and mentioned their happy hours in Venice there had been an undertone of sadness in his voice, as if those hours were numbered now. No, she must wait until he told her in his own time, but her hand went up to touch the piece of jade as if it were a touchstone that could ward off the grief of parting.

Phyllida felt impelled to wear her golden dress again that night for Piero's special party. It would always be associated with Hugh and, besides, if she wore no other jewelry at all, the jade pendant looked beautiful against such a background. She asked Maria to dress her hair very simply and add no flowers or decoration. Then, when she was ready, she went downstairs filled with excitement at the prospect of sailing out across the lagoon by moonlight.

Both Piero and Gareth admired the pendant, and when she told them Hugh had given it to her in memory of their flight from Paris, Piero glanced quickly at her face. Had Hugh already broken his news to her? But, from the calm radiance of her expression he knew that Hugh was, wisely or unwisely, leaving it until the next morning.

All Piero's other guests came to dine first and, in high spirits, they all went out to the jetty, where three gondolas were waiting to take them out to the chartered sailing boats.

The evening could not have been more perfect—a brilliant full moon shed a wide, silver pathway over the water, smooth as silk; the air was very still and almost as warm as midday.

"Fate is always kind to my parties," said Piero contentedly, and he made sure that Hugh and Phyllida were placed in the same boat, although Hugh did not actually sit beside her, but as she talked and laughed with a handsome Venetian painter, she was deeply aware of his presence.

Torcello was all that Piero had promised, the ruined church (once a monastery) bathed in moonlight and casting dramatic black shadows on the long grass surrounding it, while, in the cloister, smiling waiters in white jackets were stationed behind a long trestle table ready to dispense champagne, wine and, later, delicious lobster salad, *vol-au-vents* stuffed with creamed wild mushrooms, shrimps and chicken, followed by fresh fruit salad made from hothouse peaches, grapes, nectarines, oranges and limes. It was a good hour-and-a-half sail from the mainland and, when they had explored, carrying glasses of champagne, the guests would be hungry.

When she had almost despaired of being alone with him, Hugh subtly extricated Phyllida from two admirers and took her down to the beach.

The untrodden golden sand was still damp from an imperceptible rise and fall of the gentle tide, and her thin gold slippers had not been designed for a stroll on the shore; but she didn't care. She was alone with Hugh at last and they stood, entranced, watching the tiny phosphorescent ripples of wavelets no bigger than a child's hand. Now and then, a small fish leaped and subsided in a golden flame a little further offshore.

It was the most romantic place she had ever seen and surely Hugh must be unable to resist it. Timidly, she slipped her hand into his—if he was ever to declare his true feelings this would be the setting.

Instead, although he took her hand in a friendly clasp, he remained silent, staring out to sea. Suddenly Phyllida felt a deep anger mounting in her. Why should this man draw the very heart out of her one minute with his glowing eyes, his whole attention—not to mention the gallant rescue from Paris—then enclose himself in a casing of ice when it suited him. Oh, he could lavish affection and, most certainly kisses, on casual women, but wasn't *she* a woman, too? A woman who could make no secret of her love. In a hard little voice, she said,

"Pray, why did you trouble to draw me away from amusing companions if you want only to gaze at the sea?"

"Because I wanted to watch it with you—did you expect more?" His voice was equally hard and curt, not daring to look at her in case his control broke.

"Yes, I did." Her anger grew until she was quite beside herself, all thoughts of correctness and maidenly modesty forgotten. "One day you are all devoted attention, your eyes and voice warm with love and, in the evening, holding me close in a dance as if you were my lover! Next day you have slipped away to flirt, publicly, with some—some painted *hussy! And* call me a child when I protest! Today you showed me what you said were your 'treasured places' in Venice, gave me this wonderful present—yet now, *now* when we must be on the most romantic spot in the world . . . oh, *why don't you kiss me?*" her voice rose in a passion of frustrated fury.

Hugh stood still as stone, his fine face pale and set. "I mean to explain everything to you tomorrow, Phyllida. You will care for me no longer after that."

She turned from him and ran, stumbling a little on the shallow sand dunes, for her eyes were filled with agonizing tears, but she did not stop until she reached the ruined church. There, in the shadows of a broken tower, she sank down on the rough grass and gave way to a storm of angry weeping.

It was Gareth who found her, curled in a crumpled heap with her tears and anger quite spent. He had strayed away from the merry company, wanting to drink in the glories of this mystic, deserted island to which he planned to return many times with his paints and brushes. Seeing his sister in such a plight shocked him, and he went on his knees beside her, raising her head against his shoulder,

"Phyllida, what is it? Whatever has happened to reduce you to such a state?"

Gratefully, she leaned against him for a moment before she spoke. Then, "Do not ask me anything tonight, Gareth." She sounded infinitely drained and weary. "You have always understood me—please bear with me now, I need your help so much. Stay close beside me on the voyage back, explain that—oh, say *anything,* that I have been taken ill, faint, whatever you like. Oh, Gareth, I am so *glad* you found me, I couldn't have borne anyone else." She gave a small sigh that still held echoes of a sob.

Gareth was aghast at the change in her from the shining, golden girl he had last seen an hour ago. She must have had some terrible scene with Hugh, but he not only loved his sister dearly but understood her well.

"Leave all that to me," he said firmly. Then teasing her tenderly back to some kind of normality, he went on, "Now come on, Amazon, we must do something about your appearance! It is permitted to swoon amongst the aristocracy—but *not* to appear like a dismal, drowned kitten—you must suffer nobly with style!"

He drew her up and out into a patch of moonlight and looked her over. "Well, it might be worse. Can you coil up your own hair? Because I shall go down to the sea and soak my handkerchief to bathe your face and eyes. The saltwater will sting a bit, but it will be very reviving—you are too good a fighter to let them know you have been crying." He waited long enough to make sure that she was attending to her disheveled hair, then with bounding leaps he was down on the beach, returning in almost no time. "Press this firmly all over your face— it is wonderfully cool."

She obeyed him like a helpless child, thankful that she had insisted on wearing her hair in the familiar chignon which she could manage without a mirror. Soon her face and hair looked much as they had before, except for her pallor, which would be easily explained. Then Gareth turned his attention to her gown.

"Hm. It looks as if you had been up to no good, my

girl." He was frankly critical but it helped to brace her, as he hoped it would. He carefully adjusted the shoulders, then again went on his knees to help her in straightening the long skirt, which had twisted and creased under her in spite of her light weight. At last he was satisfied.

"That makes my story easier," he announced. "If you lean on my arm and can manage to limp a little, I shall declare that you came to explore the church alone— oh, no need to worry, I saw Hugh returning to the company some while ago when I was up here." His young voice hardened slightly on the name, for he guessed it was Hugh who had distressed her so and loyally hated him for it. "You tripped, I think, in a concealed rabbit hole and twisted your ankle so that the sudden pain made you swoon. Can you keep that up?"

"It is a perfect explanation, Gareth." She smiled up at him with a trace of her normal liveliness. "How good you are—how many times in the past have you rushed to my aid, I wonder?"

"Rot. It was you who kept me painting against all odds in Bath, so don't let's get maudlin or you'll start crying again and ruin our good work!" He held out his arm for her, then looked down into her eyes. "Remember —Amazons come up *fighting* and don't you dare to let me down!"

Her chin went up as she took his arm. "I won't—I promise. And Gareth—I *will* tell you what happened tomorrow."

When they reached the cloister the company was getting ready to go down to the boats. Everyone—especially Piero, who insisted on supporting her on the other side—was filled with cooing solicitude and sympathy over her mishap. Only Hugh remained on the outer circle, slightly aloof. Never relinquishing Gareth's strong arm for a moment she allowed herself to be placed in the finest seat, with him beside her, her still oddly slim ankle supported by cushions.

Hugh traveled in the other boat, trying his best to give his full attention to a cheerful old duchess, bubbling with gossip.

When they reached the *palazzo* it was well after one o'clock in the morning. Phyllida impetuously kissed Piero on the cheek.

"It was a truly wonderful party," she said, "and I'm very sorry that my stupid carelessness caused a fuss at the end. But thank you, dear Piero, thank you for everything." That included a very deep, tacit thank you for his tact in not asking any awkward questions, and not remarking that her ankle wasn't swollen.

To Hugh, who still seemed wrapped in an invisible cloak of aloofness, she merely said a cool "Good-night."

Then, to maintain their story, Gareth helped her up to her room, his kind eyes anxious.

"Well, we managed that but—are you *sure* you're all right, Phyllida? Oh, don't worry, I'm not proposing to pry, but it must have been something very serious to make you cry like that—you *never* cry."

"It was serious—at least to me. But that is over now, so pray don't worry. I declare, you have turned me into an Amazon again, and I shall fight all the way, if necessary, and *refuse* to give way to foolish emotion." Then she hugged him. "You have been an angel, Gareth—no girl ever had such a brother!"

He grinned, partly relieved. "No man ever had such a sister, either. Now sleep well, dear Amazon, and I'll be around in the morning if you need me, and *there's* a sacrifice for you! Giving up painting for half a precious day."

To his relief she laughed at last—not her usual joyous sound but vastly reassuring. He closed her door quietly and Phyllida was alone. She ached with weariness, yet dreaded going to bed—in the dark it would be hard indeed to banish the image of herself and Hugh on the shore.

Downstairs, Piero challenged Hugh. "I have never

known you to be cruel, my boy. What did you do to hurt her so deeply when you are determined, out of pride, to deal her a deadly blow in the morning. You will not have much time, either, since you must embark from the main quay on your boat going east."

"I shall not need much time, believe me, for the sorry tale I plan to tell her, and the sooner I am away the better," said Hugh gravely. "When she has heard it, she will be thankful that I did not respond to her request tonight that I should embrace her."

"Ah, so that was it," said Piero sadly. "Poor child, she is to suffer more painfully for your life even than you do. Have you any errands that need attending to?"

"No," said Hugh, "I have burdened you enough as it is. I sent messages today to the Prince's coachman telling him to return to his normal base in France. My baggage is already stowed on board the trading vessel that I mean to take; it calls at Constantinople within the week and I am the only passenger, so at least I shall have solitude." His voice grew bitter—almost savage. "If I have to pay court to some lush Eastern woman in order to loosen her tongue, at least I shall have decent time to mourn my exquisite Phyllida in peace."

Piero looked disturbed. "Is that a good thing, I wonder? Your visit there is of the utmost delicacy and importance, Hugh, and with a broken heart you may not be in an ideal frame of mind in which to start."

Hugh smiled cynically. "I swear that my self-control is more ironclad by now even than the righteousness of Miss Smith."

At this, Piero looked reassured. "Do not fret about her any longer. When I was certain of your date of departure I laid plans, for I must confess I am too old to support a desolate girl for long in my normally well-ordered, artistic life. No, I have asked our old friend the Princess Lilli von Löwendorff to arrive for a short visit tomorrow evening. She brings with her an elderly English governess, anxious to retire to her own land. So, between us, we shall arrange for the two women to return together to England. Of course, Phyllida's parents will be much put out by the news of their daughter's behavior but, by then, Lilli will have carried her off to Vienna—and I cannot think of a more respectable, lively companion for a tragic girl, can you?"

At last, Hugh smiled. "I have never known you to do anything that was not perfect, Piero. What a diplomat you are under that artistic exterior! Now, if you will forgive me, I shall go to my room. Sleep will not be possible, but I must decide the last details on the highly distasteful story I have to tell Phyllida tomorrow." His face saddened. "It has proved to me how truly I love her that I can blacken myself so harshly to set her free quite finally." He went to the door, then said over his shoulder, "Ask Lilli to find her a splendid young husband, a man worthy of her whom she can come to love."

He went out, leaving Piero too disturbed to bid him good-night. What an end to his carefully planned evening —when he had hoped against hope that an evening on the romantic island might change Hugh's mind a little, preventing him from cutting all his links with Phyllida so violently. But the ploy had failed.

Sighing, Piero poured himself a large brandy—most unusual, for he was not a drinking man. How he had looked forward to receiving the four young people when he received Hugh's message from Paris! True, the two young men, Henri and Gareth, had found their hearts' desire, but Hugh and Phyllida had found only pain.

"I'm getting old," muttered Piero as he carried his brandy up to bed.

Hugh extinguished all the lights and opened his bedroom windows wide, gazing out to catch a final glimpse of this city he loved so much. But soon his vision was blurred by vivid memories of Phyllida on the beach beside him at Torcello . . . golden, forbidden Phyllida reduced to pleading for the tender kisses his whole being ached to bestow.

Savagely he turned away from the window and began pacing the darkened room, rehearsing in his mind every last detail of the sordid little story he meant to tell her a few hours from now. Doubts and longings he banished sternly from his heart; it was part of his strength that whatever task he had to face—however distasteful—he did it with implacable thoroughness and attention to the smallest detail.

When dawn broke he stripped off his clothes and sponged himself again and again with bracing, icy water and shaved carefully.

Slowly he donned his traveling clothes—thick, brown breeches and boots, an immaculate white shirt and silk cravat to show that he was a gentleman, and finally a high-collared brown cloth coat. As soon as she saw him, Phyllida would know he was leaving.

He stowed his handsome evening coat of blue velvet and the silk breeches into his remaining small valise, placed his large brown cape beside it and then sat down to wait.

Maria called Phyllida at an unusually early hour, bringing a tray of coffee. Her eyes were two huge dark question marks as she delivered her message.

"Excuse, please Signorina, but Sir Hugh Abingdon asks your attention on the *terrazza*." She had learned the words by heart, for her English was still not good.

Phyllida, who was grateful for the coffee, sat bolt upright in bed.

"Tell Sir Hugh—*no*." Her eyes darkened with anger. How *dare* he send for her at this hour, presumably to chide her like a forward child. Indeed, after the long night during which her emotions had swung between shame at herself and fury at Hugh's rebuff, she felt she never wanted to face him again. At least not before the heat had cooled from both feelings.

"I said 'No,' Maria!" she repeated briskly. The girl scuttled away, her romantic, Latin heart feeling important at being the messenger in what was obviously a lovers' quarrel. Ah, the English were strange and cold in such matters, she thought pityingly. She and her own lover, Felipe, relished shouting abuses at each other, and then, momentary anger forgotten, subsided into a most loving embrace.

Hugh turned quickly when she appeared on the terrace, expecting Phyllida. Blushing crimson, Maria spoke in Italian, explaining that the signorina refused to come.

Impatiently, Hugh drew a piece of paper and a pencil from his pocket and wrote quickly, his hand a little unsteady. She *must* come.

Phyllida had risen from bed, drawing on her long, green velvet dressing robe and was brushing out her golden hair before turning to her coffee, at which point Maria reappeared and handed her the note.

Phyllida stared at it. The writing was jerky, almost nervous and not at all typical of Hugh. It said: "I implore you to come, Phyllida. I have to leave within the hour and I shall be gone for a very long time. However angry with me you are, I entreat you to allow me to bid you farewell."

She read it twice; then, without waiting to dress, she ran from the room. She had known that he must be gone very soon—but the phrase "for a very long time," tolled like a knell in her head. She could not bear it. All the base, petty feelings of the long, wasted night fell away, leaving her defenseless against the truth.

She loved Hugh in spite of everything—loved him to the point where she could not face a life without him.

Chapter Nine

He was facing the door, expecting her, but when she came onto the terrace in her simple, clinging robe, her golden hair loose on her shoulders, it struck him to the heart. She was as fresh and lovely as a delicate spring flower opening to the sun, and all his senses rebelled against the offensive little tale he had to tell her.

For her part, Phyllida stood still, shocked at Hugh's ashen pallor, the plain traveling clothes which betokened a long, hard journey rather than a luxurious coach drive to another capital.

He held out his hand and slowly she approached, never taking her frightened eyes from his face.

"Oh, Hugh, I did not realize—I so nearly didn't come!"

"I had to see you," his voice was harsh and curt. "Come and sit down, Phyllida, for what I have to say is far from pleasant."

Like someone hypnotized she took the chair he indicated, perching rigidly on the edge as though bracing herself for what was to come.

"I am returning to France," he began, "oh, not to Paris but a small town much further north. I received a desperate letter by special courier yesterday from a young lady prominent in those parts; her husband owns a big castle there and much of the land, in fact he is the *Grand*

Monsieur. A few months ago she visited her sister in Paris while I was there and," his mouth curled in distaste, "I am afraid we had rather more than a slight dalliance together. It meant nothing, believe me but, it seems, vicious tongues wagged and a very colorful story reached her husband. He is a proud, hard man she told me, and now he has decided to divorce her, naming me as the cause. They are Protestants, alas, so there are no religious problems to such an act. Now Francine is distracted, for he is so angry that he cannot humiliate her enough to salve his pride—she is being stripped of everything, thrown out of their home and left desolate and poor . . ." He paused, while Phyllida felt that ice was coursing through her veins rather than warm blood.

"She begs me to do the right thing and marry her," he went on in a voice bereft of all emotion. "Her sister will not take her in, and she has nowhere else to turn. So—I am bound to," his bitter smile wrung her heart, he was so unhappy. "It may be hard to believe, but I *am* a man of honor and my wild life was bound to catch up with me sooner or later."

Phyllida sprang up and went to him, her whole being aching only to comfort him. "Oh, *no,* Hugh—no, no, *no* . . . what is past cannot claim your whole life. I—I can't bear it for you."

With a small sigh of utter exhaustion he did what he had so long wanted to do and folded her in his strong arms, holding her close against him and resting his cheek against her silky hair.

"My little Phyllida," his voice was soft, broken. "You must know in your heart that you are my only—my sacred —love. But alas, we have met too late—I have fought against it, only God knows how desperately, for every glance from your beautiful eyes inflames my very soul. Last night, on Torcello, I was tempted almost beyond bearing but, by then, I knew what today must bring. Even before that I knew that my evil reputation all over Europe must *never* shadow your life, my darling—you are too infinitely fine and good, so I can only prove my love by giving you up. It has been a perfect dream, my dearest, but now it is over."

She rested still against his breast for a few moments, then raised her head, her eyes misty.

"Kiss me, Hugh—just once," she pleaded.

Hungrily his mouth came down on hers and, for both of them, the nearness was traumatic; passion seared through them, her own rising gladly to meet his, and the kiss grew deeper until they seemed to be one. At last Hugh managed to curb himself before this miracle of what their love could be almost made him throw every strong resolution to the winds and swear that never, never would he leave her side again.

In a small voice, Phyllida asked, "You really *must* marry this woman? It—it sounds so very final."

"It is, my darling—but perhaps it is for the best. For you must go forward into life now—perhaps mourning me for a little while as, selfishly, I hope you will. But my one hope of true happiness will lie in hearing from Piero that you have married happily, married a young man worthy of you who trails no dark shadows. Nothing, I believe, can ever hold quite the magic of first love, for it is the very peak of a magic mountain—but one can neither live forever on the peak nor by magic. There are so many sides to love, Phyllida, and although the worthwhile things may sound dull to you now, it is kindness, humor, companionship and respect that lay true foundations."

"And you?" She spoke in a flat, frozen voice. "Will you achieve any of those with Francine?"

"Oh, I shall settle to it in time. She is witty and charming and we shall do quite well, I expect, but *you must forget me soon,* my Golden Enchantress, and nurture no false hope, for there is none, none at all. I am leaving now and, I think, we shall not meet again. Stay here awhile and do not watch me go or say farewell. Piero will care for you as long as you need him."

With three strides he was gone.

151

Phyllida stood, still and cold as a statue by the balustrade, quite numb with shock. A few minutes later she saw the gondola bearing him away, out of her life, almost with indifference, for the pain, when it began, would be unbearable.

He did not look back but sat stiffly, staring straight ahead, his cape wrapped closely round him although the morning was warm.

Piero also saw him go and his fine old face etched with sorrow. It was all so wrong, so cruel when Hugh was the bravest, finest young man he had ever known and deserved Phyllida as she deserved him. When had he told her, Piero wondered, for Hugh had not confided his final plan—no doubt fearing that his close friend might try to dissuade him.

And how would he find Phyllida herself? Weeping in dire distress (which might be the best thing—better than holding the hurt pent up in her heart), or limp and swooning?

Gareth had also seen the departure and met Piero in the hall.

"Shall I go to her?" he asked, his young face deeply distressed. "I must confess, I cannot understand Hugh's attitude at all—it was so obvious that they were both deep in love when we left Paris, yet I was appalled at his cruelty last night. We are very close, my sister and I."

Piero looked at him affectionately—a gifted young man of Hugh's own caliber, but young still—so very young. He might simply inflame his beloved sister with useless rebellion.

"No, my boy, not yet. Later you will be able to help her more than anyone, I feel sure, but not before we know exactly how Hugh has taken his farewell." He smiled in gentle apology. "Oh, you may feel that I am old—an outsider, perhaps—but I know Hugh well enough to trust his judgment however harsh it may have been, and I care for your sister as if she were my daughter. Trust me not to distress her further—and not to undermine Hugh's last decision, for I know it will have caused him even more suffering than her. He is a strong man with a rigid code of honor and he will only have done what he considers right."

Gareth did not argue, for he, too, had experienced much of Piero's wisdom. He himself would have rushed to Phyllida's side blazing with anger against her seemingly unreasonable lover, and the older man was right: They must know, first, what Hugh had said.

Piero mounted to the terrace slowly, calming his mind as best he could. But he was shaken by what he found: Far from weeping or swooning, the girl stood, like a figure in alabaster, her hands clenching the balustrade cold as the stone itself. Gently but firmly he disengaged them and led her, like a sleep walker, to the cushioned settle placed in a vine arbor away from the long table.

Without speaking he chafed her icy hands and waited. At last, in a dead voice she said, "He has gone to marry a Frenchwoman. It is quite final."

This was an unpleasant shock to Piero, who knew quite well that Hugh was embarked for the East, but his face didn't alter.

"I will ring for hot coffee—you are very cold, my child."

She didn't appear to notice when he got up and went to the door, her eyes still fixed unseeingly ahead of her.

Piero said, "I hope he broke such terrible news gently—for whatever hard path life has forced him to follow, he cares deeply for you, my dear."

"Oh, he does—he swears that he loves me." Her unnatural tone warmed into aching bitterness. "He—he thinks he is not worthy of me and meant to break away anyway very soon. *Now* he expects me to go on living as if nothing had happened and to *marry!* How can I ever marry now that he has held me in his arms and kissed me ..."

Slowly the ice melted and great tears started to her

eyes. She turned pitifully to Piero like a hunted animal. "My heart will be his all the days of my life—no matter if I never see him again, Hugh's farewell kisses can *never* be replaced by anyone else!"

A flunky brought the coffee, placed it on the table and quietly departed. And then the storm broke. In a paroxysm of desolation, Phyllida let long, wracking sobs tear her body. Piero, very concerned, took her in his arms but made no attempt either to speak or to stem the flow. Painful it certainly was, but extremely necessary, for, if she suppressed her grief now, it would fester and turn to a bitterness that could blight her whole life.

Gareth appeared in the doorway, his face anxious, but by signs above Phyllida's bowed head, Piero indicated that this was not the moment for tender, possibly rebellious, brotherly sympathy. Gareth nodded and retired but, outside the door he swore very heartily indeed. By God's truth he would *kill* the fellow, run him through for reducing his proud, brave, sister to such a state! Indeed, after finding her in such a sorry plight last night he had begun to withdraw his admiration from Sir Hugh—but *this!*

As he went down the stairs he muttered accusations and curses against the handsome knight. "Why did he respond so eagerly to rescuing her from Paris if his intention was not to love her honorably? And here, in Venice, may he be damned, raising her hopes and even giving her a valuable pendant when he knew he would desert her? He is the very Devil incarnate . . . oh, if I only knew where he was heading, I swear he would not live to see this night out!"

In truth, Gareth had been shaken to the core. Although he was her elder by one year, Phyllida's fine, indomitable spirit had made her the very touchstone of his own determined fight for freedom from their stultifying family life in Bath. As long as she was on his side—his aptly named Amazon—he felt the courage to fight, knowing that he was not alone, not foolish, as his mother kept implying.

But if love could destroy her . . .

Moodily he went back to his paints, but no subject offered an outlet for his anger.

After ten minutes Phyllida's sobs slowly subsided. Exhausted of all feeling now, she rested her head against Piero's shoulder. Then she pulled herself together and looked up at him.

"Piero—forgive me. Believe me, I would have given way in the privacy of my room, but you are so very strong and comforting. I am not sure I could have survived it alone."

"Of course you could, my dear, for you are as strong as you are beautiful, but it is better to have a friend at hand." He made her lie back on the cushions, gave her his own silk handkerchief, since hers was crumpled into a small, damp ball and poured them both some coffee.

"Now drink it and no foolish protests!" He smiled down at her as he began to sip his own. "You have had the grief and the storm—oh, of course the sadness will linger for a long time yet—but from this moment on you are to look *forward*, Phyllida. Do you not see that it is the one thing Hugh wants you to do, and he is just as unhappy as you are? So listen to the plans I have made for you today: First I prescribe a morning of rest—no, no, do not protest that it is impossible! I shall order the charming little Maria to give you a warm sponge-bath, scented with oil of jasmine, that will relax you a little and soothe your eyes; then my masseur will attend you—he is a magician at easing all the points of tension in your body—especially the back of the neck. It is a new art here, in Italy, but it will become the height of fashion—in fact the effect is so soothing you may well find yourself asleep! Now do not look so apprehensive," his laughing eyes chided her. "Maria will be your chaperone and you will not remove your nightgown!"

"But—Miss Smith!" exclaimed Phyllida. "I had quite forgotten her until you mentioned 'chaperone'—oh, I declare I cannot bear even to see her today—she has always been so unpleasant about Hugh and if she should guess . . ."

"I intend to interview the good woman a little later this morning. You have not heard all my plans as yet and she will have much to think about." He took her cup, pleased to see that it was empty and that a little color had returned to her cheeks. "Early this evening my dear young friend Princess Lilli von Löwendorff will be joining us from Vienna—pray do not look so awed, my dear, she is a very minor princess, for princes and princesses abound in that country! I had guessed that Hugh would be leaving soon from one or two things he had said. Now I know that you may find Venice painful without him and I hope that Lilli may be just the friend you need."

"You mean—I might go to Vienna with her?"

"That we must see. I do not force my friends upon each other; it rarely works. But—if you like each other—it might be an ideal solution. Lilli is older than you but very gay, very much a leader in young Viennese society, and she is wise, too, for she has suffered."

"But what has she to do with Miss Smith?" Phyllida was bewildered.

"I think that woman is bad for you, my dear, and Lilli would not tolerate her for one moment. So I suggested in my letter that Lilli might find another elderly creature wishing to travel to England and in her reply yesterday she says she has just the person! So I mean to inform Miss Smith that her dearest wish is to be granted—she shall return to Bath very shortly. She will be too busy inventing many stories to tell there to pester you today, my child."

When Phyllida opened her eyes the sun was already getting low in the west and she was puzzled—surely it should be in the east, for this must be morning. She stretched, her body still rested and relaxed after the massage, which had, as Piero promised, sent her drifting into sleep. Then, suddenly, it all came back to her and she tensed. Hugh! He had gone forever this very morning, so, in some extraordinary way, she must have slept all day.

"Good—I was afraid I might have to disturb you when you looked so peaceful!" She turned her head to see Gareth sitting near her bed. Carefully, he placed a glass of iced lemon tea on the bedside table.

"Piero insists that it will refresh you—you know how partial he is to it himself."

"Gareth—do you know what has happened?"

He nodded. He was far wiser now than he had been in the morning. Piero had told him the story, but added, "I know how angry you must be, my boy, but I pray you not to distress your sister further by ranting against Hugh." He hesitated a moment, then went on, "I feel I can trust you, Gareth. Between ourselves I do not believe Hugh's story for a minute—indeed, I happen to *know* it is not true. But it was his way of setting your sister free and, believe me, I think he will suffer the most, for he loves her beyond life itself. He decided, days ago, that he would never saddle her with his reputation, and his greatest gift to her, painful though it will be for a while, was to make *absolutely certain* that she must accept the fact that he will never enter her life again."

"You mean—he was strong enough to break his own heart for her sake?" asked Gareth in amazement.

Piero nodded. "Hugh *is* very strong. Once he has decided on an honorable action that he feels is right, nothing can deflect him."

Gareth sat silent, thinking about this, remembering his first favorable impressions of Hugh, his admiration for his swift action in Paris.

"So," he said at last. "How can I help?"

Piero gave a small sigh of relief. "I knew I could rely on you. Hugh has left Phyllida to our care and the most important way to help her now is by not casting any doubts on Hugh's story. It will be hard, when we find her distraught and upset, as she is bound to be. But Hugh's reasoning is true, hard though you may find it being still so young yourself. She is absurdly young—also blessed with great strength of her own and a natural zest for life and happiness which will not be quenched for too long. Besides," he smiled, "I have summoned a dear young friend of mine to our aid. Come and meet her, for she is taking iced tea on the terrace."

Within minutes of meeting Lilli von Löwendorff, Gareth himself had quite lost his heart, not seriously or deeply, for it was impossible to be serious with such a volatile creature, but in humble hero worship.

Lilli was irresistible—her flame red hair gathered up into a topknot of cascading curls as was the fashion in Vienna at the time, her dark blue eyes, not large enough for classic beauty, sparkling with affectionate amusement at the ridiculous world around her; the small, pointed chin was clear-cut above a swanlike neck, while her delightful, slender body was dressed with the utmost chic. Nothing surrounding Lilli would ever be in bad taste. As soon as the two men appeared she held out a small, white hand eagerly to Gareth and he noticed, with artistic pleasure, that it was not laden with rings but set off by a single, sapphire solitaire of exceptional depth and beauty.

"Ah, Gareth," she cried gladly, "you must be the brother of our poor, heartbroken Phyllida." Her English was faultless, merely accented most charmingly by the slightly rolled German *r* sounds. "Pray come and sit beside me, for Piero tells me we have a serious task ahead to help our dear friend Hugh in one of his most honorable intentions."

Already bewitched, Gareth managed to protest. "I think my sister is suffering most at the moment."

"Ah—but she can be cured, I think. May I give you some of this most delicious tea? No?" She smiled at him, "I see you have the great British loyalty to your family—and very good it is, too. But I am sure she will recover, while, at his age, Hugh may not. But he is not our concern now—he always managed his own affairs. I think it would be very nice to meet your sister—I under-

158

stand she has had many hours rest under the care of Piero's expert masseur. Will you be *very* kind and take her this glass of refreshment that you will not accept? It will brace her, I promise, and I cannot accept my part in this rescue until I am sure that she and I are in sympathy."

Now, watching Phyllida, Gareth prayed that the two lovely young women would become fast friends, and he answered her question.

"Yes, I know Hugh has left—but I truly think it is too soon to talk about that now, dearest Amazon; let the shock pass a little and drink your tea, for I have news for you. It was not, in fact, Piero who sent it but his charming friend, the princess from Vienna who has just arrived."

A spark of interest came into Phyllida's eyes. "The one who may take me to Vienna? Oh, Gareth, I swear I can scarce bear the thought of looking out of my window to see the Grand Canal any longer—Venice *is* too painful already." But she obediently sipped from her cool glass.

"I have more news yet," said Gareth encouragingly. "When I came upstairs I glanced into the study and saw the dragon, Miss Smith, taking tea with a gray-haired old body. Their heads were so close, gossiping no doubt, they they never even saw me!"

"Oh, Piero is wonderful," said Phyllida gratefully. "He said the Princess was bringing a companion who would travel to England with Miss Smith—I confess, I could not stand any more of her spite against Hugh." It was difficult to say his name and her face went bleak. "Gareth, what am I to *do?*"

Deliberately misunderstanding her meaning, he said as cheerfully as he could, for his heart ached for her, "Get up now and ring for Maria, then dress as quickly as you can and come and meet the Princess Lilli—I think you will love her, Phyllida, she is not in the least grand or royal, just quite charming."

Phyllida rallied enough to tease him gently. "I see she has bewitched you already, Gareth, and that makes me curious! I will come down soon, I promise, and—and I will not behave foolishly. How could I when you are all being so very kind?"

Much relieved he went to the door. "That's my true Amazon! I think I will do a sketch of you in full armor— you would look fine in a plumed helmet!"

During her few minutes alone before Maria came, she found it hard indeed not to fall to musing—to re-membering Hugh's tragic face and his passionate kisses. But they would haunt her dreams and fill her mind when-ever she was alone for the rest of time, she was convinced. So, with a real effort, she forced herself to concentrate on choosing her prettiest afternoon gown, for she longed to make Princess Lilli approve of her and bear her away from this beautiful, cursed city where memories lurked at every turn.

Although unusually pale, she did indeed present a de-lightful picture when she went to the terrace half an hour later. As soon as she appeared, Lilli sprang up and em-braced her warmly, then held her away a little, looking at her with great pleasure.

"But *Liebling*—you are exquisite!" she cried most sincerely. "Piero said you were a beautiful girl, but to him so is that dull, cold Venus di Milo! If you decide to come with me on a visit to Vienna you will turn all heads," she laughed merrily, her blue eyes twinkling. "We are the most sentimental people in all the world, I think, living in a fairy story of music, hearts and flowers! Why, the men will drink a toast to your eyes in champagne from your own evening slipper—just like Cinderella . . . and very damp it is if you finally retrieve the slipper, I promise."

Phyllida had to laugh a little herself, Lilli's delight-ful nonsense was so infectious, so filled with gaiety. " 'Tis a shame one can't wear glass ones, but I fear we should be crippled after dancing in them!" she said.

"Not to mention splinters everywhere if your partner trod on your toes," added Gareth, beaming with pleasure at his sister's courage.

"Now—to Miss Smith," Lilli made a wry face, "for . have taken tickets for the two old souls so that they may depart from Venice tomorrow. And, now that we have met, Phyllida, I swear no one shall chaperone you in Vienna except myself! Come, we must give her no further cause for umbrage, I think."

"You mean—I should see her too?" Phyllida was aghast. "I—had hoped to avoid her for another day at least."

Lilli took her arm, smiling wickedly. "I do believe that, from what I have heard, the absurd fact that I am a princess will make her mind her tongue—besides, once you have thanked her—as prettily as you can manage— you can bid farewell to her for good. Is it not worth one small, final effort?"

Phyllida's frail courage at the moment cringed in the certainty that Miss Smith would mention Hugh offensively, today of all days—but she sensed that all three people on the terrace were trusting in her to do this thing. Her pride rose and she squared her slim shoulders.

"You are right but—please, please do not leave me alone with her."

"*Liebling,* you do not know me yet! Let us be done with it quickly and return to a glass of reviving wine before dinner." She looked challengingly at Piero over her shoulder. "We shall deserve your finest vintage, my friend, even though we *are* women!"

"I promise, it shall be ordered now," he replied.

Princess Lilli literally swept into the study with an air of grandeur despite her lack of inches—she only came up to Phyllida's shoulder. The two elderly ladies scrambled up from the tea table and the Austrian swept a curtsy, rather awkwardly copied by Miss Smith.

"Ah, my dears, I hope you have made friends." Lilli made it a statement rather than a question. Then she graciously extended her hand to Miss Smith with a dazzling smile. "We have not met, Miss Smith, but I understand you are very loyal. I know how grateful you will be turn to England, and Countess Schwarski will prove experienced traveler, so you need have no fears."

Miss Smith's small eyes literally goggled; she had not realized that her traveling companion was a high-born aristocrat. She accepted the royal hand limply, wondering whether she should kiss it.

"Now," Lilli went on briskly, "I have overlooked nothing for your comfort, I think. My personal carriage will take you down to Rome, where you will take the train to Paris—naturally I have reserved *wagons-lits,* for it is a long journey. From there you will go on to Calais and— *presto!*—by evening you will be in your homeland!" She made a small gesture of satisfaction. "It could not be more simple. Now, dear Phyllida wishes to take her farewells this evening, Miss Smith, for I believe Signor Roberti plans to escort us to a concert later on—so considerate he is, indulging my taste for music."

As she moved forward, Miss Smith's eyes regained some of their gimlet disapproval. "Well, Phyllida—I trust you understand that the report I am duty-bound to give your parents may well distress them," she sighed virtuously. "I shall pray for your soul, hoping that this is not yet another ruse under which you mean to meet that—that dastardly Sir Hugh! I would put nothing past him."

Seeing Phyllida wince, Lilli stepped in smoothly.

"My dear Miss Smith, if you are referring to my close friend, Sir Hugh Abingdon, I can assure you that he is already far away and will not be visiting us in Vienna when I take Phyllida to my palace."

"Oh, very well. I cannot doubt the word of a princess," said Miss Smith, albeit dubiously. Phyllida spoke clearly.

"I must thank you for your care, Miss Smith." The words were stilted, as if recited by a child who had learned them by rote. "Pray do not distress my parents more than you need. Tell them that, when I reach Vienna with the Princess I will write to them. I trust your journey will be pleasant."

Perhaps feeling that she had been a trifle sharp to her young charge, especially in front of royalty, Miss Smith leaned forward and patted Phyllida's hand.

"I am sure you will soon grow out of your willful ways, my dear, and I can see that you are in splendid hands now."

The Princess delivered a few more instructions to the old Countess, kissed her warmly on the cheek, then took Phyllida's arm and escorted her out.

Before they joined the men, Lilli said, "My dear, you are trembling—does that foolish old woman upset you so much?"

"Not really. It was just hearing—hearing . . ." she could not say it.

"Hugh's name?" asked Lilli gently. "Believe me, it is better so—if you truly love him, as Piero assures me you do, you do not want to push him away into the shadows, do you? Since I, too, know him well, surely it is better that we talk of him sometime? It will be bad for you to imprison him in your mind until he haunts you—besides, Hugh himself would hate that."

But it wasn't only hearing his name that had upset Phyllida and set her trembling. Plucking up all her courage, she faced her new friend, looking into her eyes, her own very troubled.

"I know that, Princess but—oh, please forgive me for daring to ask such a thing, but you are so very attractive. Were you and he . . . ?"

Lilli smiled. "I am *glad* you have asked, for now we can start with no cloud between us. No, I was never Hugh's mistress—never. He is a dear, true friend and that I value far more than any lover. Besides," her eyes twinkled, "wait till you meet my dear husband, Heinrich; he seethes with jealousy if a man even throws a flower to me at a carnival! Oh, he is very fierce, that one, but—although you may not understand at first, for he is rather grand, too—I love him." She spoke straight from the heart and Phyllida relaxed.

"How understanding you are—you see Hugh has made so much of his wild reputation, and I—I have seen him, even here in Venice scarce a few days ago, paying . . . great attention to beautiful women. Even when his eyes told me he loved me." She stopped quickly, for the memory still caused her sharp pain.

"One day," said Lilli seriously, "one day I think all will be explained and such foolish, trivial memories will have no power to hurt you anymore. Now let us go out to the terrace, we both need some of Piero's splendid wine."

During the next few days Phyllida scarcely left her room; the last of the blessed numbness caused by shock had quite worn off and her heart was rent with agony. Hour after hour she lay, clasping the jade pendant, reliving Hugh's every word, every precious kiss—the feel of his body holding her close as they danced, the unmistakable look of love in his warm, brown eyes. When the pain grew too great she tossed on the bed as if trying to free herself from the vivid memories which were all she had to live by now, murmuring wildly, "He can't, *can't* be marrying someone else—Hugh is mine as I am utterly his."

At intervals, worn out, she fell into a troubled doze, slow, hopeless tears trickling from under her closed eyelids. Lilli, with an anxious little Maria under her command, nursed her devotedly.

Then, on the fourth evening, Lilli came in followed by Maria bearing a light supper on a tray.

"Now, *meine kleine Kätzchen,* the time of mourning is over. No—I insist. Did not Hugh tell you many times that he wanted you to *live,* to regain your youth, gaiety and zest. Surely you cannot deny him this noble wish? To drive yourself on until you become a bitter, sour creature, living with nothing but past dreams will be to betray his love, his faith in your courage which he believed equal to his own? If he was able to surrender you to freedom and, eventually, happiness—oh, yes, it will come again, I swear

164

to you—are you determined to make his great sacrifice in vain?"

Phyllida lay very still, staring out at the sky beyond the window; the sun was setting and the sky was a miracle of deep blue, gold and red. At last she turned to Lilli and asked, in a small voice,

"Do you despise me very much? I—I have never been unhappy before—not like this, and . . ."

Lilli bent forward and kissed her on the cheek. "I do not feel any such thing. It was *right* that you should mourn for Hugh, but now you must put that behind you. Come, put on your robe and we will sit together by the window while we eat a little and discuss plans. Oh, *Liebling,* life is reaching out to you now—Vienna is at the height of the late spring season and you *cannot* remain sad in such a colorful atmosphere! Besides, I must return to my Heinrich and my household, and I cannot bear to miss more of the opera and the festivities before we all go off to spend summer in the mountains!"

Phyllida sat up, filled with compunction. "Forgive me —I have been very selfish, while you have been a true angel."

"Good," Lilli smiled. "My carriage will be at the quay tomorrow and we shall say good-bye to this now sad city and travel fast to one that has no ghosts—no memories—just a new world such as you have never dreamed of waiting to welcome you. Your nice brother has decided to remain here. Piero is delighted, for he has high hopes of his talent. So—all is arranged most happily. Now, come and take supper. The chef has outdone himself, I think!"

Slowly, Phyllida smiled, a spark of excitement running through her at last.

Chapter Ten

Vienna was a revelation to Phyllida. Once again she was in a world of elegant carriages and high-wheeled landaus, all decorated with coats of arms and polished like crystal. The wide streets, many tree-lined, were ornate with tall buildings all beautifully preserved and tended so that they glowed in the early summer sunlight. It was a far cry from the canals and gently decaying atmosphere of Venice. The whole atmosphere was redolent with life, gaiety and opulence.

Princess Lilli's palace was an exquisite miniature of those owned by the grander princes in the hierarchy. Set in a side street off the Ring—the most fashionable drive in the capital—it was entered through a high gate and a paved court lined with ilex trees and flowering shrubs in tall urns. Inside, it was all soothing pastel colors instead of the more flamboyant decor favored at the time, with glowing chandeliers and candelabra. Only Prince Heinrich seemed formidable: not, as Phyllida expected, a much older man, but in his mid-thirties; he had thick black curls (one quiffed on each side of his forehead), fierce blue eyes and a mustache carefully curled up at the ends. He welcomed his wife rapturously, then turned, none too pleased, and welcomed their guest with a formal bow and heels clicked smartly together in military style.

"Don't worry, Liebling," laughed Lilli as she took

Phyllida upstairs. "When I have talked to him, my Heini will be enchanted with you. I have missed him," she added simply.

She led Phyllida to a beautiful room looking out over a small, formal garden at the back where rosebeds—circular and diamond-shaped—were edged with narrow paths of immaculately kept colored gravel.

"You shall rest now, Phyllida—we have had a long journey," said Lilli. "Later, your personal maid, Gretchen, will bring you coffee and *Knödel* and unpack your valises. We shall dine at nine o'clock, as we are not going out tonight." And, kissing her cheek, Lilli whirled away, eager to be with her husband and explain their guest.

To her surprise Phyllida found she was rather tired, and the high, goose-feather bed was soft and comfortable. She dozed until a bright-eyed girl with fair hair neatly plaited twice round her head, came in with a silver tray of coffee and small cakes and lit the many candles.

Propped up drowsily, Phyllida sipped the deliciously rich Viennese coffee while a smiling Gretchen unpacked and whisked away any gowns that needed pressing.

"It is all very strange," thought Phyllida, "but I believe I am happy! Hugh lives in my heart but he cannot haunt this place at all!"

At dinner Lilli simply bubbled with wit and vivacity, and Heinrich, when not watching her with adoration, smiled kindly at Phyllida now that he had heard her story and the reason for her visit.

"We have only two weeks here, in Vienna, before we go to our *Schloss* in Styria for the summer," Lilli told her. "When it grows hot the whole of society leaves the city—oh, some travel abroad but," she smiled fondly at her husband, "Heini is a savage, I declare! He likes to fish and to hunt chamois and wild boar," she shuddered deliciously. "But life is not dull there at all—we have many, many friends, so there are parties and picnics and boating on the lake."

"In other words you still have plenty of admirers," Heinrich teased her with a hint of gruffness.

"Not this year, my darling," glowed Lilli. "They will all be round Phyllida, you will see!"

Admirers! Phyllida flinched a little at the idea. Her suitors in Bath had meant nothing, since her heart was unawakened, but now, with Hugh so vividly in her heart how could she manage the light banter and ease which society demanded?

As if she sensed this feeling, Lilli leaned across and took Phyllida's hand. "Do not look so anxious, *Liebling,* a little flirtation is no more than sunlight dancing on water, it is all on the surface and *so* amusing!"

They retired early, for, Lilli explained, from now until they left for the country, there would be little time for sleep. They were to attend balls, the opera and a grand royal dinner given by Heinrich's father. "And," she added, "we shall visit my dressmaker to order charming, cool summer gowns, for Austria grows very hot in July and August."

The first ball took Phyllida's breath away; she had thought Paris occasions grand, but this was like a fantasy. Everyone seemed to live in palaces, and the very size of such buildings was awe-inspiring and the heavy, ornate decor like nothing she had ever seen. Every wall seemed to contain floor-to-ceiling mirrors surrounded by elaborate gilt scrolls, cherubs, giant flowers, with the spaces between all dark crimson. The effect was of immense wealth laid on by a giant's hand. The ballroom itself was so vast and so filled with formal, overdressed people—some women still favored small crinolines—that she felt momentarily dizzy.

"This," said Lilli with a chuckle in her voice, "is our *'beau monde'.*" She herself looked enchanting in midnight blue embroidered with ferns in darker blue sequins, her only jewelry a necklace of perfectly matched dark sapphires and small, sapphire stars in her red hair. Instantly, while Heinrich scowled, Lilli was surrounded by friends eager to welcome her back. Deftly, Lilli turned some of the attention to Phyllida, who, in cream and gold, was like a single, cool lily in a garden of orchids.

At first the polite heel-clicking and formal bow as each man begged for a dance amused her, but she soon grew used to it. For, without exception, young Austrians danced divinely. Above all, she was introduced to the Viennese waltz—a far cry from the stately Parisian valse. She laughed as she was whirled round and round at high speed but, when the music stopped she was forced to cling to her partner's arm, for the great room did *not* stop! It whirled on round and round and up and down as well.

As it gradually stilled, a young man, much taller than herself, stood smiling down at her.

"I trust you will allow me to show you the secret of enjoying our latest dance without feeling seasick?" he asked. "But first let me introduce myself—I am Count Sebastian Grindl, Officer in the Tenth Regiment of Imperial Hussars. You, I know, are Miss Phyllida Chase from England, for it was the lovely Lilli who sent me to your rescue. She had no need," he added, his blue eyes twinkling, "for I saw you the moment you entered and determined to dance with you. Strangers we receive often, but only once in a lifetime does a goddess descend from Olympus."

Phyllida smiled at the graceful compliment—he was definitely handsome, she decided, and almost as fair as herself. "I am no goddess, I assure you," she laughed lightly. "Just an English girl feeling slightly over-whelmed!"

"That I can well understand," he said warmly. "I spent two years in England before I joined the Hussars—my father was determined I should learn the language and study your wonderful literature—but, I must confess, I found your social life very sober!"

"Oh, it *is,*" agreed Phyllida. "I—*I* must confess I

170

broke many rules and often made my mother angry.
was it so easy to say such outrageous things to a st
young man in this very formal city?

Then the musicians struck up another Viennese waltz
and Sebastian said, "Now—for the lesson," he grinned
engagingly. "Although I am doing myself a disservice, for
you will have no need to cling to my arm as you did to
Count Kinsky a few minutes ago!"

"Oh, but I shall enjoy the dance much more," she
promised.

For the first minute she obeyed his instructions
promptly: "Now—turn your head well to the left . . .
good . . . now to the right . . ." But she learned the trick so
quickly that after that she gave herself up entirely to joy
in the dance.

"That is how ballerinas manage to do so many
pirouettes without staggering hopelessly about afterward,"
Sebastian told her. "You swear you are not a goddess—
and I am very glad—but you dance like one. No, do not
relinquish my arm, I am taking you for a rewarding glass
of wine."

Phyllida looked up at him, her green eyes glowing
and merry. "I am not used to drinking a great deal," she
said demurely. "Pray remember 'sober England'! Although, I admit, I have been staying in France and Italy,
so I am becoming used to wine—a *little* wine."

"My beautiful Miss Chase, I plan to give you a glass
of our delicious Hock—very light and delicate, it could
not distress a kitten."

It *was* delicious and most refreshing; besides, she enjoyed Sebastian's company, for he seemed to cast the same
amusing glance over the world as Lilli. But she was not to
dance with him again that night, for hopeful partners
crowded round her as they had once done in Bath and,
remembering that she was the guest of a prince and princess, Phyllida felt bound not to attract attention to herself
in this most formal assembly. She must accept each in
turn.

171

Sebastian let her go with an amused, resigned, lifting of one eyebrow.

"Never mind," he said, "soon we all go to the country—my father has a *Schloss* in Styria also—and there can be no clamoring for dances there, except charming peasant celebrations where I shall have to teach you to *stamp* if your pretty feet are not to be crippled!"

That evening—or rather in the early hours of the following morning—Lilli came to Phyllida's room to wish her good-night.

"You were a tremendous success, *Liebling*—oh, I felt so proud of you! You are strong and brave, just as Piero said, and you will be feted and toasted for the rest of this fortnight. Tell me," she hesitated, "did you like Sebastian Grindl? You seemed to enjoy your dance with him and, to me, he is like a son."

"Lilli—you are not nearly old enough to feel that!" exclaimed Phyllida. "No one tonight looked more wonderful than you!"

"My dear, I am thirty-five and dote on my very own Heini; Sebastian is scarce twenty-one! Oh, he had a brief, youthful passion for me, I admit, but soon we both discovered that we laugh at the world, so, after that, we became friends. He is a near neighbor of ours in Styria and we usually see much of him—I wanted to be sure that you like him?"

"Yes—I like him very much," said Phyllida honestly. "As you say, his humor is quite charming and makes one feel . . . safe."

Lilli looked at her for a moment seriously, then laughed. "Good, *Liebling*—but do not place your heart behind iron bars. Now, we are all sleepy, I declare, so hurry into bed. Tomorrow we have the opera—for me, a treat, but possibly for you an ordeal, for its lasts many hours!"

Phyllida lay awake for only a very short time but, during the few minutes before sleep came she thought of Lilli's words. "Do not place your heart behind iron bars."

172

How could Hugh—now that she had felt his passion and knew of his love—ever be a cage?

By the end of the two weeks' gaiety they were all exhausted.

"Thank God," said Heinrich feelingly as they left the final ball. "Tomorrow I can clean my guns in peace."

"And our new summer gowns will be delivered from the dressmaker," said Lilli. "Although, really, I think we should use that new word 'dresses,' for some of them are daringly short for picnics—more like the peasants wear."

"They are lovely," said Phyllida warmly—indeed, she had never seen such delightfully free, comfortable garments before. One or two, in white muslin, were smocked at the yoke and embroidered with the local flowers— edelweiss and gentians—round the hem and sleeves.

In spite of herself she had enjoyed Vienna and the air of lightheartedness which prevailed. She had acquired several admirers who sent her flowers and sentimental heart-shaped boxes of rich chocolates covered with ribbons. Sebastian Grindl had not appeared again.

"No—he is away on maneuvers with the army now," explained Lilli, "but he will reach Styria soon after we arrive."

Phyllida was excited at the prospect of the summer holiday—it obviously meant freedom and a relaxing of formality, which she loved. And, indeed, their journey was not only festive but more like a royal progress. The weather was already very warm, so she and Lilli traveled in new, light dresses with only thin shawls, while Prince Heinrich was already in short *Lederhosen,* long socks, with a frilled shirt, and a small Alpine hat, made of green felt with a tuft of feathers at one side, which he wore at a jaunty angle. They traveled in a landau. Behind them followed two landaulettes carrying the personal servants and all the baggage.

"All we need is a post horn," laughed Lilli, "but Heini feels it would not be dignified!"

173

The *Schloss* might have been an illustration in a fairy tale—square and turreted it perched halfway up a steep hillside with a slight air of surprise. The setting sun bathed it in golden light and colored the placid lake below like a rainbow.

"Oh, Lilli," breathed Phyllida in ecstasy, "you did not tell me it was so *beautiful*."

"I never spoil my surprises," said Lilli happily. Then with a mischievous glance at her husband, she added, "To be truthful it was this *Schloss* that made me marry Heini!"

He laughed and threw an arm round her slim shoulders. Indeed, here in his beloved countryside, Prince Heinrich was a very different man and, for the first time, Phyllida knew she could be at ease with him.

Beaming servants were waiting to welcome them and there was a scent of roses and honeysuckle, for great bowls of flowers stood everywhere. Lilli took Phyllida up wide, winding stone stairs and showed her into a turret room with windows on three sides so that she had wonderful views of the lake, the gardens and the mountains.

"I hope you will be happy here, *Liebling*," she said. "Now change if you wish after our long drive, but we do not dress formally for dinner—dear Heini, it is what he hates most about Vienna!"

Spontaneously Phyllida threw her arms round her friend and hugged her. "Oh, Lilli, you are so good to me! How could I be anything but happy in this glorious place —and with you?"

Dinner was unlike anything she had tasted before. Fresh trout from the lake, followed by roast boar accompanied by unfamiliar vegetables, and a delicious sweet local to that area: sheep's cheese and thick cream, whipped together and flavored with wild honey, topped with crystallized black plums.

Alone at last in her turret Phyllida sat by an open window. The night was dark, but deep blue rather than black, with a tranquil moon reflected in the lake and stars so brilliant it felt possible to reach out and touch one.

The air was soft and sweet with the scent of flowers and new-mown grass.

"Oh, Hugh—my dear, dear love, if only you were here this would be paradise," whispered Phyllida. She had not realized until now that serenity and great beauty had the power to bring back longing so poignantly. In all the bustle and color of life in Vienna there had not been time to mourn—but here . . .

Lilli knew this, however, and, about an hour later, she softly opened Phyllida's door to find, as she expected, the girl sitting weeping quietly by the window. Lilli went over and sat on the wide window seat beside her.

"Poor *Kätzchen*," she said gently. "Heini is asleep and I felt sure that this glorious scene might make you sad—as it did me many, many years ago."

"You?" Phyllida turned to her, startled. "But you are the happiest person I have ever met!"

"Now—yes, but it took a long time to achieve. I was born not far from here—in the next valley—and, when I was seventeen I fell deeply in love," her smile was sad. "Only at that age does one feel that overwhelming passion, that complete surrender to a man, and my Jan was very good, very beautiful—and very young, too. But my parents approved—Jan's father was as wealthy as mine— so we were married. Oh, how we loved together and played house in our beautiful chalet on a hill! Children still, both of us, but so happy—so anxious to live each magic day with no thought for the future, for surely we had a perfect lifetime ahead. Only we hadn't. Jan's passion in life was climbing and when, a year later, he was invited to join a mountaineering expedition in the Bavarian Alps, he accepted and I urged him to do so, for I knew what it meant to him. I hoped I might be expecting our first child, so we agreed that I should remain at home." She paused for a long time, staring out into the night, her thoughts far away. "It was our first parting— and the last time I ever saw him."

175

Phyllida caught her breath and leaned over to take Lilli's cold hand.

"He was—killed?" she asked softly.

"Yes. It was almost winter and an early blizzard caught them on a dangerous rock face. The man Jan was roped to slipped and, in trying desperately to save him, Jan could not. They both fell hundreds of feet into a crevasse. That is all."

"But—your child?"

"No—even that was denied to me. For a year I mourned bitterly, refusing to leave our chalet and go home to my parents. I—I think I still believed, in spite of all, that he would come back . . . he was so strong, so fearless always, that I could not quite accept his death. I would sit for hours at the window, as you are doing now, gazing out over the country—hating it sometimes for being so calm and beautiful when he could no longer see it. My parents were so very kind—and quite distraught for me, so they decided to move to Vienna and take me with them.

" 'You will have no memories to haunt you there,' my mother said."

"Did it help?"

"Indeed it did. My mother had many chic gowns made for me and entertained a great deal so that we were soon welcome in society. But, as you know, I am not beautiful!" Lilli chuckled. "So, since all my 'inner lamps' were turned off, few men fell in love with me and I was thankful. Then, after three years, Mother grew impatient. She talked to me, again, of marriage . . . such wise words but I hated them . . ."

"What did she tell you?" Phyllida was curious to know what had so transformed Lilli into the glowing creature of today.

"Of what marriage can *really* mean—as it does all over Europe. Never again the sweeping, blind passions of youth, of course—but kindness, protection, companionship and above all my own place in society."

"Why! That is exactly what Hugh said to me," Phyllida's eyes were wide with interest. "It is—can it *always* be true?"

"Of course! How else could I be so very happy and contented now? I met Heini when I was twenty-six. Oh, but he was a so-serious young man, not all extravagant words and gestures like the men I met at balls. First, I grew aware of his great kindness—yes, under that fierce manner, he must be the kindest man in the world. He did not rush matters, and, gradually, my lamps began to shine again, for I wanted to please him. For a whole year we remained friends—but I found I was attracting much attention, now, from other men . . . and knew I was only utterly myself with Heini. So, eight years ago we were married and I have never regretted one single moment. Oh, although Jan will always hold a place in my heart, the memories are all tender now, no longer sad; it is like reading a wonderful fairy tale that happened to two children—for we were little more. One's first, early love never quite dies, Phyllida, but we grow older and life must go on—so why must it go on alone? I believe that is betrayal of all that early glory. Now, you must sleep little one." Lilli stood up and, bending, kissed Phyllida's forehead before slipping out of the room.

So—first these words from Hugh, then Lilli, the two people she loved and respected completely. She vowed to try, with all her strength, to follow such wise counsel.

Count Sebastian Grindl appeared two weeks later, looking bronzed and more handsome than she remembered after his month of camping with his regiment. He smiled at her.

"You see? I am in time to escort you to our first dance in the country—'ball' is far too dignified a word for the splendid stamping and yodeling that goes on. But they are far more amusing and lively. I shall teach you the steps, as I promised, and so avoid having your feet being

177

stamped to pieces—for I swear every young man for miles around will want to dance with the 'Beautiful Eenglish Meess!' "

Phyllida laughed—it was good to see him again, she found; and he, in his turn, was delighted at the subtle change in her: She no longer had that air of faint abstraction, and two weeks of fresh air, country living and, he suspected, Lilli's wisdom had done much to restore the natural glow to her eyes and cheeks. He had decided on their very first meeting that he would marry her, but, like Heini years ago, he had no intention of rushing matters. No, he would tease her, make her laugh, make her feel completely at ease with him, for he guessed that her heart had been lately broken. Now he saw that she was a spirited girl and he looked forward to planning gay adventures and surprises to restore her still further.

They went down to join a big picnic party on the lake shore. It was yet another blue, cloudless day, and the women were enchanting in their fresh sprigged muslins—some even wearing a fashionable version of the full-sleeved, embroidered peasant blouses and dirndl skirts that swung becomingly whenever they walked. But every woman, alas, he thought, wore a wide-brimmed straw hat to prevent her skin from becoming sunburned—in preparation for her return to Vienna, where pale skins were a sign of good breeding. Yet how lovely Phyllida would have become with a golden skin! More beautiful even than she was now.

When the elaborate lunch was finished and servants had cleared it away, the older members of the party were drowsy and betook themselves to the shade of a small grove of trees close by. The younger ones discussed what games they should play: pat-ball? since some had brought small, long-handled rackets and soft balls; or hide-and-seek? Or, more daringly, kiss-in-the-ring (a game as old as time itself). While they were arguing, Sebastian uncoiled his long body from a comfortable posture and, head and shoulders taller than the others, strode to Phyllida and offered his brown hand, slightly cowing the eager youths surrounding her and begging her to vote for kiss-in-the-ring.

"Come, Meess Phyllida—we are both too old for such youthful frolics! I have a whole new world to show you instead." His smile was so merry, so friendly she had to ignore his implication that she was too old for games—which, indeed, she had enjoyed vastly on other picnics.

Taking his hand she stood up, her green eyes smiling. " 'A whole new world'?" she asked incredulously. "Pray where is Utopia hiding in this valley?"

"Underneath the water," he replied, leading her to a spot where half a dozen flat-bottomed, comfortably cushioned boats were moored if the company felt like venturing out on the lake. Sebastian chose the best one with care, then handed her in, casting off the mooring rope and leaping in expertly himself and taking the oars.

"You are not expecting me to dive, I trust?" she asked demurely.

"Oh, nothing I plan is ever so drastic," he assured her. "No, your voyage of discovery merely entails your moving one of the cushions onto the wide, flat stern of the boat—there, leaning over and looking down into the clear water, I swear you will see a world you never knew existed. Besides, I think you had had your fill of callow adoration!"

"Oh—the young men are very charming," protested Phyllida lightly. "Is this merely a jealous plot?"

" 'Jealous'?" he looked indignant. "What right have I to be jealous? Certainly not. But I appreciate your intelligence and believe that not one of them would dream of taking you to explore the magic of this lake." He rowed for a few minutes and then hoisted the oars up on to the rowlocks. "At no point is the water deeper than eight feet and it is so clear that you can see right to the bottom where, amongst a forest of fernlike weeds of many colors, small fish and water creatures live busily and undisturbed. Now, place your cushion—oh, and one for me, for I never tire of watching."

Together, soon totally absorbed, they lay side by side watching what was, for Phyllida, indeed a completely new world. To his delight she threw off her straw hat, since it cast tiresome shadows, and her gold hair gleamed in the sunlight.

"Look—look at that strange little striped fish!" she cried. "Why, it is the loveliest thing I have ever seen . . . but it is *fighting* for something the new one is carrying in its mouth!"

"Life in that world is as hard as the one up here—all for survival," said Sebastian contentedly.

As each new creature came into view he described it by name with great knowledge and Phyllida was spellbound by the stories.

"How do you know so much?" she asked at last.

"Because I discovered this secret world when I was seven and have never ceased to learn more about it."

Her would-be admirers on the shore had kept an eye on the boat and the two recumbent figures lying close together astern. But when at last they returned to the party, Phyllida explained all.

"How foolish you are," she cried gaily. "Looking down into the water is more fascinating than any games, I declare." And to the wide-eyed girls she said, "You have seen no rare jewels as beautiful as the small fish out there. Oh, there are lazy, fat trout as well, but the little ones! You *must* go boating next time."

The village dance, held in a big hall festooned with colored streamers, was attended for a while by all the surrounding gentry. Traditional music was played by a fiddle, a horn and drums, enthusiastically backed by singers. Great steins of light beer were the favorite refreshment, but there was mellow wine from the last season, too. Phyllida was glad that she had been advised by Lilli to wear her sheerest muslin, for the hall was already hot and, at first, she sat with the older people watching the strange dances and Sebastian stood behind her chair, explaining them.

There was a pause and then eight men took the floor and gave an exhibition of the famous Austrian Schuhplattler dance in which they not only stamped but clapped hands together, leaped in the air striking their leather-clad thighs with resounding smacks. There was uproarious applause at the end and each man was plied with cold beer.

"You will *not* be expected to do that!" Sebastian laughed over her shoulder. "But come—shall we try the next dance?"

It was a charming country measure, danced in groups of four or six people together forming a circle, then advancing in pairs to the center, next weaving a chain of hands—very like dances Phyllida had learned as a child.

"Well—there was no stamping at all!" she told Sebastian.

"Just wait for the country version of our waltz!" he warned.

And he was right. It was a carefree, joyous affair, very fast, during which girls were often lifted right off their feet by their partners and swung high. Sebastian danced as fast as any of them but did not swing Phyllida right off her feet—at the end she was flushed, breathless and laughing.

"Next time you will be asked by one of the youths," he said, "but remember—keep your feet well under you, moving swiftly in step with the rhythm all the time. No village boy will dare to swing you off the ground, I promise."

Sure enough, a young man in *Lederhosen* plucked up courage to come and bow very low before her, his forehead perspiring a little with nervousness. Phyllida stood up, smiling, and was instantly whirled away at great speed. But she enjoyed it and, as she turned her head this way and that she was aware of Sebastian watching her with approval. How *nice* he was, she thought gratefully—but no flicker of romance stirred her heart. He was simply Sebastian, her amusing, interesting friend.

The slow, hot summer wore on gradually with charming diversions every day, although Sebastian did not attend all of them. Prince Heinrich was happy and relaxed, doing all the things he loved most—fishing, hunting and shooting with his friends. By evening he was tired and very charming to Phyllida as well as his wife. There were seldom festivities in the evening, since every household went early to bed, for, the hotter it became the earlier they rose in the morning. This enabled wives to see to the household and organize meals for their husbands to take with them while the air was fresh and cool with dew still shining on the grass.

One day Sebastian said, "Tomorrow, I shall call for you at about seven o'clock, Phyllida. I have another world to show you before the huntsmen turn to it."

"You promise there will be no shooting?" she asked. "I hate to hear the guns."

"The only sounds you are likely to hear are the cowbells and an occasional shepherd yodeling across the hill to his friend."

"Then I shall look forward to it very much."

She was ready as soon as he called for her, but he looked doubtfully at her thin summer slippers.

"I forgot to ask if you enjoy walking," he apologized, "for we are going up the hill some distance where no carriage can pass."

"I love it—Lilli and I often walk quite far in the morning. Oh, I see! You are looking at these silly slippers —how thoughtful of you. I will change at once—Lilli has given me a pair of light doeskin boots that cover my ankles and are very good when we pass brambles or nettles!"

They set off following a goat track that wound leisurely up the hillside until the smooth lake below looked quite small. The stillness was broken only, as Sebastian had promised, by the gentle sound of musical cowbells—

each one pitched slightly differently so that the farmer could round up his herd with ease, knowing if one was missing. They were beautiful, docile creatures, their hides a soft golden brown turning to cream and they gave deliciously rich milk.

"I can't believe we have climbed so high!" laughed Phyllida. "It has seeemd like no climb at all."

"Believe me, we have covered three kilometers at least—and we are nearly there." On the crest of the hill Sebastian held out his hand. "Let me steady you on the short, stony way down to where I have chosen an ideal position where we can sit—and watch."

"Yes. What *is* this other world? It can't be as glorious as the fish, I declare."

"Different," he agreed, "but just as graceful in a different way." When he had settled her comfortably on a warm, mossy stone with a grass bank behind her, he went on, "Now—we wait and watch those craggy outcrops on the wilder hills opposite."

Phyllida was utterly happy. Since Lilli had talked to her she had learned not to let the endless beauty and peace of this place make her sad—indeed, she reveled in it. The sun was warm already and her place very comfortable. Sebastian sat beside her and, although they talked quietly, he never took his eyes from the crags. Suddenly he was very still.

"Look," he said, "up on the highest crag of all."

As she watched Phyllida gave a little gasp. The most graceful creature she had ever seen, more slender than a goat and smaller, with delicate horns silhouetted against the sky, leaped nimbly from the topmost crag to a wider one a little lower down, landing perfectly with all its four tiny hooves coming together. There it waited, looking back expectantly. Soon a young one appeared at the top and, after a slight hesitation, took the same leap to land just as well.

Sebastian laughed. "It is obviously school hours for the young chamois," he said. "Aren't they a miracle?"

"Oh, they are indeed," Phyllida agreed warmly. "But —'chamois' did you say?"

"Yes."

Her sensitive face clouded. "I wouldn't have missed that for the world and yet—I almost wish I hadn't seen them. Surely Prince Heinrich and his friends shoot them, don't they?"

"At the end of the summer, yes, when the young ones are fully grown. It is a great trophy to have chamois horns on the wall!"

"You don't, do you?"

"No. It's strange," he mused. "I am a serving soldier —yet I cannot bear to kill any wild thing. My father gets very angry but he has had to accept it now."

"I don't mind when they kill wild boar—they look such ill-tempered, vicious animals when they are brought home. But these . . ." Phyllida stopped, then turned to Sebastian and laid a hand on his arm, "I am so thankful that you do not."

He was very touched but the moment broke as, suddenly, she caught sight of a strange flower close beside her on the grassy bank. She had never seen anything like it and, curious, she bent over and plucked it.

"Sebastian—what is this? See, the stalk, the small leaves *and* the flower are all the same extraordinary greeny gray white and furry, as if it were covered with down!"

His blue eyes shone with delight. "Oh, Phyllida, Austria has taken you to its heart indeed! That is an edelweiss, rare and beloved as a sprig of white heather on your Scottish heaths. Village maidens—especially when they are betrothed—will search for weeks over the hills to find one."

"Why? Except that, in a strange way, it is very beautiful."

"There is a legend attached to it: When a girl finds an edelweiss herself—it must not be a present—and cherishes it, perhaps pressing it in her Bible, as long as she keeps it her true love will never be unfaithful."

Phyllida listened, her face absorbed, then gently cradled the little flower in her long, slim hands. Watching her, drinking in her tranquil beauty, Sebastian felt a pang. Her green eyes, gazing reverently at the edelweiss, were misty with love and longing as if the flower, indeed, held magic—a magic from which he felt quite shut out.

Her heart and mind had winged far away and he knew that she did not love him.

But there is time, he thought hopefully. Plenty of time and at least I am here and he is not.

Chapter
Eleven

August turned into September; there were open log fires in the *Schloss* in the evenings, and here and there a tree was tinged with flame and gold. Autumn was creeping on and Lilli said,

"Dear Heini is set on shooting a second chamois— then we shall go back to Vienna. The winter there is the gayest, happiest time of all. There are balls, but also trotting races in the Prater, hot chestnuts roasting on braziers in the streets, fancy dress parties at Halloween— then the snow begins and it is Christmas—or, as we call it, the Feast of Saint Nicholas." Her eyes shone like a child and Phyllida felt bound to say, reluctantly,

"Lilly—surely I should go somewhere else? You have been so good, so very good to me and I have never been so happy but . . . I must long have outstayed my welcome."

Lilli looked at her in amazement. "*Liebling,* you have become my little sister, unless you wish to return to Bath I shall never part with you, except to a husband."

They were sitting by the lake and, when Phyllida didn't answer but looked pensively out over the water, Lilli added gently,

"Sebastian is much in love with you, I think—and he is rare, that one, for I believe he is good all through—and so amusing."

Phyllida turned startled eyes to her. "Oh, how dreadful—I have enjoyed his company so much but as—as a friend. I swear I would not hurt him for the world."

"You haven't," Lilli smiled. "He talked to me last week before he returned to the army, and he has no false hopes but he would make a wonderful husband, you know."

"Indeed, I *do* know. I have never liked a young man so well. He is all that you say—kind, thoughtful, reliable —but . . . I love Hugh as much as ever. You have taught me to enjoy life again, and I do, but I—I cannot imagine another love taking his place."

Lilli sprang up. "Well, I know that you have learned to enjoy things again and with that I shall be content. Come, for Heini and his friends will soon be home from hunting and there is much to prepare."

Phyllida followed her but resolved to disappear discreetly if, by chance, a lovely chamois was carried in in triumph.

She thought of Sebastian as they walked up the hill— thought of him a little sadly, for, had her heart been free, she could have loved him dearly. Only it was Hugh's dark, handsome face that filled her mind at every turn. It could not be possible that he would never enter her life again.

Vienna was all that Lilli had promised and more. A new zest was in the air as everyone returned, refreshed, from the long holiday, and conversation bubbled as experiences were exchanged. At first it was difficult to return to formal gowns and bonnets, but many new fashions had arrived in the city and charming little hats gay with feathers suited Phyllida particularly well.

Sebastian came to call, resplendent in his uniform of dark blue frogged with gold, tasseled epaulets, and tight white breeches. His busby made Phyllida laugh—unlike the British bearskin, it was short, crisp fur and fitted close to the head, standing straight up for perhaps eight inches with a cockade at one side.

"You look more of a giant than ever!" she teased.

"And why not? You have certainly grown more beautiful," he laughed back. No, she could not believe he was seriously in love with her. He was far too merry and lighthearted and she was glad. It would have been lonely without him as an escort.

She enjoyed balls much more than before. So many faces were familiar now, and in the country she had tried hard to learn German and was fairly fluent. It was on such an occasion that Phyllida met the little Archduchess Alexandra of Walden-stern.

They happened to be alone in the ladies' powder closet and both were looking in the mirror and patting their hair tidy at the same time. The Archduchess laughed.

"We are night and day, are we not? Although I am a very *small* night!" Indeed she was tiny with sparkling brown eyes in an elfin face and beautiful curly black hair. She went on, "You, I know, are Miss Phyllida Chase—I am the Archduchess Alexandra." She made a rueful little moue. "Can you imagine being married to a great statesman at seventeen! Oh, I am supposed to be so staid and proper, and *indeed* I try—but it is hard not to laugh at the wrong moment, I declare."

"Do you not love him?" asked Phyllida.

"Ludwig? I do not know—you see we are both of the royal blood and the marriage was arranged by the emperor himself long ago, while I was still a child. Oh, Ludwig is very kind—very generous, like a father. You must meet him, for he is also very splendid and very clever. I should like to invite you to visit me, but I must have his permission."

Just then Lilli came in, but when she saw Phyllida's companion her face became cold as Phyllida had never seen it.

"Good evening, Archduchess," she said distantly. "I think your husband is looking for you."

Her tone was enough and, with a last, wistful smile at her new friend the young girl hurried away.

189

"Lilli—*why?*" asked Phyllida, puzzled. "I have never seen you really displeased with anyone before."

Lilli smiled again. "I am not displeased, but she is not a suitable friend for you, *Liebling*. The Archduchess Alexandra is already a scandal, a shameless flirt and a very, very naughty girl; her poor husband suffers much from her antics, for he is our greatest statesman dealing with foreign affairs and should have a gentle, modest wife who could be a perfect hostess."

"His wife is very young," protested Phyllida, "and I do not think she is very happy."

"There you are!" exclaimed Lilli. "She has known you scarce five minutes and already such indiscretion! Disgraceful. No, Phyllida, I regret I must forbid such a friendship. Why, I declare, your reputation would be in ruins once it became known."

Phyllida glimpsed the little Archduchess at many functions, but neither made any attempt to talk together. Besides, Phyllida felt a pang for the handsome, graying Archduke, his chest covered with dazzling decorations, medals, and the royal purple sash over his left shoulder; he looked tired and careworn.

One evening Prince Heinrich was to attend a reunion dinner for all his hunting cronies of the summer. Since he was not at all jealous of Sebastian Grindl on Lilli's account (indeed, she had confided her hopes that the young Count would marry Phyllida), he gladly agreed to the young man escorting both ladies up the Danube to a *Heurige*—a country festival to celebrate the coming of new wine from the vineyards.

"It will be very gay—very amusing," cried Lilli, "and we must wear country dresses under our cloaks, for, although the *Heurige* is held out-of-doors on a platform by the river, it will become very hot with all the dancing and drinking, not to mention the singing, in which everyone joins."

Sebastian, too, had dressed simply and, as he handed them into his carriage he said,

"Of course, if you wish we can drive all the way along the riverbank, but it is only a half-hour journey on the boat and, in autumn, the Danube is very quiet, very calm."

"Most certainly we shall go by boat," laughed Lilli. "Whoever heard of arriving at a *Heurige* in a carriage?"

After a short drive they came to a bridge where, at the foot of some stone steps, a wide, comfortable barge was moored, decorated with flowers and colored lanterns; about twelve people were already seated, all of whom Lilli and Sebastian knew, and the oarsmen wore *Lederhosen,* and flowers in their hats so that everything was very festive.

As soon as Sebastian's guests were seated they set off. Phyllida was amazed at the great width of the Danube, for she had only driven over it in the past.

"It is indeed wide," said Sebastian, "and, in winter it roars along like a lion! Very turbulent and often partly frozen."

"And is it really blue? It is hard to see in this light."

"When it appears blue, you will know that you are in love," he laughed. "That is another of our legends."

The *Heurige* was already in full swing when they arrived. The platform, built out beyond an old inn, was hung with more colored lanterns, some made like bunches of grapes, and a trellis stretched over the top was festooned with vines. There were several long, scrubbed trestle tables ranged on each side, every one laden with smoked hams, sausages of all kinds and homemade bread, while great wooden casks of must—as the new wine was called, for it had not yet completed fermentation—stood round at regular intervals with pewter goblets set ready.

The band was impressive—three fiddles, a harmonica, two cornets, an upright piano and drums. Most of the guests were young, but some older people had brought whole families, and all, without exception, wore gaily patterned peasant dresses or embroidered blouses and wide, swinging skirts. The men were in *Lederhosen,* tall socks and frilled shirts.

Unlike the country folk, no one was shy and, in no time, Lilli and Phyllida were besieged with eager young men who whirled them round with such cheerful abandon they grew quite flushed and breathless. When at last they sat down laughing, Sebastian brought goblets of wine.

"The whole object of a *Heurige* is to make everyone thirsty," he laughed. "Do not be alarmed, Phyllida, it will not go to your head."

Cautiously she took a sip, then smiled. "It is nice," she said. "A little sharp but very fresh."

During an interval when everyone was laughingly exhausted, the pianist struck up some of the famous old songs—all with a catchy lilt but very sentimental.

"What did I tell you?" said Lilli. "We are *all* sentimental here—hearts, flowers, young love and wine are our lifeblood, I declare!" And she sang merrily, swaying her body from side to side like everyone else.

About midnight some of the youths were very flushed and growing rowdy, so Sebastian decided it was time to leave. By then Phyllida's fair hair was in charming disarray and she looked like a nymph, as ardent partners had crowned her with vine leaves and one had hung a garland of gentians round her neck.

"Oh, I have never enjoyed myself so much," she declared as they boarded the barge. "But what a sight I must look!"

"Indeed, you do," chuckled Sebastian. "Like a pagan goddess, this time, running free through the forest—and more beautiful than ever!"

He guided her back to the stern of the barge, beyond the oarsmen and the rest of the company. A cool breeze stirred the night and it was welcome after the heat of so much dancing.

He watched her in silence for a little while, then, keeping his tone light, he said, "You must know that my heart is at your feet, Phyllida. Will you consider marrying me? Oh, not immediately, but soon? I shall always cherish you, you know—and, besides, we are always so happy together."

Instantly she became grave and very still, her green eyes dark and wide. At last she turned to him:

"I—am very fond of you, Sebastian; indeed, I am happier with you than anyone I have ever known but . . . oh, I would not hurt you for the world!"

"Forgive me. I spoke too soon." He gave a rueful little laugh. "I believe those foolish love songs carried me away. But do not spurn me utterly, I beg. It shall make no difference to our relationship, I give you my word. Just let me hope a little."

In an agony of remorse she slipped her arm through his. "If I were free, I would sooner marry you than any man and—perhaps . . ."

"That is enough—more than I deserve," he interrupted quickly before she could say any more. "I shall go on hoping but, I swear, I will not mention it again until you give some sign. Now, let us rejoin Lilli and the others."

When they returned home Prince Heinrich was still out and Lilli, still excited, twirled lightly round the hall. "Oh, what *fun* that was, I declare. I have not been to a *Heurige* for some time and had forgotten how much I enjoy them. You were a great success . . ." she began, then noticed Phyllida's strained expression. "Why, *Kätzchen*, what is it—did you not enjoy yourself, too?"

"Indeed, I did but—on the boat coming back Sebastian proposed to me, and I—I fear I have hurt him. I did not refuse him outright, but how can I ever accept when I still love Hugh with all my heart?" she asked passionately.

"But, *Liebling,* he is *married* now—you told me so— and has taken farewell of you forever."

"I know," Phyllida twisted her hands together wretchedly. "And I know it is foolish but—even now, after all these happy months with you, I cannot quite believe it. Something tells me that it is not over, that he will come back into my life even if it takes years. Things happen—oh, pray do not think I wish his wife ill, for I do *not*. But—things can happen; she may find she does not love Hugh after all or—or she might become ill. Anything is possible."

Lilli sat down on the big carved settle. "Come, join me for a moment before we go upstairs. Listen, Phyllida, and remember that I know Hugh well. He not only told you of his marriage, but also said he could never marry you in any case, since he would not inflict his dreadful reputation on you ... and, my dear, it *is* shocking. You may not believe it now, but if you were married to him I fear it would become a grave burden, meeting you at every turn. Could you endure such bitter, spiteful arrows and still respect him? I doubt it, no matter how much you loved him. No, he meant it when he said his great wish was for you to meet a really worthy young husband and settle down—and who could do better than Sebastian? You are already such close friends and he amuses you; he is trustworthy, rich, a man due to inherit great possessions and he will be finished with his time in the army within a year now. Above all, he is *kind* and will love and care for you all his life. What more can you ask?"

"Nothing," said Phyllida in a small, despairing voice. "I know how stupid and ungrateful I must seem but—I *cannot* tear Hugh from my heart, and Sebastian truly deserves the very best."

Lilli decided to say no more that night and they went to their rooms. There in her boudoir, while waiting for her husband to return, Lilli wrote a long letter to Piero—a letter which gravely disturbed him. When he received it he declared to Gareth,

"I am going to England. No, I cannot explain my reasons at present, but I may be gone two weeks or even more. When I return I shall expect you to have completed two more fine paintings, for then you will have enough for an exhibition and nothing will please me more than to launch you as my protégé at the Accademia di Belle Arti."

Gareth flushed with pleasure, but protested, "Oh, not there, Maestro, surely? You have taught me so much but I am only worthy of a *small* exhibition at first—somewhere that will not attract such august notice."

"Nonsense," retorted Piero briskly. "You have great talent now, my boy, and no pupil of mine skulks in the backwaters!" After which he departed to order his packing and the arrangements for his journey.

The Christmas season was arriving in Vienna, and Phyllida felt the greatest upsurge of excitement she had known since her early childhood even though Christmas in Bath never quite came up to her expectations.

Sebastian kept to his word, and, to her relief, after a slight embarrassment on her part at their first meeting after his proposal, he reverted to being her close, amusing companion, giving no further hint of his feelings.

He had escorted her to the famous trotting races in the Prater gardens, where Prince Heinrich ran two splendid teams of high-trotting ponies—and won.

"They are almost like ballet dancers!" exclaimed Phyllida. "Their steps are so high, so graceful and, I swear, in perfect rhythm with each other. How is it managed?"

"Constant training," said Sebastian. "But, if you have enjoyed them I will show you something even more magical in the equestrian field."

"Can there be anything more magical?"

"I think so. Wait and see."

To her astonishment he took her to a grand building where they entered a ballroom as ornately decorated and chandelier-lit as the rooms in which they danced. The difference was that the whole central area was covered with light sand and there were seats ranged all round the walls.

"This is the training ground for our most famous team of horses—the Lippizaners. More perfectly matched, even, than the trotting ponies, although each one will give an exhibition of dressage separately. When they tour Austria—for they are almost worshipped—they appear together, of course, and often in the open. But here it is their school."

He led Phyllida to a splendid vantage point and she watched, entranced, as each animal—without apparently any directions—gave the most graceful performance she had ever seen.

"How is it done?" she asked when they left, glowing with enthusiasm.

"The only way to great achievement—training," repeat Sebastian. Then he added his only personal compliment for a long time: "Just as you have achieved perfect social poise and all the graces under Lilli's subtle tuition—you are truly perfection, Phyllida, even amongst royalty."

She blushed and thanked him most sincerely.

Then the snow began to fall, light, dry with often brilliant cold sunshine turning it into crisp diamonds. It was mid-December and time to think of Christmas shopping. At that time the famous Viennese Christmas Market opened every evening. There were hundreds of open-air stalls, shielded by tarpaulins and gay with lanterns, which sold Christmas bibelots: cheap jewelery, sugar hearts on ribbons decorated with religious medallions; there were miniature, crude figures of Saint Nicholas in white robes wearing a bishop's miter and carrying a tall crook, and a terrifying little figure with a lolling tongue of bright scarlet.

"What on earth is *that?*" asked Phyllida.

Both Lilli and Sebastian were eager to explain the custom.

"Why, it is Grampus," cried Lilli, "the devil who appears at children's parties every Eve of Saint Nicholas, to pounce on the children, accusing them of being very wicked during the year—not worthy of any gifts."

Sebastian laughed. "It is a terrifying custom, I must

admit, and usually under the scaly costume, hideous mask and forked tail is a normally loving papa or uncle or an elder brother. It reduces young children to hysterical sobs of terror—but the older ones know that in a few minutes he will be banished by the coming of Saint Nicholas, bringing his blessing of forgiveness and his acolytes bearing a huge sugar cake covered with candles."

"And, behind him is drawn a great sack full of lovely presents," added Lilli. Then she chuckled ruefully. "Of course the youngest children have usually to be taken from the room, screaming with fear by then, but it is felt that eventually it does teach them to repent of their mischief before forgiveness comes."

Phyllida shuddered. "I hope I never see a Grampus!"

"Oh, sometimes they attend balls," said Sebastian airily. "But grown-up people seldom have hysterics!" He presented them each with a magnificent sugar heart and a figure of Saint Nicholas. "These will protect you from the taunts of the Devil!"

One morning Phyllida asked Lilli if she might borrow the carriage for a short, private shopping trip into the city. She particularly wanted to buy very special presents for Lilli and Prince Heinrich in thanks for all their kindness, and she thought a small present for Sebastian would not be out of place. Also she felt bound to send a parcel to her parents, since her father had continued to send her a generous allowance and their mutual letters seemed to have healed much of the breach between them. Gareth, too, and Piero must have gifts.

"Of course, *Liebling*—in fact you could not have chosen a better day, for I have hundreds of tedious greeting cards to write to all our relations and friends," said Lilli.

Every shop in Vienna was lavishly decorated, giving full rein to national sentimentality. Highly colored cribs were surrounded with cotton wool snow bespangled with tinsel, stars and colored candles. Saint Nicholas usually presided over the Holy Family as though he had engi-

197

neered the miracle personally. Christmas trees, bedecked with glass baubles and colored lanterns stood in tubs along the streets—in fact, Vienna was *en fête,* with shoppers laughing and sometimes singing carols as they went home laden with bulky packages.

Phyllida gave the carriage driver directions—first she wished to go to a silk merchant in the Ring. When last there, choosing materials for new ball gowns, Lilli had lingered longingly over a bale of rare emerald silk shot with gold—then decided on a less expensive faille.

"It is absurd, perhaps," she explained, "but my Heini is so very generous always that I try hard not to squander his money."

Now she should have an ample length of the emerald in which she would look superb. For Prince Heinrich, too, there were many beautiful silk cravats to choose from.

Phyllida was utterly happy, her cheeks pink in the crisp, cold air, and her gold-mesh purse amply filled with the schillings she had saved carefully for this expedition.

She leaned forward eagerly, noticing that Sebastian's regiment of Hussars was on sentry duty at the Royal Palace, but he was not among them. The Ring was unusually busy with fine carriages traveling both ways and, at one point, they were all brought to a standstill as the royal coach with liveried outriders passed by. Casually she looked into the carriage beside her, wondering if it carried one of her acquaintances.

Then her heart stood still and she turned deathly pale. Inside, a tall, dark man was bending most solicitously toward his charming companion and, as Phyllida stared, hypnotized, unable to look away, she recognized them both. The man was Sir Hugh Abingdon without a doubt, and the blushing girl, laughing up at him most provocatively, was the little Archduchess Alexandra.

Phyllida felt trapped in a nightmare.

"Please turn round," she called sharply to her driver. "I have suddenly been taken ill and must go back!"

Alarmed at her tone, the driver executed a highly

skillful, if dangerous, turn and spurred the horses with his whip. As soon as they stopped Phyllida sprang out, stumbling a little, and without even thanking the driver she ran through the high gate and into the house, stopping for nothing until she had reached her room.

There she flung herself full length on the bed, face down, as her slender body became wracked with sobs. Lilli, surprised to hear the precipitate rush up the stairs, went to see what had happened. Had there been an accident? When, filled with concern, she sat on the side of the bed, trying to take the shaking girl in her arms, Phyllida turned savagely away, unable to speak for the wildness of her grief. For half an hour Lilli waited, helpless, stroking the golden hair and totally baffled.

At last Phyllida lay still, her face still hidden. Slowly, in a low, strange voice, husky with tears she said,

"He has lied to me—all the time Hugh was *lying!* He broke my heart, took my whole life away with *lies!*" She stopped and lay still, as Lilli's own heart sank. She had known that Hugh was paying a lightning visit to Vienna on his way to England, but had implored him to run no risk of being seen by Phyllida and he had promised— while asking tenderly after her.

At last Phyllida turned over on her back, her lovely face ravaged with suffering. "He was making love, quite shamelessly, in a carriage to the Archduchess Alexandra! He did not feel me so near, nor even turn his head to see whether *anyone* was watching such a shocking display! Oh, I hate him, hate him, *hate* him! He must have invented that loathsome story about having to marry some Frenchwoman just to be rid of me and *I believed him.* Oh, Lilli," she seemed to see her friend for the first time, "I no longer want to live—indeed I cannot, not with such burning daggers in my heart! You are so kind but, please, leave me now, and let me die."

Lilli stood up, her voice calm and practical. "Nonsense, Phyllida, no one has ever died of a broken heart. You have had a terrible shock, I agree, but Hugh always warned you of what he was. Now, I shall send for a potion and then stay beside you until you sleep." She crossed the room and pulled the velvet bell rope. When Gretchen appeared, staring, alarmed, at the figure in such disarray on the rumpled bed, Lilli gave her precise instructions in a low voice and, sensible, she scuttled away to carry them out.

By then Phyllida lay limp and, as Lilli eased her out of her coat, she responded like a doll. "When Gretchen returns and you have drunk the potion she will help me to undress you, *Liebling,* and then, while I watch over you, you will sleep."

" 'Sleep'?" echoed Phyllida stupidly. "I shall never sleep again."

Lilli ignored this and removed her shoes.

"Sleep is the most merciful gift the good God ever gave to the world—when you wake the shock will have passed, I promise, and you will be able to think rationally again. Oh, yes, it has been a most cruel blow, I agree, but you are *strong,* Phyllida and, when you are able to see it in proportion, you will view things quite differently."

Phyllida drank the potion obediently when it came. It was very strong, a recipe Lilli had taken gratefully from her mother during her own time of bitter mourning. And, almost before they had undressed her and wrapped her in her nightgown, Gretchen discreetly changing the wet, tear-stained pillows, she was asleep.

When she woke, three hours later, Lilli was still sitting patiently by her side. Phyllida reached out a grateful hand and, in her normal voice, said,

"How good you are, dearest Lilli, and how patient! I—feel quite calm now. Just very tired and sad."

Lilli smiled tenderly. "Of course you are sad, *Kätzchen*—being set free by force is far from easy. But we shall not discuss it again today. Like any deep wound, the heart must be left in peace to heal—and yours will, my very dear girl, for you are so young and the world lies ahead of you, filled with life and warmth and so many people who care about you."

"Yes," Phyllida managed a wan little smile. "I expect, in time, I may even marry Sebastian."

Lilli sat up sharply. "But not as a stopgap, something to salve your pride—he is too fine a young man for that!"

Phyllida felt drowsy again, and murmured, "No—never like that. But, since my heart is empty—quite empty —I may even love him in time. . . ."

Chapter Twelve

Lilli and her husband gave a magnificent party on the Eve of Saint Nicholas. A splendid Yule log burned merrily in the big open fireplace, sent specially from the estate in Styria and almost the length of a young tree. A Christmas tree stood in the hall, gay with candles, tinsel and gifts for all the guests wrapped in colored paper and tied with ribbons. The whole house was decked with sweet-smelling evergreens, holly and mistletoe.

They had already given Phyllida her Christmas present—a new ball gown in leaf green, embroidered with tiny rhinestone flowers, and she wore it that night with deep pleasure.

The dining table was set for fifty guests with finest gold plate and gilt candelabra with red candles; at every place there were little silver *bonbonnières* filled with sugared almonds and nuts, and tall damask napkins folded in the lotus shape stood in one of the many crystal glasses beside each setting. The sideboard groaned with great dishes of hothouse fruits, cold sweets and crystal flagons of red and white wine. At ten o'clock, as the company took their seats, roast turkeys, skillfully carved already by the chef but pressed back into shape, would be served garnished with tiny, sizzling brown sausages, bacon rolls, five different kinds of stuffing; roast potatoes, and several fresh green vegetables, including hothouse asparagus, as well as cranberry sauce, apple sauce, bread sauce and rich gravy, would be handed separately by a dozen flunkies.

But, before this there was a ceremony during which a group of cloaked carol singers came in, and stood round their choirmaster to sing, in perfect harmony, favorites such as "Tannenbaum, mein Tannenbaum," and "Silent Night," being rewarded afterward by mulled wine and hot mince pies.

"It is like England," said Phyllida ecstatically to Lilli, "yet far, far more wonderful! It is, I declare, the Christmas I have always dreamed of and never had until now!"

Lilli looked at Phyllida with pride. The beautiful girl had shown her spirit, indeed, since her heartbreak over Hugh, never showing her grief and making a noble effort to appear even happier than usual in public. In fact, Lilli was not sure exactly how Phyllida felt inwardly now, for she never pried. But Phyllida's green eyes were glowing, and a smile came readily to her lips.

Just before midnight all the Catholics present went in carriages to Stefanskirche for midnight Mass, to return later and continue the festivities. But Protestants and others stayed behind to dance. Among them was Sebastian Grindl and, after an exhausting polka he led Phyllida under a mistletoe bough.

"I can resist no longer—may I give you a Christmas kiss, Phyllida? Oh, it is traditional, I swear, and need mean nothing—except to me."

To his amazed delight she turned a radiant, willing face up to him. "With all my heart, Sebastian!"

He kissed her very gently, almost reverently, restraining his longing for her. Afterward she still stood, holding his hands.

"How dear you are—how very dear," she said softly.

His heart leaped and he asked: "Is it possible—are you giving me the sign I have prayed for, ever since the *Heurige?*"

"I—think I am, yes," she said simply.

"Oh, my Phyllida—will you truly consider marrying me?"

A flicker of fear crossed her face but she said, "I beg you not to rush things, Sebastian, but I know nobody, now, whom I should be prouder to marry."

When Lilli returned from Mass they sought her out and told her the news. For a moment she looked very serious, then, hugging them each warmly she declared, "I am so happy for you, my dear children, so very happy. But—let us keep it a secret between ourselves until the excitement of Christmas has died down, shall we? Besides, I must invite your parents, Phyllida, for your father will wish to discuss matters with Sebastian's father in the proper, decorous way, as is only right. I will ask them to come at the end of January, if it suits them, and then we will give a grand ball and announce your betrothal."

"I have promised Phyllida not to rush matters," said Sebastian solemnly, although his blue eyes shone with pride. "And I will not. Just to be with her, often, is all I ask at present."

Lilli looked at him fondly—how wise he was for his years, how very sensitive. With a pang she hoped that he would not, after all, have his heart broken. She had had no reply as yet from her long letter to Piero and, although Phyllida showed such a brave face to the world, there were moments when she sat staring into space when she thought she was unobserved.

So Christmas passed in a welter of goodwill, affection and gifts.

On New Year's Eve, Sebastian brought Phyllida a small package. Inside she found an exquisite diamond ring and looked up at him, startled.

"Oh, Sebastian—it is so perfect but . . . I cannot wear it, not yet."

"You will see that it is strung on a fine chain for the present, my love—pray wear it round your neck sometimes until I have the right to place it on your finger. I tried to find an emerald worthy of your eyes but no such stone has yet been found, I think."

That evening Lilli and Phyllida found themselves alone before dinner, as Prince Heinrich was still dressing. Phyllida looked pale and a little distraught.

"Lilli, I am afraid," she said abruptly. "Oh, I care deeply for Sebastian, indeed I do, but—Christmas quite carried me away I believe."

"You mean you still love Hugh in spite of everything?"

"Yes," replied Phyllida, very low. She stood up and began pacing the room, almost talking to herself. "When the first shock had passed, I found myself making excuses for him. After all, bending over the Archduchess was not truly serious, not nearly as marked as the attentions he paid to the woman in Paris, or the one in Venice. Perhaps he *did* lie to me about his marriage, but, as you reminded me, he was determined to free me in any case because of his reputation. So why shouldn't he flirt a little? After all," he voice grew bitter, "I have done something far worse, for, although I *will* marry Sebastian he will never possess my whole heart."

"Oh, *Liebling*." Lilli was very distressed—distressed for both young people. "There is a whole month yet before we need to make any public announcement, and who knows what may happen in that time?" Then she added slowly, "I think you may discover that you love Sebastian more than you think now. Marriage between close friends can bring a depth of love far beyond mere passion."

"Perhaps it will," said Phyllida, but her tone was flat.

Fortunately January was a busy month, filled with social engagements. Mr. and Mrs. Chase wrote most amiably to Phyllida and told Lilli that they would be delighted to be her guests from January 28. Sebastian had asked his parents to come to Vienna at that time, too, and, when he hinted that he might become betrothed to the charming Miss Chase whom they liked, they were pleased.

Everything was *en train* and Lilli decided to hold the ball on February 3. Why, *why* did Piero still send her no news?

When the engraved invitations to the ball arrived, headed by a royal crest, Phyllida helped Lilli to address them. But soon she looked up, puzzled, yet secretly relieved.

"You do not mention that it is to celebrate a betrothal?" she said.

"Of course not! It would be most incorrect before your father has given his consent!" retorted Lilli. Later, to her husband, who was in on the secret, she showed some of her inner anxiety. "Heini, I am worried; somehow this match is not quite right."

"Nonsense, my love," he said cheerfully, for he thoroughly approved. "You were not sure that marrying me was 'right,' were you? Yet look how well it has turned out. Do not fret, my beloved, everything will arrange itself most happily, you'll see."

Sebastian noticed, with a trace of unease, that Phyllida spent little time with him alone, but she seemed quite happy and always had a hundred reasons that seemed logical. After all, she was busy preparing for her parents' visit, and Gareth, too, was coming from Venice. "Remember, I haven't seen them for many, many months," she reminded him. "I want to have everything perfect for our reunion."

Gareth was not arriving until the eve of the ball—he had urgent work to finish, he explained. So Phyllida met her parents alone. At first all three were a little ill at ease, having been apart for so long and Mrs. Chase was frankly overcome by being a guest of Prince and Princess Löwendorff.

"Mercy, Phyllida, you live in royal style now! And you have changed a great deal, I swear. You are no longer the wild girl so alarmingly described by Miss Smith. Indeed, you are a perfect lady, I do declare—and soon to be a foreign countess, too," she sighed sentimentally. "We shall see little of you at home after that, I fear."

"Oh, Sebastian and I will visit you often, Mamma," cried Phyllida, touched by how timid her once stern mother had become.

"But you will not want a house in Bath, I think."

"No, dear Mamma," said Phyllida seriously. "Sebastian has a fine house here, in Vienna, and big country estates, which he will help his father to manage when he leaves the army. No, Bath would not be—wise," she added slowly.

Mr. Chase, in his own quiet way, was also mightily impressed and, when he met Sebastian, more than satisfied. "You have chosen well, my daughter—a fine young man. I am sure his father and I will have little to arrange. All this puts my modest fortune to shame!"

"No, no, Papa." Phyllida kissed his cheek warmly. "And you have been so very generous to me always—I hope I have not caused you much anxiety?"

"Some," he smiled ruefully. "And I missed you, my dear."

"I know. But we shall often meet after—after my marriage. And you will be so proud of Gareth—even Mamma must be—for I declare he has become quite a famous young painter in Venice; quite rich, too, for he soon plans to buy his own house there."

Mr. Chase sighed. "I failed you both badly, I fear."

"*No,* Papa—you always understood that we had to go away, to find our own ways of life."

"Yes. That young man who caused all the trouble—Sir Hugh Abingdon—I have heard strange rumors about him of late."

"Pray, pray tell me, Papa," she begged eagerly.

He smiled. "A lawyer never passes on rumors, my dear—I feel they have been foolishly exaggerated."

She said no more, for, indeed, she found that she did not wish to hear terrible news of Hugh's behavior now, of all times.

The meeting between her own and Sebastian's parents went very smoothly. A marriage settlement was quickly agreed on and, although Mrs. Chase was unusually silent with the Duchess, feeling her social airs and graces would be pretentious amongst such august company, they seemed to like each other.

"She was quite homely at times," exclaimed Mrs. Chase to her daughter. "She has promised me some delicious Austrian recipes, which one would not expect to be the province of a duchess!"

"Oh, no, Mamma," Phyllida laughed. "At home, in Styria, she loves to supervise the kitchen, and her preserves and jellies are famous among their friends. She is not 'grand' at all! She will teach me, too."

Day followed day, bringing the ball ever nearer. Phyllida alternately dreaded it and longed for it to be over. Once publicly betrothed to Sebastian there would be no going back. Besides, he was so tender and considerate that her warmth toward him grew. She would, indeed, be *safe*. From what, she dared not contemplate.

Lilli had insisted that she have a new gown for the great occasion. She and the dressmaker insisted on white, especially as the Duchess had given Phyllida a simple but extremely fine diamond necklace to complement her ring. When he heard of it, her father insisted on paying for the gown, which touched her deeply, and when it was delivered on the morning before the ball, Phyllida was delighted with it. It was very simple, almost bridal in its purity of color and line. As a betrothal gift Prince Heinrich and Lilli presented her with four diamond stars for her hair.

"Once you are betrothed, *Liebling,* you will be established as a woman, no longer a girl, and expected to deck yourself more grandly. Phyllida," she paused, her eyes worried, "you *are* sure, are you not? There is still time, you know."

Phyllida turned to stone. "I am absolutely sure, Lilli. My feeling for Hugh will gradually fade, I know, and—

and Sebastian is so very kind. He has promised that we need not be married for a year if it pleases me. He deserves so much more than I am giving at present, but it will come—it *must*." Her voice held a note of desperation. She dared tell no one—not even Lilli—that her dreams had become tormented with longing for Hugh. It was "first love," as everyone had told her, and a haunting that would take long to fade into gentle lavender and ribbons.

After Gretchen had helped her to dress, and tiered her hair into a fit setting for the glowing stars, she fastened the diamond necklace round her throat herself, praying that she might prove worthy of such gifts after all. It was still early, but she could not stand the silent loneliness of her room. Lilli and the Prince would be downstairs already, she knew, seeing to all the final arrangements. They were both in the hall as she came slowly downstairs—Lilli regal in a gown of silver brocade and her husband resplendent in blue satin, his breast covered with many decorations. He stepped forward gallantly, bowed and kissed both her hands.

"A snow bride crowned with sunlight," he said approvingly.

Lilli kissed her. "Poor *Kätzchen*—pray do not feel so nervous. It is a great strain, this moment, I well remember —but soon all will be laughter and gaiety. Besides," she smiled, "you are not the only early arrival. Sebastian is here, in Heini's study, hoping to place his ring on your finger. Do you have it?"

Phyllida held out her slim hand, realizing she had done wrong to put it on herself. Quickly she slipped it off. "I will take it to him now. And, oh, how can I *ever* thank you both for all your care and kindness to me?"

Lilli slipped an arm through her husband's, who smiled down at her. "My dear, we are both true Austrians at heart! We dearly love happy endings! Now, go to Sebastian, for he is impatient and we have many details to see to."

Sebastian, in full dress uniform, came eagerly forward

to welcome her, as the vision that was Phyllida came through the door.

"My dear, dear love—I did not dare to hope—but you are here already!" He held her at arm's length and looked at her before smiling broadly. "And so ethereal I scarcely dare to touch you!"

Smiling, she held out her palm, the ring resting on it. "I shall not melt, I swear."

He took it, then kissed the palm on which it had rested. Phyllida was thankful, for a little shiver passed through her which he did not notice. The ring! Once on her finger her promise would be final.

Suddenly they were both startled and alert. A great pounding came on the front door. Footmen rushed to see the cause of such a disturbance and the Prince and Lilli followed close behind, dismayed. The great door opened and all at once many voices were exclaiming—above them all rose the voice of Sir Hugh Abingdon, ragged and desperate with pleading.

"Am I too late? I have traveled without pause, day and night, to reach here in time—free, at last, and able to tell Phyllida the whole truth . . . but if she is truly happy, I will leave."

Forgetting Sebastian—to her later shame—Phyllida ran to the door on winged feet. Stunned, she and Hugh stared at each other across the hall, forgetting everyone around them. His face looked younger, despite fatigue; it was at last unguarded, open, and his warm, chestnut eyes glowed wtih love. With a little, strangled cry, she sped straight into his arms, her own eyes blinded by tears.

Caring nothing for his dusty cloak or her white dress, Phyllida leaned against his dear breast as his arms held her—so strong, so tender.

Suddenly they were interrupted by her mother's sharp voice coming from the stairs.

"Sir Hugh Abingdon! How dare you show your face here—and on such a night! Release my daughter *immediately!*"

At that, Piero and Gareth, who had traveled the last part of the journey with him, stepped forward. Gareth, his face wreathed in proud smiles, went to greet his parents, saying clearly so that everyone could hear,

"Have patience, Mamma, it is no longer *Sir* Hugh, but *Lord* Abingdon!"

Phyllida gasped and looked up into Hugh's gently amused face. "Do not fear, Phyllida my beloved, it is only another trophy to lay, at last, at your golden feet— if you are sure I am still welcome?"

"'Welcome'? Oh, *Hugh!*" Her tears shone in the wide green eyes.

"Not only is he made a baron, but he was too modest to wear this—now I insist!" Piero drew a square leather case from his pocket and opening it, a dazzle of precious stones on a ribbon sparkled with life under the chandelier.

"What is it?" asked Phyllida tremulously, feeling that the moment had brought too much joy already.

"It is the Most Royal Order of the Garter—bestowed on Hugh but four days ago, which is why his journey had to be taken at such breakneck speed." He offered it to Hugh, his face beaming with pride and delight. Hugh released Phyllida for a moment. Then, taking the splendid order in his hands, he bent forward and placed the rich ribbon round her neck. Her slim hands flew up to touch the wonderful jewel. Then she looked up at him, by now quite dazed.

"A high title—now this! Oh, Hugh, how did it all come about?"

Here, Piero intervened, joining Lilli and Prince Heinrich.

"I know—if you will allow yourself to be kidnapped —Hugh wishes to tell you his story alone. And I shall take much pride in telling our dear friends here."

"I am going to swoon," declared Mrs. Chase in an agonized voice. And did. Mr. Chase and Gareth attended to her with the smelling bottle and a fan from her reticule.

Lilli was smiling—all else forgotten except the happiness of Phyllida and, at last, the honors duly bestowed on a dear friend.

"May I kidnap you, Phyllida?" asked Hugh diffidently. "I know it is wrong of me on the eve of this ball—Lilli, can you spare her for, perhaps, two hours?"

She came forward, both hands outstretched. "With all my heart, Hugh—I am so thankful, so very thankful for you," then she glanced at Phyllida. "My dear—have you forgotten poor Sebastian?"

Instantly Phyllida's cheeks flushed with shame. "Oh —how cruel of me—how unforgivable. Hugh—please promise not to disappear, I shall be but ten minutes, but I fear I have dealt a terrible blow to Sebastian, and he has been such a true and faithful friend."

She found Sebastian standing with his back to the fire. His face was a little pale, but his eyes held no reproach.

"So, dear Phyllida, your heart was not quite free after all?"

"No, Sebastian," she answered gravely. "And, once he came, I could neither hide my heart nor cheat you of the full happiness you so richly deserve. I don't expect forgiveness, for that could never be possible, but think kindly of me later on, for I swear I would never have deserted you once our troth had been sworn."

Sebastian smiled and took her hand. "Sit by me for a few moments, Phyllida, and listen. I have always known that you could not give me all your heart, and ever since you finally accepted me I think I have always known that it was just a dream, too perfect to come true—a star I could never reach."

Phyllida felt overwhelmed by so much adoration. "Oh, my dear, I can scarce bear to take my own happiness at the expense of your sorrow—so do not grieve for me, Sebastian, you are so very good and fine. Indeed you are the best friend I have ever had."

He smiled. "Pray, allow me to grieve a little—but I do not begrudge you one moment of your happiness, Phyllida. Now go to him, for you have waited a long time, I think."

She stood up then, and bending down she kissed his forehead. "I know that you will find the love you deserve," she said.

Unclasping the diamond necklace his mother had given her, she placed it on a table nearby and slipped from the room.

Hugh was still in the hall, surrounded, as Piero told the story from the time he had left Venice himself to entreat the Prince to give Hugh his freedom at last. Hugh's eyes implored Phyllida to hurry back so that they could escape.

Gretchen was tidying her room when Phyllida ran in, her face radiant.

"Oh, Gretchen, hurry and help me." She was already struggling impatiently out of the white ball gown. "Get out my dark green morning gown and a cloak—any cloak so long as it has a hood to cover my hair."

Gretchen stared at her, thunderstruck, then at the blaze of jewels hanging on her breast instead of the chaste diamond necklace.

"Oh, quickly, quickly! I will tell you everything later—but this is almost the happiest hour of my life! I am going out."

The young maid, speechless, hurried to do her bidding.

"I cannot take off this decoration—it means too much. I will wear it under my gown until I return." She quite forgot the diamond stars in her hair and so did Gretchen. In five minutes Phyllida was ready and flew out of the room and down the stairs, pulling up the hood as she went.

Hugh came to the foot of the stairs to meet her, his

hand outstretched. "You are as rare in changing your clothes swiftly as in everything else." He tucked her hand through his arm.

"Forgive me, Lilli—Prince Heinrich; we shall be back, I promise, and come to the ball."

Then they were outside in the dark, starlit street.

"Do you mind walking—it is not far?" asked Hugh. "There is a small *Weinstube* I know, owned by a dear old friend, and it will still be almost deserted at this hour."

"I declare, I would gladly walk to the moon if you asked me to!"

"Wait, Phyllida," he said solemnly. "Wait, until you have heard my whole story before you make such rash promises."

So they walked in silence, then entered an oak door lit outside by a lighted bunch of grapes, and in no time the smiling, white-haired owner had welcomed them, taken Phyllida's cloak, and installed them in a small booth at the end of the narrow room.

Hugh sat opposite her, almost unable to believe the miracle that she was truly there—that she still loved him.

"Tell me," she pleaded, "I have tried so hard to tear you out of my heart—indeed, I almost succeeded after seeing you driving in the Ring with the little Archduchess, and I accepted Sebastian. But deep down it was useless. Surely we have belonged together from the very beginning."

"And that is where I will start," he said. A flagon of fine red wine and two goblets were placed before them and then the tactful old man, smiling, went away as quietly as he had come.

"The story starts when I was twenty," began Hugh. "I was my father's only son and had been brought up very quietly on our country estate, at Abingdon Grange, where I had tutors, and my father himself taught me riding, shooting and how to manage our land. I knew nothing of the fashionable world, but he decided I should spend a year at Court, learning a little more about life and, hopefully, finding a suitable young wife," he chuckled. "Well, you know yourself how foolish those young girls are! Besides, my mother was a witty, cultured woman with the same spirit as you, my darling, so I chose to hold aloof. This made me a great favorite with the Prince, who always wanted me near him. Then, one night, he unfolded a plan—a daring challenge for me to take up."

"You mean all your travels have been in his service?" asked Phyllida.

Hugh nodded, and his face darkened. "I had no idea that I was entering into such bondage. At the time it seemed an exciting adventure—a chance to see the world and meet many beautiful women. But, first, he insisted that I gain a reputation as a rake—a shameless flirt and a gambler. Indeed, he spread many of the stories himself!"

"How selfish," she exclaimed. "Did he expect you to find many beautiful women for his *pleasure?*"

"No, no. My missions were strictly diplomatic and very, very secret. There was much unrest in Europe and the nearby East and his ambassadors were finding getting information difficult. So, His Highness decided that for me to contact wives and mistresses of statesmen and, through them, give and receive messages, would provide an excellent cloak for the purpose. I was to flirt with them, flatter them—but nothing more, I swear, my darling—until they agreed to help me. And it worked. The Prince also established certain trusted contacts for me in every country—people such as Piero and Lilli, who could give me the necessary introductions."

"But surely the statesmen minded you courting their wives?"

"Not once they received my messages, which often helped them to make decisions they had not understood were possible before. And," he smiled ruefully, "I was surprised at how gladly bored women enjoyed being in on high secrets—and keeping them, too." He went on: "When I was twenty-five I knew that my parents were distressed by my shocking reputation, so I asked the Prince to release me. In truth, the missions had grown irksome, and some women demanded more of me, which I could not give. He refused. And then I met you . . ."

He paused and leaned across the table, taking both her hands. "You were the girl of my dreams, Phyllida— the first woman I had truly loved. But, by then, I felt so unworthy I felt that I *must* set you free for your own sake. I had learned such iron discipline over my emotions by then that I tried hard—you know how I tried!"

"Only it was too late from the very beginning, my beloved," she said softly.

"When Gareth begged me to help him in rescuing you from Paris, I went to the Prince, determined to insist on my release . . . but he had gout and was in a waspish temper. Instead, I asked him to let me use his coach in France—I hinted that I needed it for a personal assignation, that my heart was a little involved and that I might disappear for several days. I added that I hoped to restore my honor in her eyes. I didn't think he heard that, for he started laughing. Then he said his mind was set on my vital mission to the East, which could and, indeed, did avert a petty war." Hugh's mouth twisted in bitter anger. "I hated him deeply in that moment—particularly when he sneered at my wish to restore my honor—at which point he laughed again and asked *what* honor had I left to save by then? So—he grudgingly allowed me twelve days in which to take you to Piero Roberti, after which I was to sail for the East."

Phyllida's eyes darkened. "Oh, Hugh, that dreadful story of being forced to marry a Frenchwoman—of your past having caught up with you! It broke my heart, I swear, for deep down I had a sure instinct that you were good, and true and most honorable. Yes, even after watching you at the opera and, later, with that painted creature in Venice, that instinct only faltered before asserting itself more strongly than ever. But Piero and then Lilli, your friends, helped to persuade me that your one wish was for me to forget you—to marry a worthy man 'trailing no shadows,' as you once said. Well, I, too, tried. It was only after seeing you in Vienna with the Archduchess that I could bring myself to accept Sebastian . . . knowing that I should never love him as he deserved. It was a wicked thing to do."

"No, Phyllida, you see, I *did* love you enough to want your happiness, and by then I despaired of ever being free from the Prince. But Piero and Lilli have proved their magnificent friendship and loyalty to us both, my love. When Lilli told Piero that you still loved me, he went to England, to the Prince, and made that selfish man feel almost ashamed of himself!" He smiled. "That is an unheard of achievement! So, when I returned from the East via Vienna, where I had one final, vital report to be passed to the Archduke through his gay little wife, I found the Prince in a very different frame of mind!"

"My darling—I shall hate him for the rest of my life! What a price he made you pay for your noble deeds and self-sacrifice! If that is treason, I don't care!"

"He has done little to earn your loyalty," said Hugh, his eyes at last shining with amusement. "Well, I found Piero still at the royal elbow, prodding and prompting him to bestow absurd honors on me which would proclaim to the whole world that I had never been the wicked man they thought."

Phyllida undid the neck of her gown and drew out the Order of the Garter—she kissed it reverently, then insisted that Hugh put it round his own neck.

"My dearest, it has warmed my very soul to wear it, but now I want everyone to see it, to honor you as I do, and it will make me so proud, so *very* proud of you."

Reluctantly he did her bidding. A silence fell between them—a silence filled with the great depth of their love, which needed no words but communicated itself by their eyes as it had first done so long ago over tea at the Grand Pump Room Hotel in Bath.

At last Hugh gave a low, contented laugh. "My golden girl—I can scarce believe, even now, that you are with me—and your glorious hair so fittingly bedecked with stars!"

Phyllida's hand flew to her hair and she blushed. "Goodness! I changed from my ball gown with such unseemly haste I had quite forgot them! They were a gift from Lilli and the Prince." She added hastily, "Not Sebastian. Blessedly, he had not yet given me his ring, and I took off the diamond necklace that his mother gave me."

Hugh recaptured her hand and gazed long and deeply into her shining eyes.

"Oh, Phyllida—I feel so very humble after all the suffering I have caused you but . . . will you do me the greatest honor of all by becoming my wife?"

"Do you need to ask the question that I answered with all my heart long ago?" she said simply. "You would have been the husband of my heart all the rest of my life, even if our paths had never crossed again."

He moved from his place opposite to sit beside her. "I swear I shall die if I cannot kiss you now," he said huskily. And, in the candlelit booth, screened from all eyes, he took her in his arms. Their kiss was long and tender with none of the desperate passion they had shown on the terrace in Venice when he took his leave. For now a golden future stretched ahead in which their mutual passion would have full rein with, at last, no more secrets, no partings.

As he released her gently, Hugh said, "I have presumed a little, my darling, for I cannot bear to see your finger empty of my claim." He drew from his pocket a ring, which he slid slowly on her finger.

Seeing it in the candlelight Phyllida gasped with pleasure. It was the emerald that Sebastian had failed to find—a flawless stone that mirrored the deep green of her eyes. She raised misty eyes to his.

"Hugh—it is so perfect, so very beautiful . . . I have no words."

"Words are never necessary between us," Hugh said happily, his gaze reflecting the delight he felt from seeing it on her hand. "Now, we must drink our own private toast." He poured wine into each goblet. "Herr Schrube will be hurt indeed if we ignore his hospitality!"

With joyous gladness they drank to the future. Then Hugh said,

"Princess, do you not think we should go to the ball? I fear we have lingered long past the two hours I promised Lilli, but we owe her so much, besides which we both have to change to do her honor."

Phyllida sighed. "Yes. Yes, indeed we should go. Although all I want is to be with you, my own dear love."

With a note of thankful triumph, he said, "But this is no parting, my heart—nor will there ever be a parting in future. It is the *beginning* of one life together from now on. Pray, let me give you my arm, Lady Abingdon!"

"With all my heart, My Lord!" she laughed, and together they went out into the still, blue night.

ABOUT THE AUTHOR
Caroline Courtney

Caroline Courtney was born in India, the youngest daughter of a British Army Colonel stationed there in the troubled years after the First World War. Her first husband, a Royal Air Force pilot, was tragically killed in the closing stages of the Second World War. She later remarried and now lives with her second husband, a retired barrister, in a beautiful 17th century house in Cornwall. They have three children, two sons and a daughter, all of whom are now married, and four grandchildren.

On the rare occasions that Caroline Courtney takes time off from her writing, she enjoys gardening and listening to music, particularly opera. She is also an avid reader of romantic poetry and has an ever-growing collection of poems she has composed herself.

Caroline Courtney is destined to be one of this country's leading romantic novelists. She has written an enormous number of novels over the years—purely for pleasure—and has never before been interested in seeing them reach publication. However, at her family's insistence she has now relented, and Warner Books is proud to be issuing a selection in this uniform edition.

ROMANCE...ADVENTURE...
DANGER...

THIS TOWERING PASSION
by Valerie Sherwood   (81-486, $2.50)
500 pages of sweet romance and savage adventure set against
the violent tapestry of Cromwellian England, with a magnificent
heroine whose beauty and ingenuity captivates every man who
sees her, from the king of the land to the dashing young rakehell
whose destiny is love!

THIS LOVING TORMENT
by Valerie Sherwood   (95-745, $2.75)
Born in poverty in the aftermath of the Great London Fire, Charity
Woodstock grew up to set the men of three continents ablaze
with passion! The bestselling sensation of the year, boasting 1.3
million copies in print after just one month, to make it the fastest-
selling historical romance in Warner Books history!

THESE GOLDEN PLEASURES
by Valerie Sherwood   (95-744, $2.75)
From the stately mansions of the east to the freezing hell of the
Klondike, beautiful Rosanne Rossiter went after what she wanted
—and got it all! By the author of the phenomenally successful
THIS LOVING TORMENT.

LOVE'S TENDER FURY
by Jennifer Wilde   (81-909, $2.50)
The turbulent story of an English beauty—sold at auction like a
slave—who scandalized the New World by enslaving her masters.
She would conquer them all—only if she could subdue the hot
unruly passions of the heart! The 2 Million Copy Bestseller that
brought fame to the author of DARE TO LOVE.

DARE TO LOVE
by Jennifer Wilde   (81-826, $2.50)
Who dared to love Elena Lopez? She was the Queen of desire and
the slave of passion, traveling the world—London, Paris, San
Francisco—and taking love where she found it! Elena Lopez—
the tantalizing, beautiful moth—dancing out of the shadows,
warmed, lured and consumed by the heart's devouring flame.

LILIANE
by Annabel Erwin   (91-219, $2.50)
The bestselling romantic novel of a beautiful, vulnerable woman
torn between two brothers, played against the colorful background of plantation life in Colonial America.

AURIELLE
by Annabel Erwin   (91-126, $2.50)
The tempestuous new historical romance 4 million Annabel Erwin
fans have been waiting for. Join AURIELLE, the scullery maid
with the pride of a Queen as she escapes to America to make her
dreams of nobility come true.

THE BEST OF REGENCY ROMANCE FROM WARNER BOOKS